MW01001870

Saudi Arabia

Saudi Arabia

GENE LINDSEY

HIPPOCRENE BOOKS
New York

For information, address:
HIPPOCRENE BOOKS, INC.
171 Madison Avenue
New York, NY 10016

Library of Congress Cataloging-in-Publication Data
Lindsey, Gene.
Saudi Arabia / Gene Lindsey
p.   cm.
ISBN 0-87052-998-6
1. Saudi Arabia.   I. Title.
DS204.L46   1991
953.8—dc20   91-9062
CIP
Printed in the United States of America

The following publishers have generously given permission to use material and quotations from their works: *Shorter Encyclopedia of Islam,* edited by Hamilton A.R. Gibb, Cornell University Press, 1965; "American Culture in Saudi Arabia," by Solon T. Kimball, *Transactions,* New York Academy of Sciences, 1965; *The Science of Man in the World Crisis,* by Ralph Linton, Columbia University Press, 1945; "Cultural Factors in Managing an FMS Case Program: Saudi Arabian Army Ordinance Corps (SCOP) Program," by Maj. Joseph R. Mayton, U. S. Army, Defense Systems Management College, 1977; *Peoples and Cultures of the Middle East,* edited by Ailon Shiloh, Random House, Inc., 1969; *Islam in Modern History,* Wilfred Cantwell Smith, Princeton University Press, 1957; *Saudi Arabia; Its People, Its Society, Its Culture,* by George Arthur Lipsky, Human Relations Area Files Press, 1958; *Arab Mind,* by Raphael Patai, Charles Scribner's Sons, 1973; "The Influence of the Arabic Language on the Psychology of the Arabs," by E. Shouby, *Middle East Journal,* 1951; *The Cultural Environment of International Business,* by Vern Terpstra, Southwestern Publishing Company, 1978.

To my father, Carl Lawrence Lindsey

ACKNOWLEDGMENTS

I would like to acknowledge the great debt owed to John A. Campbell for his extensive support and to Jani Giles for her continuous encouragement.

Special thanks are owed to Helen Fordelon and Enya Ylagan for their editorial assistance and tireless support.

Thanks also to David H. W. Edwards and Craig Wilson for their critical review, to Maria Julita Tolentino, Gina Tamayo and Ana Villarama for their secretarial support, and to my friends in Saudi Arabia for their valuable contributions.

Although I am indebted to those above for their generous aid in producing this book, they should not be held responsible for its contents.

CONTENTS

MAPS

PREFACE

*I*n August 1990, the United States began airlifting American combat troops to Saudi Arabia. By the end of August, thousands of American troops were encamped in the harsh desert between the Saudi oil fields and the Kuwaiti border to prevent Iraqi troops from invading Saudi Arabia.

Why did Saudi Arabia ask for help from the United States? How do Saudis treat the Americans? What is it like there?

This book describes many of the events leading up to the current crisis in the Middle East. It also explains those factors which interact to form the Saudi Arabian culture and its impact on Americans. Many of these factors are based on attitudes and values which have evolved over thousands of years. Therefore, it is necessary to understand how they evolved to learn why things are as they are today.

Chapter 1

Sudden Significance

*T*wenty years ago, most people were not even aware of Saudi Arabia. If they were, they associated it with sultans, harems and camel-riding sheiks. The Saudi culture was of passing interest to scholars and romantics, but of no more importance to the West than that of Polynesia—until it was discovered that the desert nomads were pitching their tents on sand dunes that covered seas of oil.

During the 1970s, the Saudis continuously increased their oil production and raised their prices until money from the West was pouring into the magic kingdom faster than wealth had ever changed hands before. The Saudis took the money and went on a gigantic spending spree, buying luxuries and improving their country in one of the most ambitious development programs ever attempted.

Saudi Arabia advanced more rapidly than any country in modern history, and by 1981, it had become one of the richest, most important countries in the world. It controls over a quarter of the world's diminishing oil reserves, has billions of dollars worth of Western investments and is the center of the religion of a billion people. It also influences world economy, the productive capacity of dozens of industrial nations, and the policies of fifty Muslim countries. Every day, Americans buy over $40 million worth of oil from Saudi Arabia, a kingdom threatened by pan-Arabists and religious fanatics. Because the denial of Saudi oil would cause economic chaos, the United States is militarily involved in this unstable region, in a conflict which biblical evangelists predict will turn into Armageddon.

Once they realized how much oil and money the Saudis had, Western countries, companies and workers flocked to the kingdom to get a piece of the action. The United States and British governments gave the Saudis large loans, military assistance, economic advice, and managerial support. Other governments curried favor with the Saudis to obtain contracts for their countries. American, Asian, and European companies rushed into the lucrative Saudi market to get multibillion-dollar contracts. Millions of workers from all over the world responded to employment advertisements promising high pay and adventure to work in Saudi Arabia. But they all encountered problems due to their ignorance of the Saudi culture—the Saudis wanted modernization without westernization. The governments were thwarted, many companies failed, thousands of Western workers gave up and returned home, and military assistance was only partially effective.

Most Westerners still do not realize that the Saudi culture is an entirely different way of life. Its roots reach directly to the ancient Semitic culture of the Babylonians and Aramaeans described in the Old Testament of the Bible.

Many Saudi values are the same as those of their ancient Semitic ancestors, whom they claim descended from the prophet Abraham through his son Ishmael around 1700 B.C. Their value system remained intact, enforced through Bedouin custom for thousands of years as the nomadic people survived a harsh, unforgiving environment. It remained intact despite the attempts of the Greek, Roman, Byzantine, and Persian empires to change it. Their value system matured and blossomed during the Dark Ages of the West when it was incorporated into the Islamic religion. It then became formalized and remained intact despite further attempts by Christian crusaders, Mongolian invaders, Portuguese traders, and British imperialists to alter it.

The Saudis of today live by, and are extremely proud of, these values which shape their entire way of life. They believe their system of values is the only morally correct one and continue to resist attempts to change it. Consequently, Saudis think, express themselves, act, live, work, and solve problems differently from people and governments of the West.

This difference in beliefs and values makes it extremely difficult for Westerners to deal with Saudis because most Westerners cannot understand Saudi behavior or predict their actions.

Differences are significant throughout the spectrum of Saudi culture. Their physical environment is barren, their society is nomadic, and they practice a religion rarely observed in the West. Their history is a tale of family and tribal feuds and their late-blooming economy is based on a single resource—oil. Their foreign affairs consist more of rhetoric than of action. Their government is a family affair and their laws are based on vengeance. Their archaic language is almost unsuited to modern times and their citizens are only now beginning to receive a secular education. Their technology superimposes state-of-the-art on the primitive because their psychology causes them to distrust innovation. Their conduct of business is slow, frequently illogical and frustrating to Westerners. But it is a culture undergoing rapid change in response to both internal and external forces.

The kingdom is extremely remote and its cities are built on harsh, hot, desert sands. The distance from the United States is so great that only the special Boeing 747-SP can make the fourteen-hour flight without refueling. The harsh terrain can tear up a new set of truck tires in a day; the ever-present sand makes it almost impossible to maintain sophisticated military equipment, and the extreme heat makes metal so hot to touch that most maintenance has to be done late at night. Consequently, the United States had to create the Rapid Deployment Force with supplies based at an Indian Ocean island, to be able to provide the capability to respond to a Middle East crisis.

Saudi society is composed of proud nomadic Bedouin and their urban-dwelling sons who put tribal identification and family loyalty above all else. The population is so small that Western companies contracted by the Saudi government have had to import millions of expatriate workers.

Islam is more strictly observed by the followers of Muhammad in Saudi Arabia than anywhere else in the world. Religion so totally dominates life that Western governments and companies find it extremely difficult to accomplish anything in the country during the annual one-hundred-day-fast and pilgrimage period which marks the observance of two of the five pillars of the faith.

The country derives its name from the al-Saud dynasty which came to power after two hundred years of tribal warfare. Saud family members select the king, run the government, and control everything that goes on in the kingdom. The distinction between the Saud family and the government is so vague that it is often referred to as "the only family-owned business in the United Nations."

Saudi Arabia's unique government is a benevolent dictatorship which totally integrates church and state. It denies personal freedoms guaranteed by Western democracies, yet provides social benefits only dreamed of in the West. Saudi Arabia is ruled by a king who has absolute power and issues royal decrees to enact regulations not covered by Islamic law. It is also a government that had to clean up its act after a period of total corruption and bureaucratic incompetence.

Rather than a constitution, the law of the land is the Islamic Sharia which governs the lives of Saudis and expatriates alike. It is a harsh legal system in which the accused is guilty until proven innocent, and many acts considered legal in the West are serious crimes, subject to punishments which are banned in the West.

The Saudis pride themselves on having a way with words when speaking the complex, exaggerative Arabic language. Arabic, with its strange hypnotic quality, has not changed for fourteen centuries, cannot be directly translated to or from English, and is the source of frequent contract disputes between Saudis and Westerners.

During the past twenty years, the Saudi economy has gone from rags to riches. In 1964, the kingdom's revenues were less than $400 million a year, its cities were connected only by markers in the sand, and its people were dirt poor. By 1981, its oil revenues had reached $400 million a day, it had a nationwide network of roads, and one of the highest per capita incomes in the world. But as the kingdom increased its revenues at a fantastic rate, it caused worldwide, double-digit inflation and almost destroyed the global economy.

While the Saudi economy mushroomed, it delicately balanced its foreign affairs. As an Islamic country, it sides with its Islamic neighbors in a continuous cold war with Israel by boycotting Western products related to Jewish interests and occasionally embargoing oil shipments to countries which support Israel. Yet its participation in Arab-Israeli wars has been minimal, and it continually seeks the latest military weaponry from the United States to defend itself from its Islamic neighbors.

During the economic boom, Saudi Arabia bought hundreds of billions of dollars worth of complex, state-of-the-art technical equipment, but its people were so illiterate that the kingdom had to depend on expatriates to operate it. The Bedouin lacked the knowledge and skills required to function in an industrial society and no schools existed to train them. Their need to know how to use modern technology was so great that the Saudi government began an education program to train the entire population in twentieth-century skills.

The installation of massive amounts of high technology in a seventh-century environment produced a strange mixture of old and new, where Cadillacs are driven with the same reckless abandon as camels. It is a land where the 6,400-year-old lunar calendar is used to coordinate communications with a satellite system launched from the American space shuttle by a Saudi prince, and royal prayers for rain are coordinated with the kingdom's meteorological computer center to assure their success. The rate of acquisition of technology is so rapid that the kingdom lacks the capability to use and repair it.

The Saudis' lack of technological skills is a result of their mind set, derived from their Bedouin heritage and religious conservatism. The religious conservatives reject innovative ideas, such as the earth being round, as deviations from the true faith while maintaining their Bedouin distrust of strangers who would attempt to convince them otherwise. Their Bedouin pride prevents them from admitting they are wrong. Their mind set compounds the problems of Western organizations and technicians brought to the country to implement complex modernization projects.

In fact, Saudi business is done with such slowness and is so frustrating to Westerners, that the first Arabic words they learn are *enshAllah bukra* (if Allah wills, [it will get done] tomorrow). The lack of a trained work force, support services, accurate information, and Saudi managerial skills, cause many projects to take three times as much money and effort to complete as they would in the United States. Consequently, many Fortune 500 companies abandoned their attempts to enter the market. The culture shock is so great that over one-third of the Westerners, who go there to get rich, quit before the expiration of their one- or two-year contracts. Many quit during the first week.

The winds of change which profoundly altered Saudi Arabia in the recent past will continue in the future in response to numerous forces. Saudi Arabia must deal with the greed and envy of its neighboring Arab countries, continue its role as an Islamic leader, respond to the pressures of the Organization of Petroleum Exporting Countries (OPEC) and the industrialized world, and continue its plans to become totally self-sufficient. It must also deal with internal pressures to become more westernized, democratic, and secular.

Until twenty years ago, the behavior and actions of Saudi Arabia were of little interest to the West. Now the way the Saudis think, express themselves, act, live, work, and solve problems is suddenly significant. What Saudi Arabia does can affect the future of the entire world!

Chapter 2

CITIES IN SAND

*S*audi Arabia contains some of the harshest, bleakest desert and mountain terrain in the world. It has no permanent rivers or lakes and has only occasional water holes and wadis, or dry river beds. Yet despite its severity, it has a serene type of beauty: a timeless quiet in which the brightness of the sands is contrasted against the starkness of the mountains and blue cloudless skies, where the moon and stars appear in crystal clarity when the darkness of night quickly overtakes the blazing sun.

The kingdom is in the center of what geographers call the Middle East, but the United States State De-

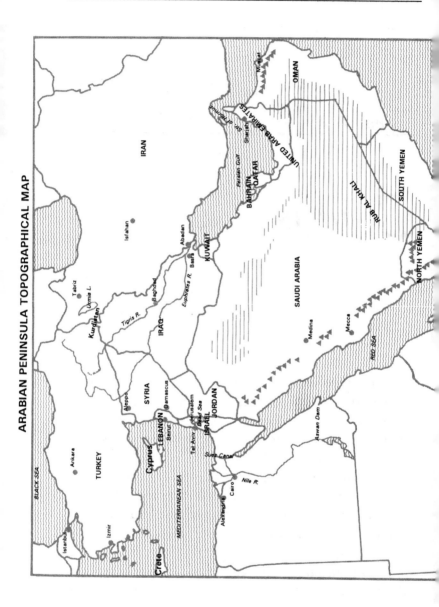

ARABIAN PENINSULA TOPOGRAPHICAL MAP

partment calls the Near East. The region includes the countries of southwest Asia and north Africa and is usually meant to describe the countries from Libya on the west to Afghanistan on the east.

Saudi Arabia is southeast of Europe, northeast of Africa and southwest of Asia. Its nearest borders are about eight thousand miles from the United States, eight hundred miles from Russia, sixteen hundred miles from China and about twelve hundred miles from both Italy and India. Politically, the country is bounded on the north by Jordan and Iraq, on the northeast by Kuwait, to the southeast by Qatar and the United Arab Emirates and to the south by Oman and Yemen. It occupies four-fifths of the Arabian peninsula; a wedge-shaped subcontinent bounded on the west by the Red Sea, on the south by the Arabian Sea and on much of the east by the Persian Gulf. The northwestern part of the peninsula extends to the Mediterranean Sea and forms a land bridge between the continents of Africa and Asia. The northern tip of the peninsula and the land to the northeast is known as the Fertile Crescent because of its numerous rivers and the cool breezes which blow from the Mediterranean Sea.

The kingdom of Saudi Arabia, containing an area of 873,000 square miles, is equal in size to the eastern United States and is almost as large as Europe. The jagged Hejaz mountain range runs parallel to the Red Sea and reaches its greatest height of thirteen thousand feet in the southwestern corner of the peninsula. The base of the Hejaz mountains juts further southwest toward Africa to choke off the Red Sea at the twenty-mile wide Strait of Bab al-Mandab. A lower range of bare mountains cuts across the southern part of the peninsula parallel to the Arabian Sea, flattens, and curves north along the eastern coast where it rises to ten thousand feet. The edge of this range reaches into the sea toward Iran and almost closes the Persian Gulf at the thirty-mile-wide Strait of Hormuz. The southern interior third of the country consists of the largest desert of towering, windblown sand dunes in the world. The Saudis call it Rub al-Khali (the empty quarter).

The central portion of the peninsula, Nadj, is an arid, eroded plateau which gradually slopes from west to east. Coastal plains are adjacent to the Red Sea and the Arabian Sea, while the coast of the Persian Gulf consists of mud flats, salt marshes, and mangrove swamps. The Red Sea, formed by continental drift, is very deep but filled with treacherous coral reefs. The Persian Gulf is shallow, filled with silt from the Tigris and Euphrates rivers, and is strewn with sandbars and reefs.

Saudi Arabia is effectively an island. It is surrounded on three sides by water and cut off from the Fertile Crescent in the north by desert sands and barren rocks. In the days of sail, the seas surrounding Arabia were formidable barriers, the Gulf of Aqaba to the northwest is 20 miles wide and the Red Sea and Persian Gulf are about 120 to 150 miles wide. With jet aircraft and modern ships, the seas are no longer a barrier. Dhahran is about 120 miles from Iran, Jeddah is 120 miles from Sudan and 250 miles from both Egypt and Ethiopia.

Over 90 percent of the land is too arid for cultivation and it is scorchingly hot. During the day, temperatures can reach 165°F in the sun and over 125°F in the shade. At night, in the winter, it can dip to 30°F. Rain is scarce in central Arabia. Some parts receive two to six inches per year; other parts do not get any. It is usually years between rains in the Rub al-Khali desert. There is little life other than in isolated areas where ground water is near the surface in wadis or oases, where date palms and grass grow. The rest of the land is baked dirt, rock, and sand with only occasional stunted tamarisk and acacia trees and prickly saltbushes to break the monotony. Somehow sand cats, oryx, cheetahs, leopards, and badgers manage to find food to survive. Scorpions, vipers, cobras, rats, jackals, and birds also manage. Camels thrive and wander aimlessly through rock and sand, and across roads in front of speeding vehicles.

The southwestern mountainous tip of the subcontinent receives rain from monsoons blowing off the Indian Ocean. The rains make this region relatively fertile and green with juniper and wild olive trees growing on the slopes. From October through April, the winds blow steadily from the northeast. In May, the winds change direction and become stronger. By June, they blow from the southwest at gale force. Then they moderate and continue to blow from the southwest until September when the direction begins to change back to the northeast.

During late spring and early summer when the winds blow from the north, suffocating sand and dust storms called *shammals* spring up and carry dust thousands of feet in the air. The brown dust clouds reduce visibility to several yards and penetrate everything, leaving gritty silt. When the wind blows from offshore, it absorbs the moisture from the Red Sea and Persian Gulf and causes swamp-like humidity in Jeddah, Dhahran, and other nearby land areas.

Saudi Arabia is divided into five major administrative provinces: the northern, the central (Nadj), eastern (al-Hasa), western (Hejaz) and southern (Asir). Its population is clustered into two large cities, three smaller cities, several large towns, and villages.

Its largest city, Riyadh, has the highest urban growth rate in the world, and is expanding northward at the rate of two miles per year. It now has a population of about 1.7 million. Its mud houses and modern twenty-story office buildings are located on the high desert plateau inland in the east central part of the country. Its name means "the gardens" because of the palm groves and wells in the area. Riyadh is the capital and financial center of Saudi Arabia and contains most of the kingdom's new government offices and supporting organizations.

The second largest city, Jeddah, is thought to have been founded by Phoenicians in 2000 B.C. and has an estimated population of about one million. It sits on the Tihama coastal plain adjacent to the Red Sea in the west central part of the country about 500 miles west of Riyadh. Jeddah, with its modern high-rise office buildings, neon signs, shopping malls, and beautiful palaces, also contains picturesque shuttered houses built of teak and coral blocks. It is a seaport, the official port of entry for pilgrimages to Mecca, and the commercial capital of the kingdom. The bustling city of Jeddah is also the site of a forty-foot-long grave claimed to hold the remains of Eve, the mother of mankind.

Mecca, with its 460,000 inhabitants, is the religious center of the Islamic world and site of the forty-acre Grand Mosque which can hold 320,000 persons at prayer. It lies in the desert foothills adjacent to the Hejaz escarpment, about 40 miles inland southeast of Jeddah.

The prophet and founder of Islam, Muhammad, is buried at Medina, another religious center. With an estimated population of 320,000, it is located inland on a fertile plain 220 miles north of Jeddah.

Perched in the cool mountains a mile above sea level, just east of Mecca, is Taif, with a population of 250,000. It is an agricultural area with ancient stone watch towers, mud houses, and splendid new hotels and government buildings used as the Saudi capital during the summer.

Abha has around 40,000 people and is located high in the rugged mountains about 300 miles south of Jeddah. It is an agricultural center of terraced farms, and houses made of mud with horizontal rows of projecting stones. The residents share the area with tribes of baboons which raid the farms and throw rocks at people. Abha is just east of and above the Asir national park on the coastal plain.

Jizan, with its conical mud buildings, has a population of about 25,000. It is a small port, fishing center, and farming community situated on the Red Sea coastal plain about 375 miles south of Jeddah at the southern tip of the kingdom.

Dammam, al-Khobar, and Dhahran are adjacent modern cities with a combined population of 250,000. They are located in the coastal plain next to the Persian Gulf in the oil production and distribution area, about 230 miles from Riyadh. Dammam is the main Persian Gulf port and is near Ras Tunurah, the world's largest deep water port. Al-Khobar is a major trade center. Dhahran is the site of the headquarters of Aramco which, with its 55,000 employees, is almost a separate country; so much so, that its employees refer to themselves as "Aramcons" rather than Americans or Saudis. Dhahran is also the home of the University of Petroleum and Minerals, located on the highest Saudi point on the Persian Gulf, 350 feet above sea level.

Hofuf is a major agricultural area with about 100,000 people, found at an oasis in the al-Hasa province about 100 miles southwest of Dhahran.

During the last decade, millions of tons of sand were moved at the small fishing village of Yanbu to enable the development of a major $40 billion industrial city with a population of 100,000. It is located on the coastal plain adjacent to the Red Sea, about 220 miles north of Jeddah.

A billion cubic yards of sand were excavated at Jubail during the same period, to enable the creation of another major $40 billion industrial city next to the Persian Gulf, about 75 miles north of Dammam. By 1995, it is expected to have a population of about 90,000.

A third extensive construction effort in the sand created King Khalid Military City as a major base to protect the kingdom's northern borders. Located inland about 200 miles north of Riyadh, it contains training areas, barracks, armories, an air base, civilian housing, schools, hospitals, and supporting infrastructure to accommodate 70,000 people.

The cities are linked together and to neighboring countries by a 57,000-mile network of new highways and paved roads. Modern roads connect Jeddah, Riyadh, and Dhahran, run up the west coast from Yemen to Yanbu, parallel the Persian Gulf from Kuwait to Qatar, skirt the Rub al-Khali desert from Abha to Riyadh, and connect the capital with Jordan through al-Buraydah, Medina, and Tabuk.

Jeddah, Riyadh, and Dhahran are served by large international airports, and twenty smaller cities have domestic airports. Saudi Arabia also has three seaports on the Persian Gulf at Dammam, Ras Tunnurah, and Jubail, and five on the Red Sea at Jizan, Jeddah, Rabeigh, Yanbu, and al-Wejh. In addition, it has a railroad which runs from Dammam to Riyadh.

The area south of Dhahran to Harad contains the world's largest oil field, whose flares can be seen for 50 miles at night as they burn off unused natural gas.

SAUDI ARABIA

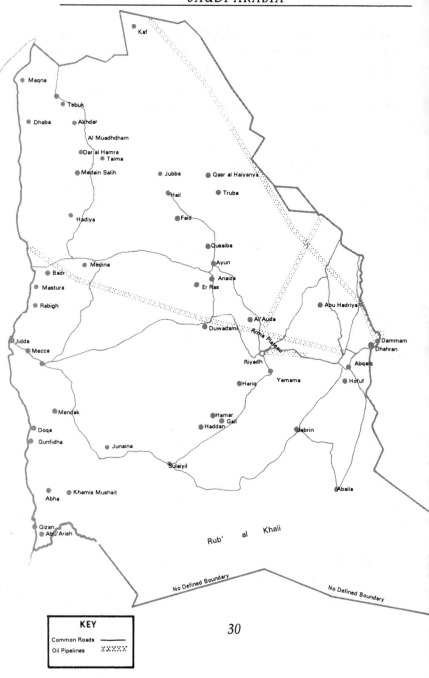

Kaf

Maqna

Tebuk

Dhaba   Akhdar

Al Muadhdham

Dar al Hamra
Taima

Medain Salih   Jubba   Qasr al Haiyanya

Hail   Truba

Hadiya   Faid

Qusaiba

Medina   Ayun

Badr   Anaiza

Mastura   Er Ras

Rabigh   Abu Hadriya

Al Auda

Duwadami   Arma Plateau   Dammam
Dhahran

Jidda   Riyadh   Abqaiq

Mecca   Yamama   Hofuf

Harig

Mendak   Hamar
Gail
Doqa   Haddan   Jabrin

Qunfidha   Junaina

Sulaiyil

Abha   Khamis Mushait   Abaila

Qizan
Abu'Arish   Rub'   al   Khali

No Defined Boundary   No Defined Boundary

30

KEY
Common Roads ———
Oil Pipelines xxxxx

SAUDI ARABIAN POLITICAL MAP

Pipelines stretch from the oil producing center of the eastern province to refineries at Riyadh, Ras Tunnurah, Jubail and under the Gulf to Bahrain. Another pipeline stretches 1,000 miles to the Mediterranean Sea while two others cross the peninsula to Yanbu.

Between these areas, Bedouin tribes continually move their flocks of sheep and camel herds five to ten miles per day in search of muddy water and patches of grass as they have done for the past four thousand years.

Chapter 3

*B*EDOUIN SONS

*A*t first sight, Saudi society has the visual impact of a biblical movie with men wearing scarves on their heads and white flowing robes, and ladies swathed in black showing only their dark eyes. The similarity ends with the sight of Cadillacs, Mercedes-Benzes, and high-rise hotels. It is a society of people practicing traditional Bedouin customs, and foreigners building things the local people have never seen before.

In appearance, most Saudis are olive-skinned with black, wavy hair; but descendents of captured

Crusaders may have blond hair and blue eyes, and those of African ancestry are dark and negroid.

Saudis are officially discouraged from wearing Western clothes in the kingdom, and usually wear their traditional dress. The men wear loose fitting *thobes* which allow maximum air circulation for cooling. Thobes are plain white, ankle-length, long-sleeved shirts buttoned at the neck. On their heads, they wear white skull caps over which they wear *gutras* (white cotton or red-and-white-checked wool head cloths). The gutras are held in place by *agals* (black, doubled-rope-looking rings). They wear leather sandals, held to their big toes by large loops. In winter, they may wear Western sport coats or brown or black wool cloaks with gold-braided edges, called *mishlahs*, over their thobes. Saudi men wear very little jewelry, but often wear solid gold watches and carry small strings of worry beads.

The Saudi clothing is impractical for heavy manual labor. Thobes restrict men's movements and have to be held up to enable them to climb steps. Gutras restrict peripheral vision, and the ends can get caught in machinery. The leather sandals flap as they walk and provide little protection for the feet. Foreign contractors have insisted that Saudis wear Western clothes for their protection while working in construction and around heavy equipment. Yet, they often wear gutras under their safety helmets or wear sandals while moving heavy objects.

Saudi women wear black cloaks or capes called *abayas* over their heads, which cover their entire bodies. Most women also wear black translucent veils over their faces, a custom the Ottoman Turks introduced to Arabia. The women wear their black capes and veils even when sitting in the sun on a public beach with their families. The custom of wearing veils is not practiced in the southern Asir province and is more relaxed in Jeddah than in conservative Riyadh. Saudi women wear gold necklaces, bracelets, and rings; and occasionally, Westerners notice spiked heels and designer jeans under the abayas.

The clothing presents a peculiar problem to Westerners: all Saudis look alike. Since all men wear identical white clothing which covers everything except their faces, hands, and feet, differences in hair color or length, types of clothing or other distinguishing features are not noticeable. From the back it is impossible, and from the side it is difficult, to identify a Saudi. Expatriates gradually start studying the Saudis' builds, facial shapes, skin colors, and types of mustaches and beards to be able to identify one from the other. Since the women are totally covered, the only thing Westerners can tell is their relative height. The inability to quickly recognize Saudis in group situations frequently leads to embarrassing moments. During the opening ceremonies of the new Jeddah airport, a Western consul spent five minutes referring to a bodyguard as "Your Royal Highness" before the crown prince arrived.

Although it is hard to tell from the way they are dressed, Saudi society has four classes of people, with an extreme range of class difference. Sunni Muslims are distributed between a very small upper class, a small but rapidly growing middle class, and a large lower class. An even lower social class is formed by the 250,000 Shiite Muslims that live in the eastern province. The royal family and rich merchant upper class live in huge palaces and grand estates. The administrative, professional, and merchant middle class live in small to medium-sized apartments and villas. The Bedouin farmers, taxicab drivers, and truck drivers of the lower class live in tents, tin-can shanties, and mud-brick houses. The Shiites live in a range of middle and lower class housing.

The Shiites are not trusted by the government and are regarded as the lowest class because of their extremist beliefs, political instability, and trouble making. Every year on the anniversary of the death of their sect's founder, they mourn with self-flagellation, demonstration, and riot. The Shiites have disrupted oil production, looted banks, burned cars, and shot it out with the police.

Somewhere between 7 and 10 million Saudis live in the parched land, but nobody really knows how many there are. In 1962, the government guessed that the population was 3.3 million. In 1973, the government tried to conduct a census and came up with a population of 5.9 million. For some unknown reason, an official government publication quoted the population in 1975 as 7,012,642! However, Western experts estimate the Saudi population to be under 10,000,000. The different population estimates create further enormous statistical errors.

The Saudis are shifting from herding to higher paying professions. In 1974, half the Saudi labor force worked in agriculture, but many Bedouin have since left to take construction jobs. The government recently estimated that there are about 1.5 million Saudis in the labor force: about 425,000 are in agriculture; 315,000 in construction; 210,000 in commerce; 190,000 in services; 100,000 in transportation and communication; 45,000 in manufacturing; 45,000 in mining; and 20,000 are employed by utilities. The government itself employs about 275,000 Saudis: 85,000 are in administration; 62,000 in education; 20,000 in health fields; and 110,000 in the military.

Since 1980, the shift in professions caused rapid urban growth. The proportion of the population living in cities and towns has increased from 35 to 60 percent as the Bedouin have left the desert.

The Bedouin way of life began evolving before the first settled civilizations appeared within walking distance of the desert dwellers.

Primitive men lived near lakes and streams during the Ice Age in what is now Rub al-Khali Desert. As the water vanished, the people moved to the shore of the Persian Gulf near what is now Dhahran, which some archaeologists believe might have been biblical Eden. About seven thousand years ago, they came into contact and traded with the Ubayds who lived in the north by the Euphrates River in what is now Iraq.

Around 4000 B.C., the Ubayds evolved into the Sumerian civilization. Within a few hundred years, the Egyptians happened along the Nile River and shortly after, the Harappan civilization appeared near the Indus River in what is now Pakistan. Around 2500 B.C., these civilizations made dams and canals to irrigate fertile farm lands and built cities of permanent houses. The Sumerians built the walled cities of Ur and Erech; the Egyptians built Memphis; and the Harappans built Mohenjo-Dara and Harappa.

As the civilized people farmed the lands and built their cities, they invented the wheel and ox-drawn carts. They made kilns to fire pottery and smelt metal and fashioned tools and weapons out of copper and bronze. They made jewelry of silver and gold. They divided their labors and bartered their services to each other and soon specialized in farming, raising cattle, firing bricks, constructing houses, building boats, crafting jewelry, and making tools and weapons.

Then, they developed written languages. The Sumerians and Harappans used pictographs to illustrate ideas. Later, the Sumerian pictographs turned into cuneiform writing with wedge-shaped characters which they recorded on clay tablets. The Egyptians refined the pictographs into standard hieroglyphic characters which they wrote on paper made from strips of wet papyrus.

The civilizations began studying the nature of things and recording their findings. They studied the heavens and used the stars to help them navigate at night. They learned how to count, calculate and keep track of time. The Sumerians developed a 354-day lunar calendar that started circa 4400 B.C., and the

Egyptians invented the solar calendar. Within a short period, they began to teach their knowledge to others and developed great libraries of technical and historical knowledge.

They evolved as organized societies of ruling kings and developed beliefs in systems of gods which they held responsible for anything that they did not understand. The Sumerians worshipped a supreme god called Baal; the Egyptians held a supreme god named Ammon; and the Harappans believed in a supreme mother goddess called Shakti. The ruling monarchies integrated religious beliefs with their laws and promised good fortune and eternal life to those who complied. The religions soon provided the divine justification of their right to rule and spiritual rationale for their laws.

When their religious beliefs became more structured and their technology improved, the civilizations used their highly developed skills and organizational abilities to build great temples to their gods. The Sumerians built huge, brick pyramids called ziggurats. The Egyptians built an enormous statue of the sphinx and a smooth-sided pyramid which is still the largest stone building in the world. The Harappans built a holy city filled with brick temples.

As these civilizations became more advanced, their demands for other commodities increased and merchant traders traveled greater distances to meet those needs.

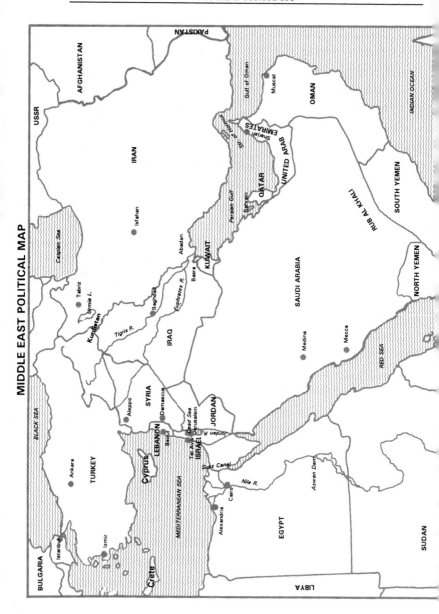

MIDDLE EAST POLITICAL MAP

The traders used their ability to navigate, and knowledge of the monsoon cycle of changing wind direction to sail great distances. The Sumerians sailed through the Persian Gulf and the Egyptians sailed through the treacherous Red Sea to trade with the Harappans and each other. During their travels, the sophisticated Sumerians traded with the primitive people who lived on the shores of the Arabian Peninsula.

Some of the primitive people on the Arabian peninsula settled in small villages. In the east, they lived in mud huts by oases. They lived off dates from palm trees, farmed small plots of land irrigated with water carried from the oases, and fished in the Persian Gulf. A few exchanged water and dates with Sumerian traders for metal knives, pottery, and spices. In the southwest, a different people clustered together in small villages of mud and stone huts which shielded them from the monsoon rains. These people dug shallow wells to get water trapped after monsoons drenched the mountains. They harvested wild seeds and resins from trees and used rocks to make walls for narrow hillside terraces where they farmed vegetables and spices. The remainder of the people of the Arabian peninsula were simple nomads.

While the Sumerians, Egyptians and Harappans tilled their rich irrigated soil and developed their sophisticated societies, the people of central Arabia had to take what little they could get from the parched earth. They were unable to settle and build cities, evolve divisions of labor, develop a written language and bodies of knowledge, or create elaborate religions.

The nomads had to continually move their herds of sheep, goats and camels from water hole to water hole to find grass to feed their animals. They lived in black goat hair tents with sides which were opened during the day to allow ventilation and closed at night to hold in the warmth. The tents were partitioned in the middle to provide living quarters for the men on one side and space for women, children, baggage, food and cooking on the other. These people endured the burning-hot sun, wind-blown sand, freezing-cold nights, hunger, and thirst. Often, they went for months without water, living only on milk, butter, cheese, yogurt, and dates. They had no means to improve their environment and took no aspect of survival for granted.

By around 2500 B.C., some of the nomads had tamed camels. The socially superior Bedouin, whose name comes from the Aramaic word *badawiyin*, revolved their lives around the animals. These people comprised large, highly mobile, warlike tribes who took pride in their herds of camels and their ability to extort tribute from weaker tribes and enforce claims to water holes and oases. The socially lower, yet respectable, sheep and goat herdsmen had smaller tribes and were often clients of the Bedouin. At the bottom of the social scale were groups of slaves, itinerants, and lowly born who served as artisans and servants. They were treated as inferiors by the well-born tribes who would not intermarry with them or consider them as equals in combat. However, as a group, all levels of nomads despised villagers.

The villagers, who were tied down to tiny plots of land on which they worked hard to raise their food, likewise hated the nomads. The nomads, especially the Bedouin, frequently attacked the villagers to steal their food. The villagers surrounded their small houses with high mud walls for protection from Bedouin attack. When the Bedouin were unable to take what they wanted, they traded meat, wool, milk and camels with the villagers for fruit and vegetables, and goods made from metal, wood, and textiles. The villagers practiced the customs of the Bedouin, but the Bedouin rejected the ideas acquired by the coastal villagers during their trade with other peoples.

The Bedouin's life depended on their camels. The camels, from the Aramaic word *jamal*, were single-humped dromedaries which could go without water for six weeks in the winter and three days in the heat of summer. The camels drank twenty-five gallons of water at a time and stored great quantities of liquid in their stomachs. If forced to desperation, the Bedouin cut open the stomachs of their camels and drank the liquid to survive. The females were prized for their greater endurance, but on special occasions a young male camel was roasted for a feast. Nothing was wasted. The camel's hair was used for making rope and cloth. Its skin was used to make water bags, its dung was used as fuel for fires and medicinal purposes and its urine was used as shampoo. The Bedouin also depended on the camel for their livelihood. Each family raised twenty to fifty camels per year for trade. If the weather was good, they prospered. If it was bad, they raided more fortunate tribes and stole their camels.

Because of the camels' speed and infrequent need for water, the Bedouin ventured deep into the desert and ranged over large territories. In summer, large groups of Bedouin camped at tribally owned wells and in winter, they split into smaller groups and camped deep in the desert which provided pasturage after the fall rains. Often, their migrations covered two thousand miles per year.

The family was the basic unit of existence. A man could not survive alone, but a larger group could scarcely be supported by the harsh terrain. The members of the family unit were dependent on each other for their very existence. They had to trust each other, but they did not trust anyone else.

Families were dominated by men, and groups of related families were ruled by male heads of clans. The men fought battles, hunted, tended animals, and socialized with men of other families. The women lived together closely, as the men were often away, and pitched the tents, gathered firewood, prepared food, and raised the small children. They wove hair cloth and made it into rugs, tents, and saddle bags. They also treated animal skins and made them into water bags, buckets, camel troughs, cradles, and saddles.

Male children were necessary for continuance of the families and were given preferential treatment from birth. Female children were an accessory. If the male-female balance of the family was threatened, newborn females were buried alive.

When the male child was about four, his father eased him into the men's world to develop his character. The boy had his own way while under the care of his mother, whose basic task was to give him what he wanted and make him happy. The men's world was very different. The boy had to learn to serve his father and to obey his commands. He learned that although all females were supposed to do his bidding, all men older than he, including brothers or cousins, were his superiors. He also learned that he could treat boys younger than he as inferiors, although not quite as inferior as women. It took years for the boy to adjust from being spoiled by his mother to assuming his role in the men's world. In the meantime, the father whipped or slashed the boy with a knife to discipline him and harden him for his future life. The boy was expected to acquire courage by learning not to show fear of punishment or pain.

Courage was important because the Bedouin had to protect himself from attack in order to survive. This was achieved with the support of his family. His survival was based on family cohesion, solidarity, and shared responsibility. To have family support, the Bedouin had to adopt the family's code and values to the extent that he identified his own interests and loyalties with those of the family. The older the Bedouin became, the more he felt the pressure to conform. Older men eventually became sheikhs, the heads of families or clans, and had to set the example of how younger men should act.

Families grew into extended family networks or clans of several generations. When an old sheikh died, each of his married sons became the leader of a new family unit which in turn would grow into a clan. Each clan took the name of an ancestor, and the name of the family was preceded by the word *al* (the). As the number of clans grew, they comprised a tribe of related families headed by a tribal sheikh. If a tribe grew large enough, part of it left and became an independent tribe. Whenever a tribe divided, one part kept the ancestor's lineage name and the other adopted a new name. So, all tribal groups consisted of a lineage stock and related families. The Bedouin identified with, and took great pride in, his lineage name. Since the beliefs and politics of tribes were associated with their lineage, the Bedouin made sure to learn the details of his ancestry so that he did not get killed by his grandfather's enemy.

A tribal sheikh was selected from among the lineage segment of the tribal group. He was generally the oldest or most important member who was chosen by close kinsmen and approved of by the rest of the tribesmen. But a younger son or nephew with luck, superior intelligence, or better fighting ability could be chosen over a less-qualified older son. When several strong candidates wanted to be sheikh, the followers of the challengers often formed separate new tribes. Those who remained were expected to be devoted to the new leader.

The sheikh ruled by consent and held his position through the strength of his personality and the wisdom of his judgments. If he lost consent of the tribe, he was deposed. The sheikh exerted his influence over the tribesmen as the leader of the *majlis* (council). The sheikhs held daily open sessions during which tribesmen discussed all matters of importance, and individuals appeared to present problems, or state grievances. It was the duty of the majlis to solve problems, settle disputes, and make tribal decisions. The clan majlis included all adult males, but the most senior and respected members had the greatest influence. It was the sheikh's job to try to obtain a consensus. When disputes could not be settled within the clan, they were referred to a majlis at the tribal level which was composed of representatives of all the family units.

Tribal law was based on the principle of recompensing the victim, rather than punishing the criminal. It was a principle which led to a tendency to argue and haggle over the value of things while having little regard for the feelings or rights of others. Two witnesses were required to establish guilt. If that failed, the accused was subject to trial by ordeal, such as walking on hot coals.

Loyalties and rivalries were so intense that even closely related tribes were frequently at war over access to water, or engaged in blood feuds.

Conflicts within tribes could often be mediated by individuals who had blood ties in both groups, but conflicts between tribes were not usually settled through negotiation. They were settled through blood feuds carried out by the *khamsah* (group of five). The khamsah consisted of a man's kin through five degrees of relationship, including relatives as remote as second cousin. If a man was murdered, his relatives in the khamsah were expected to retaliate. The members of the offender's khamsah, who shared collective responsibility for his acts, could legitimately be killed in revenge. The offender and his khamsah normally fled to seek refuge with a distant tribe, from where they tried to arrange payment of blood money after the victim's khamsah cooled off.

Bedouin tribes claimed territories in which they had exclusive use of pasturage and water. Family lineages within each tribal group owned wells or oases where members of the lineage families settled and tended date trees and plants. The tribal territories could be rented by other friendly families and tribes except during extreme drought. The tribes usually tried to maintain a wide circle of friendly relations to have maximum available resources in time of need.

However, Bedouin alliances were fickle; they were made and abandoned as opportunity presented itself. Tribes united against a common foe could quickly begin fighting among themselves.

They took great pride in demonstrating their manhood and bravery by the good clean fun of stealing from each other. Their favorite pastime was raiding enemy tribes and carrying off their herds of camels and horses. All able-bodied men and boys participated in the raids which were usually held in the spring when there was grass for grazing. The raids took several months and covered very long distances to make it difficult for their victims to retaliate. When raids were successful, the spoils were divided among the raiders during the victory celebration. Songs were improvised that grew into legends describing the cunning and bravery of the raiders. Often, the herds were stolen right back in counter raids by the victims.

Raiding and tribal warfare followed a strict set of rules based on the Bedouin sense of fair play. Raids could only be made after a declaration of war and only on those who could fight back. Raids were not conducted between midnight and sunrise, as a man's soul was supposed to have departed from his body while he slept. Bedouin were expected to run, if outnumbered, rather than stand and fight. It was forbidden to kill the wounded or prisoners. Women and children were spared and often given stolen camels to ride to the safety of another tribe.

The Bedouin were feared and respected, and their values served as the ideal for all other peoples of the Arabian peninsula. Their values were expressed in proverbs such as, "Better to die with honor than to live in humiliation," and "Nothing humiliates a man like being subject to someone else's authority."

They were the original macho men and had a very strong, complex sense of honor. It was honorable to display loyalty to the family, and to be virile and have many sons. It was honorable to do work that would not dirty the hands; but it was dishonorable to engage in dirty manual labor, such as farming. It was honorable to participate in raids, to be brave, and to defend oneself. It was also honorable to behave with dignity, and be hospitable and generous.

The male Bedouin wore his honor like a suit of armor, with face being its outward appearance. He hid his weaknesses, risked danger, and endured pain to prevent loss of face. He had to save face at all costs. If he did something dishonorable, he could save face by keeping it secret; but if it became known, his face was blackened (lost). Therefore, lying was justified to save face, and it was a duty to save somebody else's face. If the Bedouin lost face, it reduced his self-respect; so great efforts were needed to restore honor if it was lost.

Honor was the collective property of the family. If any family member brought dishonor on himself, the whole family was disgraced. It was the duty of the men of the family to assure that no member committed an act which would disgrace them. They had to govern their own behavior and protect the sexual honor of the family's women. If a man's dignity was threatened by a woman's loss of honor, her brothers and father had to kill her to remove the stigma from the family. They would then try to kill her lover to take blood revenge on him for causing the death of a member of their family. This led to many bloody tribal feuds over insults or slights to women.

The Bedouin's self-respect was so sensitive that he was extremely wary of being slighted and often imagined personal insults where none were intended. To restore his dignity, he put up a great show of reaction and erased slights with appropriate revenge. By defending his dignity, he compelled others to respect him, thereby restoring his self-respect. The Bedouin did not allow anybody to insult him and get away with it.

Since the Bedouin needed respect, he tried to do things to impress others. The easiest way of earning respect was to be hospitable. The Bedouin was judged by his graciousness and generosity as a host. The guests were expected to accept invitations and gifts to avoid a show of disrespect. Hospitality to a guest was an absolute duty. The Bedouin had to display his generosity even if it meant that he had to kill his last camel to serve his guests. If a stranger, or even an enemy, accepted an invitation to a meal, the Bedouin regarded it as his duty to protect the guest's life with his own.

As Bedouin tribes slowly expanded in central Arabia, other Bedouin migrated north and absorbed the culture of the Sumerians. They formed a rival kingdom called Akkad and around 2350 B.C. the Akkadians warred against Sumeria and took control of Mesopotamia. The Akkadians melded with the Sumerians and by 2000 B.C., they developed a more advanced civilization centered in Babylon.

Around 1200 B.C., the Sabaean civilization evolved in the southwestern mountainous region of Arabia, known as Saba (Sheba). The Sabaeans built large stone dams and irrigation systems which enabled them to raise cereals, myrrh, incense, coffee, and other spices. The Sabaeans migrated east along the Arabian Sea to settle in what is now Yemen and Oman, and west across the Red Sea to settle in what is now called Ethiopia. Saba grew into an important commercial center around 950 B.C. and traded with countries as far north as Israel.

The Sabaeans were referred to in the Bible as "Arabs of the South" and traced their ancestors back to Himyar. They lived in densely populated towns and spoke an Amharic language. The Bedouin were called "Northern Arabs" in the biblical book of Genesis. The Bedouin spoke the Semitic Aramaic language and traced their ancestry to Ishmael, the outcast son of the biblical prophet Abraham. The word *Arab* first appeared in an Assyrian inscription of 853 B.C. which described a gift of camels to a group of Assyrian princes. Other Assyrian and Babylonian inscriptions record the purchase of camels from *Aribi* and *Aribu* rulers and tell of raids into the Aribi land. During the sixth century B.C., the Persians began to refer to the peninsula as *Arabaya*.

Ancient traders landed their ships from the Indus valley and Africa at a harbor at the southern tip of the Arabian peninsula (now called Aden). The goods were carried overland through the mountains to Saba for trade. The southern Arab merchants relied on the camel caravans of the northern Arab Bedouin to carry their cargos of spices to the markets of the Fertile Crescent. The Bedouin organized caravans of hundreds of camels and developed a network of routes through the deserts. The main route led from Saba through the mountains to the desert town of Najran, through Mecca and Yathrib (now called Medina) and via different branches into Damascus, Israel, and across Sinai into Egypt. Other routes branched off at Mecca and ran northeast to Babylon, Mesopotamia, and the Persian Gulf.

The Bedouin caravan camps at the northern edge of the Arabian desert became permanent around 800 B.C. and evolved into the Nabataean civilization. The Nabataeans controlled all the territory from Yathrib to Damascus and Palmyra (in what is now Syria). They carved their capital, Petra, in the cliffs of an almost inaccessible valley in the Jordanian desert, and carved another large town called Madain Salih in cliffs two hundred miles north of Yathrib. The Nabataean cities controlled the northern caravan routes and became major commercial centers. They charged caravans for safe passage through their territory and sold them water and supplies.

As the years passed, the Nabataean civilization disappeared when the caravan traffic dwindled and Roman legions captured their cities. Much later, the Sabaean civilization was destroyed by earthquakes and mudslides. But the Bedouin continued to raise camels, run caravans, and raid each other. Their tribes grew larger, their beliefs grew stronger and their loyalty to their families grew more intense. Bedouin tribal identity provided the only cohesive force in the country until it became Saudi Arabia.

Although tribal influence has declined somewhat, it is still a strong unifying factor. There are about one hundred major tribes. The Anazah tribal federation which includes the 75,000-strong Rwala tribe of the Saud family is the largest and most influential. Many Bedouin sheiks live in cities and lobby for their tribes with the government to obtain subsidies and social services. Since tribal support can increase the power of princes or senior government members, great efforts are made to keep the tribesmen happy.

Family loyalty is the most powerful force. Family members take care of each other's welfare, including grandparents, aunts, uncles, and cousins. Younger members take care of the elderly and three generations often share the same house—the parents, children, married sons and their wives, and grandchildren. The Saudi is known by the family to which he belongs, and his loyalty and duty to his family are greater than any social obligation.

Saudis are very status conscious. Traditional Saudi status is based on family and age, but status is also accorded those who are wealthy or who have influential friends. However, a poor sheikh of a Nadj tribe, the ancestral home of the Saud family, is socially superior to a rich Jeddah merchant. Governmental emphasis on education has also caused the possession of a college degree, particularly an advanced degree, to accord high status.

Status is very important in the selection of marriage partners. The ideal partner is a first cousin. A Saudi proverb says, "He who marries not his cousin deserves to have only girl children." Other family or tribal members may also be desirable, but mates from other tribes are not acceptable unless they are socially equal or superior. A Saudi man cannot marry a Westerner or other non-Muslim unless she converts to Islam.

Saudis are not allowed to date, but since telephones have been installed in the kingdom, young men spend hours illegally calling their sisters' girl friends, and women call men who have slipped them notes with their phone numbers.

Parents select mates for their children since marriage is more than just the union of two people; it is the inclusion of the wife into the husband's family. Saudi women can exert tremendous influence within the family. In some cases they even rule the house. So, wife selection is very important to the entire family of the prospective groom. When a young man is deemed ready, his mother may start the search. Often, the two young people are not acquainted and do not even meet until the marriage ceremony.

When the right bride is found, the prospective groom must pay her a *mahr* (bride price) before they can be married. The bride price provides for her security in case she loses her husband. In 1982, the bride price was about fifty camels or $10,000 and thousands of young men could not afford to get married. In compassion for the frustrations of young Saudis, the government gave them the money to get married. In 1983, the price of brides had dropped to about $8,500 for virgins and $6,000 for non-virgins.

After the parents arrange the marriage, Saudis have their most important social event, a three-day wedding ceremony. On the first day, a sheep is sacrificed to bless the occasion and a women's party is held at the bride's home. Electric lights are strung from the house to the surrounding walls and the party is held outside. The women dance together to small bands, gossip, and nibble snacks. During the party, the women show off their fine dresses, hair styles, and jewelry to their friends, and mothers and sisters check out the other women as prospective partners for their sons or brothers. On the second day, there is a men's party at the groom's house. After the blessing, the men drink tea and coffee. They may watch belly dancers shimmy to the music of a small band. They may also do their traditional sword dance, singing, swaying, and swinging their sword blades to the beat of drums. That night, the marriage is consummated and afterwards, the groom holds the nuptial sheet aloft to prove her virginity and his virility to a mixed party of men and women. On the third day is the bride's party when she is given gifts, money, and gold.

Deaths are observed more somberly. A Saudi is buried on the day of his death. He is wrapped in a shroud and carried on the shoulders of his male family members and friends to the edge of the desert where he is buried in an unmarked grave.

These events occur during the early evening when it is cooler. Saudis rest during the extreme heat in the early afternoon. They stop what they are doing at the noon call to prayer and resume several hours later after the mid-afternoon call to prayer. During this period, they eat a large meal and take a nap. In the evening, after the sun sets, the cities come to life.

Saudis love to visit and talk to each other, at home, at work, and when in town to shop; so many customs have evolved around this pastime.

Coffee drinking is the leading custom. The coffee-serving ritual is a traditional form of hospitality. First, a few coffee beans are lightly roasted in a long-handled iron skillet over an open fire. After they have cooled in a wooden dish, they are ground in a stone or brass mortar and pestle. A long-spouted, brass coffee pot is filled with water, put on the fire and brought to a boil. The grounds are poured in and the water is brought to a boil three more times. The strong coffee is poured into a pot containing some ground cardamon seeds. The greenish, unsweetened coffee is then served in tiny china cups. When a guest drinks the contents, the cup is refilled until he signals that he does not want any more by holding the cup out and shaking it from side to side.

A favorite Saudi custom is to have a traditional Bedouin feast. The family and guests sit in a circle on rugs placed on the ground, with one leg curled under them and the other knee raised. They visit for a while, snacking on dates and drinking sweetened tea. They use unleavened pita bread to scoop up and eat *homus* (a paste made of garbanzo beans) and *tabullah* (a salad made of chopped lettuce, parsley, tomatoes, mint leaves, green onions, and bulgur wheat). When it is late, they feast. The main dish is a whole roast lamb, served in a brass bowl on a bed of rice pilaf mixed with raisins and pine nuts. The brass bowl is placed in the center of the rugs. The lamb's eyes are offered to the guest of honor and the guests reach in with their hands, rip off and eat pieces of the tender sweet meat. When the meal is over, the guests are given rosewater to wash their hands and face, and an incense burner is passed around for men to soak their beards in the smoke. The guests leave as soon as the meal is finished.

Another Saudi custom is smoking the *huqqah* (water pipe) which many expatriates call a "hubbly-bubbly." The huqqah has a brass water chamber that sits on the ground with a tall, ornate brass pipe rising out of it that has a small grate in a ceramic cup at its top. A long, yarn-covered wire hose with a rosewood mouthpiece connects to the chamber below the water level. After the chamber is filled with water, pieces of smoldering charcoal are put on the grate and covered with fruit and tobacco to make the pipe ready to smoke. Suction through the hose causes the smoke to be drawn down the pipe and filtered through the water before it enters the hose. The smoke is mild, yet its effects are powerful.

Saudi men smoke their huqqahs at home, in coffee shops, and in public gathering places in town, in the desert and at the edge of the sea. They sit on cushions placed atop high, sofa-like wooden benches with several other men and share the pipe. They pass the hose from man to man, always careful to point the mouthpiece away from the person to whom the hose is being passed.

In the late afternoon and evening, Saudi families take to the sidewalks surrounding park areas and beaches to enjoy the cooler evening air. They spread rugs on the sidewalks and sit and talk or play cards. On Friday afternoons, they often drive into the nearby desert for leisurely picnics.

Another custom is visiting the *suq* (bazaar). Although there are a number of Western-style, air-conditioned malls, department stores, and supermarkets in the larger cities, there is usually one main suq in the oldest section of each city. Prices are established by bargaining with the merchant, and are usually lower than in other types of stores. Suqs have hundreds of open shops or stands carrying a variety of merchandise. There are vegetable suqs, spice suqs, meat suqs, silver suqs, gold suqs, hardware suqs, junk suqs, and everything-in-between suqs.

The old suqs are labyrinths of promenades, alleys, and pathways that wind between buildings and are covered with awnings and roofs of assorted materials. The entryways frequently have little outside cafes where shoppers can enjoy a glass of tea or juice and watch the crowds. People of every description wander through the suqs jabbering in their own tongues and wearing their native dress. There are Saudi men and women of all ages in white thobes and black abayas; groups of Pakistani men in pastel-colored baggy pajamas; Yemeni men in green plaid skirts and wide leather money belts; Sudanese, Ethiopians, Eritreans, and Afghanis in robes with rags wrapped around their heads; Egyptians in safari suits; and Europeans and Americans in suits and jeans.

Tiny Yemeni men, with ropes around their foreheads, carry parcels as large as refrigerators on their backs for a few Saudi riyals. Graceful Ethiopian women with brightly colored, flowing dresses carry large baskets balanced on their heads. Young Saudi men sidle up next to Saudi girls, who are with their parents, and drop folded notes containing their names and phone numbers hoping that the girls will pick up the notes and call them.

Old money changers sit around ancient, unguarded open safes displaying hundreds of thousands of dollars worth of different currencies, including stacks of uncirculated American $100 bills. Expatriate workers from Australia to Zanzibar crowd around them and buy their native currencies for a small fee.

In the gold suqs, millions of dollars worth of beautiful eighteen and twenty-four-karat gold necklaces, bracelets, rings, coins, and bars are arranged in the windows for sale by gram weight at Zurich daily closing prices. Nearby jewelry shops glitter with solid gold, diamond-studded Rolex watches, huge diamond, emerald, and ruby rings, and other baubles. Submachine gun-armed police lean against walls trying to stay awake as they gaze at the shoppers.

Old men sit on the ground whittling little sticks of *rak* wood, about the size of a pencil, which they sell in small bunches to Saudis to use for cleaning their teeth.

In some small shops, men make and sell long-spout brass Arabian coffee pots; in others, men make water pipes. Small bakeries prepare pita bread by placing dough on top of a rounded concrete dome heated from below, so the bread falls off when it is done.

Hungry shoppers can buy a taco-like *shawarma* and watch the vendor slice pieces of beef and lamb from a blazing vertical spit, chop it up with seared tomatoes and onions and stuff it into a piece of pita bread.

In other parts of the suqs, shops filled with sacks of unground aromatic spices and exotic herbs, like frankincense, myrrh, and cinnamon, fill the air with their fragrance. Larger shops have stacks of Persian and Afghani rugs and carpets. Smaller stalls have bolts of material, suitcases of all descriptions, leather money belts, gun belts and holsters. Others sell hand-made black coral jewelry, metal boxes, brass pots, redwood tables and room dividers, as well as mass-produced Japanese stereo radios, tape cassettes and toys.

The vegetable suqs are located in large fields where vendors set up tents and cloth-covered stands, trucks unload their produce, and shoppers park their cars. Vendors hold up fruits and vegetables and shout their asking prices. When a shopper passes their stand, a nearby vendor shouts a lower price, and the first vendor may counter with an even better price. If the shopper is interested, he can pay the asked price or make a lower offer. Yemeni men follow the shoppers around and carry all their purchases.

Serious shopping is a challenge to Westerners because many stores carry strange combinations of unrelated merchandise. One store might carry perfume and radios, but no other electrical or cosmetic products. Shops also carry parts of products normally sold as complete assemblies in the United States. An American engineer bought a garden hose to wash his car and found that it had no fittings to attach it to a faucet. A Canadian doctor had to make trips to three stores to get the parts to make an electrical extension cord. He bought the wire in one store, the plug in another, and the receptacle in a third.

Western women have similar shopping adventures. They make many expeditions and experiment with a variety of foreign products to find foods to suit their tastes. When they finish shopping, their cupboards may resemble a cornucopia containing American peanut butter, English crackers, French soups, Polish sausages, German grape juice, Chinese rice, Italian tomatoes, Danish butter, Syrian water, Argentine beef, and other foods from around the world whose labels are printed in their native languages.

After shopping adventures, expatriates often dine out. In addition to Arabic foods, there are Chinese, French, Italian, and so-called American restaurants, including the Colonel's Kentucky Fried Chicken. Some of the restaurants are interesting and serve excellent food; others are incredibly bad. In Jeddah, there is an excellent Italian restaurant that bakes pizza in an open-hearth fireplace. Several blocks away, there is a great Mongolian barbecue and a good steak house. Hotels such as the Riyadh Marriott have chic and expensive dining rooms where meals are preceded by "Saudi champagne" (apple juice mixed with club soda) and strolling Filipino guitar players serenade the diners. Those with strong stomachs can try eating fiery hot Thai food or go to an Arab restaurant and try their luck eating dark, stringy camel meat.

There is a wide selection of restaurants because there is a large variety of expatriates. Around 3.5 million foreigners work in Saudi Arabia, mainly in Riyadh, Jeddah, Dhahran, Yanbu, Jubail, Taif and King Khalid Military City. The foreigners make up a large lower class and a small middle class.

The lower class foreigners are generally in the kingdom in single status and live in tents, makeshift huts, dormitories, or in crowded apartments. They do most of the unskilled, and some skilled, jobs in the kingdom. During the past decade, the bottom of the lower class was made up of over 500,000 Yemenis, 100,000 Koreans, and Chinese, Afghanis, Omanis, Ethiopians, Eritreans, Somalians, and Sudanese who are laborers, drivers, and construction workers. The top of the lower class included about 300,000 Egyptians, 200,000 Filipinos, 150,000 Pakistanis, 100,000 Palestinians, Syrians and other Arabic speaking peoples. These people were nurses, secretaries, clerks, mechanics, maintenance men, hotel employees, and food preparers.

Middle class foreigners are in married or single status and live in villas or apartments. If single, they are usually housed two or three to a dwelling. The middle class does most of the technical, professional, and managerial work in the kingdom. The bottom of the middle class consists of Indians, as well as Egyptians, Jordanians, Palestinians, and other Arabic speaking peoples with college degrees. These people are trained technicians, professionals, teachers, engineers, medical specialists, and doctors. The top of the middle class consists of about 30,000 Americans and 70,000 Canadians and Western Europeans who are senior technicians, managers, professionals, and doctors.

Expatriates of the various nationalities stick with their own people in their segregated company compounds where they have partial seclusion from the Saudi culture. Although Arabic-speaking Muslims are integrated with the Saudis, they are not accepted socially. Social acceptance comes only by being born a Saudi.

There is limited social interaction between Saudis and foreigners at the same class level, and almost none between class levels. There is social interaction between the foreign populations that speak the same language. Americans interact in English with Britons, Canadians, Western Europeans, Filipinos, Egyptians, Indians, and with some Saudis. But northern Arabs consider Saudis to be lazy, ignorant, and crude.

Saudis say their northern neighbors are just jealous of their oil. Saudis look down on Egyptians, Orientals keep to themselves, Filipinos travel in packs, and everybody looks down on Yemenis.

The Saudis view expatriates as a temporary economic expedient. They would prefer to have an all-Muslim work force, but the Muslim world cannot provide the skills which are needed, and Arabs from other countries are regarded as a potentially dangerous political force that threatens their security. So, Westerners are hired to develop and manage the most important projects.

The Westerners are there for the money! They are tolerated only because they are needed, but are considered a threat to Saudi values and viewed as uncaring, greedy opportunists. The Westerners feel the discrimination, have concerns about their well-being, and worry about their safety in the event of a civil uprising or attack from a neighboring country. They are a small minority group with "guest" status and have less rights than Mexican migrant farm workers living in the United States. They stand out as being inferior outsiders because they do not wear Saudi clothes, speak their language, practice their customs, or share their Islamic faith.

Chapter 4

*F*OLLOWERS OF MUHAMMAD

*M*uhammad preached that all men must submit to Allah. His teachings are embodied in a religion called *Islam*, from the Arabic word which means "to submit," and his followers are called *Muslims* (those who accept and submit to the will of Allah). Islam is based on values thousands of years old and governs all aspects of life. It is the religion and way of life of a billion believers in seventy-two countries throughout the Middle East, Africa, Europe, Russia, and the Far East. Saudi Arabia is where it started, is the center of its practice, and is the keeper of the holy places for the rest of the Islamic world.

Islam is more strictly observed in Saudi Arabia than anywhere else in the world. Its practice is heavily enforced through daily prayers, participation in month-long fasts, religious propaganda, and the threat of death for renouncing the faith. It is also enforced by a network of fanatics called *mutawijah* (religious police) who are guided by the Public Morality Committee. The Religious Police enforce public observance of Islamic rituals so zealously that even the most faithful Muslims complain to the king. Westerners and more lax Muslims dread the thought of attracting their attention and getting arrested.

During recent years, *Ulama* (religious scholars) have blamed Saudi moral laxity on the presence of Western expatriates and condemned modernization as anti-Islamic. The kings took actions to maintain the strict observance of Islam by issuing warnings to young Saudis not to become lax in dress or behavior. They also instructed government officials to stop work and pray together and made employers responsible for the prayer observance of their employees.

The influence of Islam is everywhere and is felt continuously. Religion is never far from the minds of Saudis and it is deeply ingrained in their thinking. Men quote the Koran in business discussions, and government letterheads carry the Islamic creed. People constantly use the expressions *Alhamdulilah* (praise be to God) and *enshAllah* (if God wills) in their conversations. The skylines of the towns and cities are dominated by minarets with the crescent symbol of Islam atop their spires. From the crack of dawn to the dark of night, the calls to prayers from the mosques echo through the towns. Men born in Mecca display their piety with three deep scars on both sides of their faces. Islam is a, if not *the*, major part of their lives. Their devoutness is habitual and automatic as well as purposeful and conscious. There are no formal clergy in Sunni Islam. Ulama serve as preachers and teachers, but it is up to each Muslim to pray directly to Allah and follow the tenets of Islam to achieve salvation.

The followers of Muhammad believe that he was the last of a series of prophets and that his teachings are the final revelation of God. Their Koran, which they believe to be a replica of the book made in heaven, cites the first prophet Ibrahim or Abraham seventy times in twenty-five chapters.

Islam, Judaism, and Christianity agree that Abraham was a tribal leader who lived in the ancient city of Ur outside Babylon around 1700 B.C. The Bible says that Abraham made a covenant with God (whom the Jews call *Yahweh* and the Muslims call *Allah*) to go to a place to be shown to him and make a great nation that would forever have a special relationship with God. Abraham led his followers to Canaan where he built an altar to Yahweh at a sacred site of the supreme Canaanite god, Baal, and renamed it Ur Shalem (now called Jerusalem). There was a great drought and famine at the time, so Abraham led his tribe further southeast into Egypt where the pharaoh Rameses let them settle. Soon afterwards, Abraham and his wife Sarah were evicted from Egypt by the pharaoh and they returned to settle in Jerusalem.

The Bible says that he then had a child by his wife's Egyptian maid, Hagar, whom he named Ishmael, whose descendents Yahweh said would make a great nation. Later, his wife Sarah had a child, called Isaac, about whom Yahweh said, "To your descendents, I will give this country from the river of Egypt to the Great River, the river Euphrates." Several years later, Abraham cast out Hagar and Ishmael and they went to live in the Paran desert. However, the Koran says that Abraham migrated with Hagar and Ishmael to Mecca where he was directed by Allah to build an altar called the Kaaba.

After Rameses died, Abraham's tribe was forced to serve the pharaohs. Around 1235 B.C., after centuries of slavery, the Bible says that the prophet Moses was told by Yahweh to lead his people out of Egypt. Moses, who is mentioned thirty times in the Koran, led them into the Sinai desert. As Moses led the twelve tribes to their promised land, the Bible says that he was summoned to Mount Sinai where he made a covenant with Yahweh and was given ten commandments that his people had to live by. The Ten Commandments became the cornerstone of the Jewish religion.

Joshua, the successor to Moses, led his people into Canaan and captured Jericho and the surrounding villages. After the tribes, which became known as Israelites, settled in Jerusalem, they were invaded by blonde Indo-European Philistines. King Saul led the fight against the Philistines and was succeeded by David as the second king of Israel.

David unified the Israelites into a fierce fighting force and strong nation and ruled the area from the Euphrates River to Sinai. Around 1000 B.C., David rebuilt the small village of Jerusalem into a fortress city and made it into his capital which he called Zion. In 963 B.C., David appointed his son Solomon to be the third king of Israel.

Solomon enlarged Zion and, according to the Bible, was told by Yahweh to build a "house of the Lord" on Mount Moriah. He built a magnificent temple of limestone and cedar beams above a massive, hollowed-out black boulder said to have magical powers. The temple was used to house the ark of the Covenant and became the focal point of the Jewish religion. King Solomon had gold mines in southern Arabia and became known for his wealth and great wisdom. When the Queen of Sheba heard of Solomon's wisdom, she brought a large caravan with gifts of gold, jewels and spices a thousand miles north to Israel "to prove his wisdom with hard questions."

As the Israelites settled in Jerusalem, an Aryan tribe of Medes settled across the Red Sea from Arabia and became known as Persians. The Persian prophet Zoroaster founded the fire-worshipping Zoroastrian religion whose god was Ahura Mazda, and was taught by priests called magi from the holy book, the Avesta. The Zoroastrian Persians quickly grew in strength and conquered their way east toward the Indus valley and north toward Anatolia.

When these Persian ancestors of Iranians moved to the west, they encountered the Semitic Assyrian ancestors of the Iraqis near the Tigris river and began a conflict which has never really ended.

The Persian king, Cyrus, later overran Mesopotamia, eastern Arabia, and the lands along the Mediterranean. He then carried armies in ships from Persia through the Red Sea to conquer Egypt and end the 2,900-year reign of the pharaohs. By 500 B.C., the Persian Empire occupied all the lands from Pakistan to Egypt and from Russia to Ethiopia. Their armies of occupation spoke the Persian language, practiced Zoroastrianism and spread their culture throughout the empire.

After their partial defeat by the Persians, Greek sailors began exploring the Red Sea and Persian Gulf to probe the Persian defenses. As the Greeks recovered, young King Alexander conquered the Balkans and grew in power. By 325 B.C., Alexander the Great's armies had captured the entire Persian Empire. As he won new lands, he forced his victims to convert from the Persian culture to Greek culture. He changed the names of their cities and built new ones with temples to the Greek gods to spread the Greek language and way of life. Northern Arabia was exposed to Greek culture, but very little of it reached the Bedouin of central Arabia whom the Greeks called *Saracens* (the people of the desert).

By the second century B.C., Alexander's descendants had learned of the changing direction of monsoon winds and began to sail fleets of ships to Saba with the westerly winds, and back to Egypt when the winds blew from the east. The Greek fleets reduced the need for Arabian camel caravans and started the decline of the Nabataeans.

During the first century B.C., the Persians wrested control from the Greeks and recaptured the eastern portion of their former empire while Roman legions attacked the Greeks in the west and captured Anatolia, Mesopotamia, Syria, Egypt, and north Africa.

The Romans marched into the interior of Arabia and seized the Nabataean cities of Palmyra and Petra, incorporating them into their province of Arabia Petrae. Rome then shipped twelve thousand legionnaires to Yanbu in 24 B.C. and marched them southward along the Red Sea coast to capture Saba which they called Arabia Felix. But the thirsty, exhausted Romans were wiped out by the camel-mounted Arabs when they approached the mountainous terrain of the Sabaeans.

The Roman conquerors also forced their culture on their victims and built new cities and huge temples in the Middle East to hasten the conversion from Greek to Roman culture. They let the Idumaean Herod run the Judean part of Israel. Herod rebuilt Jerusalem and ruled it with an iron hand, but could not get the people to accept Roman culture.

During Herod's reign, the prophet Yeshu, or Isa as he is called in the Koran, was born in Nazareth near Jerusalem. Ancient teachings had predicted the coming of a *messiah* (king) and many greeted his arrival as a time of change. As the prophet Yeshu grew older, his teachings attracted a wide group of followers who believed in Yahweh. The Romans, who believed Jupiter to be the supreme god, considered Yeshu's teachings as a challenge to their authority. When he continued to incite the people, they brought him to Jerusalem and executed the thirty-three-year-old prophet.

The Jews, as people from Judea were called, kept their faith in Yahweh and refused to obey the Roman decree to worship the mad emperor, Caligula.

In A.D. 66 they revolted and ran the Romans out of Jerusalem. When the next emperor, Nero, learned of the uprising, he put it down with fifty thousand Roman troops. The Jews rebelled again in the year 132 and regained control of Judea. Three years later, the Roman legions returned, killed over six hundred thousand Jews and leveled Jerusalem. They renamed it Palestine after the earlier Philistines and built a temple to Jupiter in its place. The Romans tried to end the foolishness by selling most of the Jews into slavery and deporting them to Arabia, Babylon, Spain, and Egypt, and resettling their land with other peoples. From that time forward, the Jews were a homeless people.

After Yeshu was crucified, his following continued to grow and spread throughout the Mediterranean. A Greek Jew, named Paul, organized Yeshu's teachings into a separate Jewish sect called the Nazarenes. Paul taught that Yeshu was the son of Yahweh and had ascended to heaven from Jerusalem after he was executed. His teachings said that man had to believe that Yeshu was also Yahweh to have life after death. During the second century, the Nazarene sect was formed into a new religion. They used the Greek name for Yeshu the mashiah, *Jesus the Christ*, and created the religion of Christ, or Christianity.

The Romans, who could not tell the difference between Christians and Jews, persecuted both groups. The Christians continued to be persecuted by Romans until after 313 when Constantine was converted to the new religion.

As Rome decayed from internal corruption and attack from northern European barbarians in 324, Constantine became the new emperor, fled to Anatolia, and founded his new capital Constantinople on the site of the old Greek colony of Byzantium. Constantine then began forcing his subjects to practice Christianity and combining its teachings with Roman law to regulate all aspects of life from wages to sex. His universal, or catholic, practice of Christianity later became known as Catholicism.

The Byzantines, as Constantine's subjects came to be called, controlled the southeastern half of the former empire. Their new culture spread into northern Arabia, Mesopotamia, Palestine, most of north Africa, Spain, Greece, and the Balkans.

Christianity and Judaism spread deep into Arabia during the fourth and fifth centuries. Najran, Aden, Sana, and Hadhramaut became Christian centers as tribes of southern Arabia and the kings of Ethiopia converted to Christianity. Large populations of Jews lived in Yathrib and Saba. In the beginning of the sixth century, the Jewish king of Saba attacked Najran and massacred many Christians. The Christian Ethiopians retaliated by crossing the Red Sea, crushing the Sabaean army and establishing Christian control over southern Arabia.

During the emergence of Christianity, the Persian Sassanids conquered the Parthians and integrated the Zoroastrian religion with their government. The Sassanids expanded their empire to the north and west for several hundred years by taking lands held by the Byzantines. By the sixth century, the Sassanids controlled the eastern coast of Arabia, as well as most of Mesopotamia, and eastern Anatolia.

As the Byzantine and Sassanid empires expanded, the Arabic language began to be widely used and became the main language of Arabia.

At the end of the sixth century, the Arabian peninsula was a power vacuum between the Christian Byzantine Empire in the west and the Zoroastrian Sassanid Empire in the east, which were continuously at war with each other. The Zoroastrians controlled the eastern coast of Arabia; the Christians controlled the extreme north and south; but isolated central Arabia was still controlled by the animistic, Arabic-speaking Bedouin.

Bedouin beliefs, values, and attitudes had not been affected by external influences. Their lives were regulated by *sunna* (the customs and practices of their ancestors), and they prayed to groups of rocks and trees. Their common gods were Manat, Uzza, and Allat, and their highest god was called Allah. The

Arabs of the coastal villages and farming areas of the south had been influenced by outsiders. The coastal Arabs accepted the Zoroastrian, Jewish, and Christian beliefs of their Sassanid Persian conquerors and Jewish and Christian colonies. By the seventh century the raids by Bedouin intensified into religious wars. It was in this environment that the prophet Muhammad emerged.

Muhammad was born in A.D. 570 in the wealthy town of Mecca in southwestern Arabia that dominated the caravan routes between India and the Mediterranean. The Mecca oases had been a holy place for many years and contained a collection of sacred stones in a shrine called the Kaaba. Many tribes made annual pilgrimages to worship the idols and rocks—including a large black stone which was probably a meteorite. The tribes observed a holy truce in the sacred area surrounding the Kabaa. The Quraysh tribe that ruled Mecca enforced the peace and traded with the visiting tribes.

The Prophet was born into a family of the Quraysh. His father died before his birth, and his mother died when he was six years old. He was raised as a poor orphan by his grandfather and uncle. As a child, he was sent to live in the desert with a Bedouin family from whom he acquired their customs, learned to endure the hardships of nomadic life, and gained rhetorical skills in Arabic. Muhammad became a caravan trader and visited Christian, Jewish, and Zoroastrian towns in his travels. When he was around forty, he retired in Mecca and spent a lot of time alone in a cave on Mount Hira.

Around the year 610, Muhammad began to hear a voice in the cave which he said was the angel Gabriel giving him messages from Allah. He told his wives and friends that Gabriel said Allah was the creator of man and the source of all knowledge. Muhammad began preaching his message to others after later revelations told him to proclaim that Allah was the only god. He preached that believers in Allah were "the best of peoples evolved for mankind, enjoining what is right, forbidding what is wrong, and believing in God." He preached that those who believed in Allah and totally obeyed his commands would live in paradise after death; a paradise with gardens amidst streams of running water.

The preachings of Muhammad reflected the beliefs of the time and combined concepts borrowed from Judaism and Christianity with traditional Bedouin practices to create a new Arabic religion. He taught that loyalty should be to the faith instead of to the family. He taught that women had the right to own property, receive inheritance, and obtain divorce; but left men as protectors over women. He also taught that those who believe in Allah should give part of their wealth to the poor.

Muhammad's following grew among the slaves, the poor, the women, and a few influential men of Mecca. But he made many enemies. He threatened the peace and prosperity of Mecca by proclaiming that Allah was the only god, and threatened the rich by insisting they give part of their wealth to the poor of other families. Most Meccans, including members of his own family, scoffed at Muhammad and opposed his teachings.

The leaders of Mecca put up with Muhammad's threats to their well-being for ten years. The harder he preached, the stronger they opposed him. Finally, the opposition grew so strong that Muhammad's followers were harassed, abused, and tortured. In the fall of 622, Muhammad sent seventy of his followers to safety in the northern town of Yathrib. Then Muhammad learned that his neighbors were planning to kill him so he and his closest friend, Abu Bakr, also fled to Yathrib. His escape is called the Hegira and was the turning point in Islam.

Muhammad and his followers quickly established themselves in the old white-walled city by building their first mosque, or place of worship. Muhammad began preaching to the townspeople and used the hypnotic power of Arabic to sway his audiences. Soon, he succeeded in gaining new converts. As his following grew, he started preaching to Yathrib's large population of Jewish merchants and farmers. He tried to convince the Jews, whose practices he had adopted, that he was the latest prophet of their religion. But the Jews laughed at him and ridiculed his teachings. When Muhammad's following grew large enough, he took over Yathrib and forced everybody to practice his new religion.

The Prophet taught that the world was divided into *dar al-Islam* (Muslim territory) and *dar al-Harb* (hostile territory), and that the two parts could only exist in a state of war. It was their duty to wage *jihad* (holy war) on *kafir* (non-believers) and convert them to Islam. Muslims who died in the battle would become martyrs and receive special privileges in paradise. He told his followers to give the non-believers the choice of conversion or death.

Muhammad then tried to convert Yathrib's Jews to Islam, but they refused. After his followers chopped off the heads of about eight hundred Jews, he decided it was a waste of manpower. Muhammad told them to spare Jews and Christians, whom he called "people of the book," because their scriptures contributed to Islam. Muhammad ruled that Jews and Christians could live according to their religious laws in their own communities as inferior subject peoples if they recognized Muslim authority, paid special taxes, and did not try to convert Muslims to their faith. He then married two beautiful Jewish widows, whose husbands he had killed, to demonstrate his forgiveness of the Jews for refusing to convert. Muhammad's followers celebrated by changing Yathrib's name to *Medina* (the city of the prophet).

After being rejected by the Jews, Muhammad modified the practice of Islam to make it different from the Jewish Talmud and more uniquely Arabic. He changed the day of congregational prayer from Saturday to Friday, the direction of prayer from Jerusalem to Mecca, the number of daily prayers from three to five, and the call to prayer from the sound of gongs to call by *muezzin* (caller of daily prayers). He also banned wine-making and gambling and declared

Ramadan (a traditional sacred season) as a month of fasting.

Muhammad's followers began to record his teachings, which they believed were revelations made to him by God through the angel Gabriel. Their holy book, the Koran, borrowed much from the Bible. It cites the stories of the creation of man and the Great Flood several times. The Koran tells of the relationships of the prophets Abraham, Moses, David, Solomon, and Jesus with Jerusalem, and also links Muhammad with Jerusalem.

The Koran says that Muhammad was taken by the angel Gabriel from his cave in Mecca to Jerusalem. There he was taken aloft by the angel from the sacred rock where King Solomon built the Jewish temple. As he ascended on a "ladder of light," he passed through the "seven heavens" to stand in at the presence of Allah. After receiving instructions from Allah, he was brought back to the sacred rock in Jerusalem. Then he returned to Mecca on the angel's winged horse.

The Prophet's followers collected his sayings and actions into a work called the Hadith. The Koran and Hadith combined together with Bedouin customs and practices made up the Sunna, the spiritual and social guide to the conduct of Muslims.

After he got Medina running the way he wanted, Muhammad began expanding his influence. He waylaid a large Meccan caravan and killed or converted its drivers. The Meccans got even by raiding Medina and wounding Muhammad. Muhammad and his

Bedouin followers renewed their efforts and made raids farther and farther from Medina and killed or converted everybody they found. Gradually, he took control of west central Arabia.

In January 630, the sixty-year-old Prophet rode into Mecca leading an army of ten thousand followers. Muhammad called himself the "messenger of Allah" and challenged the Meccans to accept him as their leader or die. The Meccans surrendered without a fight. The Prophet destroyed the stone idols in the Kaaba and used their names as "ninety-nine attributes of Allah." He proclaimed that the large black stone in the Kaaba was the sacred altar to Allah and that Muslims should make pilgrimages to it. He also forbade all others to enter Mecca.

With Mecca under his control, Muhammad sent his growing armies slashing their way through the south and east. Soon, he dominated the people of most of Arabia and made Islam their total way of life.

In April 632, Muhammad returned to Mecca, stood on the side of Mount Mercy and gave a farewell sermon to the pilgrims. The ailing Prophet told them of the last revelation he had received from Allah, saying, "This day have I...completed my favor upon you, and have chosen for you Islam as your religion." Muhammad returned to Medina and turned over prayer duties to his father-in-law and friend, Abu Bakr. In June 632 the prophet Muhammad died.

After his death, loyal Muslims mounted a series of raids on tribes that had seceded from Islam to bring them back into line. The raids soon spread east past the converted tribes and escalated into an all-out holy war against the Sassanid Persians. The Muslim Bedouin, still called Saracens by their enemies, dashed into enemy camps during sandstorms and cut down their surprised victims before they knew what had happened. They quickly conquered and converted the Persians in eastern Arabia and moved north. In 635, the Muslim Bedouin tore through the Byzantines in Damascus, adding new converts to their ranks. The next year, the Arab army defeated the main Byzantine army. Part of the army crossed the Tigris river in 637, overran Persia and reached the Indus valley in 643. The rest of the army turned west. In 640, they took Alexandria and by 650 they had captured all of Egypt.

The explosive growth of Islam catapulted Mecca into prominence as the political and religious center of the expanding Arab Empire. Muslims from all parts of the empire traveled to Mecca to make their pilgrimage to the Kaaba and discuss administrative matters. As Mecca grew in stature, villages and towns along Arabian caravan routes became important as pilgrim resting places.

Jeddah sprang into prominence as the port of entry for Mecca. The harbor, which was only a break in the coral reefs, was visited by ships carrying pilgrims from India, Persia, and Egypt who brought goods to trade before they began their two-day walk to Mecca. Pilgrims who journeyed to Mecca in camel caravans also went to Jeddah to trade and visit the grave of Eve. Soon, Jeddah was regarded as another holy city and became the major port on the Red Sea, and the trading center of Arabia.

As the Arab Empire expanded and the power of its leader grew in importance, a feud, which had started after Muhammad's death, erupted and resulted in the permanent division of Islam. Muhammad's favorite daughter, Fatima, claimed that her husband Ali should have been made *caliph* (successor to the Prophet) as his hereditary right. Muhammad's youngest widow claimed that Abu Bakr, whom her husband had chosen to lead the prayers, should be appointed caliph. Those closest to Muhammad agreed with the widow and ruled that Abu Bakr, who was a *Sunni* (follower of the Prophet's path) be made caliph. The *Shiites* (followers of Ali) were very disappointed and angry, but decided to wait and see who was appointed next. Ali was bypassed again in the year 634 when Umar succeeded as second caliph, and in 646 when Uthman of the powerful Umayya family of Mecca succeeded as third caliph.

Ali was named fourth caliph in 656, after Caliph Uthman was killed by fellow Muslims, but Muhammad's widow and Uthman's nephew blamed Ali for the assassination. Muawiya Umayya, the governor of Syria, refused to accept Ali as caliph and revolted. Ali moved his capital to Mesopotamia to put down the rebellion and was murdered in 661. Muawiya Umayya in Damascus then claimed he was caliph. Ali's son, Hussain, the grandson of the Prophet, fought the claim and led his father's supporters in a counter rebellion until he was killed by the Umayyads at Karbala near Babylon.

The Shiites cursed the Sunnis for having caused Hussain's death and for recognizing the caliph in Damascus. The Shiites refused to recognize the new Umayyad caliph or anyone else who was not a direct descendant of the Prophet. Instead, they appointed their own leader called an *imam* and formed a separate branch of Islam. The Shiites prayed to Ali and Hussain, worshipped their graves as shrines, and whipped themselves to atone for Hussain's death as a martyr. The Shiites were extremely emotional and violent and believed it was Allah's will to dedicate themselves to the punishment of their enemies. They became dissenters and revolted against the ruling class in the Islamic world, and still continue their tradition of fanatical violence.

The divisive rebellion also shifted control of Islam from the orthodox Sunni Muslims of Arabia to the worldly Sunni Umayyads of Damascus.

The new Arab Empire became larger than the Roman Empire and continued to grow until 732 when the Muslims were defeated by the Christian, Charles Martel, at the Battle of Tours in central France. At that time, the Arab Empire extended about five thousand miles from France through Spain, North Africa, Egypt, Palestine, the Arabian peninsula, Syria, Mesopotamia, eastern Anatolia, Persia, Afghanistan, and into central Asia into what is now Russia, Pakistan, and India.

Twenty years later, the Umayyad caliph was killed in a revolt led by Abu al-Abbas. The Abbasids,

Christians, Jews, new converts and the combat-trained Turkish Mamluk slaves resented the rotten treatment they received from the high-living Umayyads. After rallying the classes together and defeating the Umayyads, Abbas moved to Mesopotamia to be closer to the center of the Arab Empire and used one hundred thousand craftsmen to build a new capital. The construction of the beautiful city of Baghdad ushered in the golden age of Islam.

The Arab Empire was held together through the common practice of Islam and prospered through trade. The Muslims adopted parts of Persian, Byzantine, Greek, and Indian cultures and integrated them into a way of life which led to great achievements. Muslim scholars collected knowledge from everywhere in the empire and combined it to develop advanced practices of mathematics, medicine, and technology. Writers created epic poems and stories, and artists refined the arts of calligraphy and mosaic. They used their new architectural skills to build the graceful mosques which still stand in Seville, Cairo, and Istanbul. They took the dome from a Byzantine shrine in Baalbek and used it as a roof to cover the massive black boulder in Jerusalem from which Muhammad said he rose to heaven. That shrine, called the Dome of the Rock, still stands and is the third most sacred place in Islam.

The good life of the Abbasids lasted until 809 by which time their previous piety had turned into such open drinking and sexual promiscuity that their more devout subjects rebelled again and fragmented the empire. Spain was taken over by a surviving Umayyad. Afghanistan and northern India came under independent Muslim rulers. Persia, Morocco and Tunisia became separate Shiite kingdoms. Eastern Arabia and part of Oman came under control of a Shiite sect known as Qarmatians. Egypt and Syria came under the rule of another Shiite sect called Fatimids.

During the next 120 years, the Shiites widened the breach with the Sunni Muslims and tried to take control of Islam. In 878, the twelfth Shiite imam disappeared and local holy men called ayatollahs assumed leadership in his place. The ayatollahs claimed that the imam would reappear in the future as *mahdi* (savior) to bring "truth, justice, harmony and prosperity to the world." The Shiite ayatollahs also preached that only they could help their followers obtain salvation. The Shiites accepted these teachings and allowed the creation of a religious hierarchy which opposed the secular authority of the state. In 930, fanatical Qarmatian Shiites attacked the ruling Abbasids in Mesopotamia and then stormed Mecca. They massacred fifty thousand Sunni pilgrims, broke the sacred black stone loose from the Kaaba and carried it to their Persian Gulf stronghold.

When the Arab Empire crumbled into weak factions, its former enemies wreaked their revenge. A large tribe of Seljuk Turks from central Asia converted to Sunni Islam and captured Persia, Mesopotamia, Syria, and Palestine. The defeat of the Byzantine army in Anatolia prevented Christians from making pilgrimages to Jerusalem and caused them to unite against the Muslims. Pope Urban II called for the kings of the European states to drive the infidel Muhammedans or Musselmans out of the holy lands. In 1096, a motley band of European Christians began a series of crusades to free the Holy Land. The Crusaders slogged through Europe to the Bosporus, invaded through Byzantine Anatolia and killed friend and foe alike as they battled their way to Jerusalem.

The Turkish Muslims counterattacked viciously, and Christian knights who were the tolerated "people of the book" became non-believing kafirs to be killed or driven off. The first crusade was defeated in 1144 after years of merciless fighting. Three years later, Emperor Conrad III of Germany launched the second crusade and liberated Jerusalem. They held it until 1187, when the crusaders were slaughtered by one hundred thousand Turkish troops at the Battle of Hittim and Jerusalem was recaptured by the Muslims. The third crusade, led by King Richard of England, ended after his defeat by Saladin, the Fatimid sultan of Egypt and Syria.

While Syria and Palestine were under siege by Christian crusaders, Genghis Khan led thousands of northern Asian Mongols riding into Persia. The Mongols overran the Seljuk Turks in 1211 and devastated Persia. In 1258, they invaded Mesopotamia and destroyed everything in their path. They demolished Baghdad, killed the Abbasid caliph and hundreds of thousands of his followers and turned the Middle

East's largest agricultural area into desert and swamps. Then the Mongols rode into Syria, rolled over the Turks and joined up with the crusaders in Palestine.

Baybars, the Mamluk Turkish sultan of Egypt and Syria, brought the Egyptian army into Palestine, defeated the Mongol armies and started destroying the crusader forts. By 1270, Baybars had forced the crusaders out of their fort towns along the Mediterranean coast and gained control over the west coast of Arabia, Egypt, Palestine, and Syria. The Mamluk sultanate continued to rule the area for the next 250 years and taxed the trade between Europe and India to support its armies.

As the thirteenth century drew to its end, a Muslim Turk named Othman and his tribe rebelled against the Seljuks in eastern Anatolia. The Ottoman Turks crossed the Bosporous and invaded the Balkans. As they learned to use guns and cannons, the Ottomans continued their expansion into Europe and the countries surrounding Anatolia. In 1453, the Ottomans devastated the Byzantines, captured Constantinople and ended the 1,100-year reign of the Byzantine Empire.

The European Christians renewed their efforts against the Muslims and began an all-out effort in the Iberian peninsula. Finally in 1492, Ferdinand of Spain rallied the Christians together to end eight hundred years of Muslim occupation.

The Muslims retaliated by refusing to sell Indian spices to Iberia. The Christians responded by search-

REGIONAL POLITICAL MAP

ing for a sea route to India. In August 1492, Queen Isabel of Spain financed an Italian named Columbus to find a new way to India. Columbus sailed westward and, instead, discovered a new continent. In 1498, after decades of exploration, the Portuguese Vasco da Gama opened a new route to the Far East by sailing around Africa. The sea route to the Far East was cheaper and safer than Middle Eastern land routes, and was quickly filled with Portuguese traders.

In 1500, Christian Portuguese traders reached the Arabian seas and started looting Muslim merchant ships. They set up a trading center at Goa on the Indian coast in 1510 and began building forts to defend their sea lane to India. Then, they invaded the Arabian coast, slaughtered the Arabs and built a series of forts in Muscat, Aden, Bahrain, and Hormuz. The Mamluk sultan in Egypt responded by sending a Muslim fleet to end the Portuguese menace. The Portuguese joined forces with the Christian king of Ethiopia and tried to land at Jeddah to capture Mecca. The Mamluks prevented the invasion but permanently lost control of the Indian Ocean. The Arabian caravan trade dropped off, the Mamluks lost their caravan tax revenues, and their armies deteriorated.

The Ottoman Turks continued to fight their way west and defeated the Mamluks. By 1520, the Ottomans had carved out another Islamic empire that extended from Vienna south to Aden and from the Persian border west to Morocco. The Ottoman sultan made his capital in Constantinople and was caliph of western and northeastern Arabia, Yemen, western Persia, Anatolia, Mesopotamia, Syria, Palestine, Egypt, north Africa, and Balkan Europe. His empire was ruled by Turkish royalty, controlled by an elite corps of Turkish troops called janissaries, and administered by Turkish bureaucrats.

After the caravan trade diminished and the Turkish sultan became caliph, the practice of Islam in central Arabia totally disintegrated. The Bedouin reverted to their former animistic beliefs of worshipping trees and rocks. Mystics called Sufis, claiming to talk with Allah through seances, were regarded as saints. Eventually, the Sufis and their mystical beliefs replaced Islamic principles for the people of Nadj.

Around 1725, a religious scholar named Muhammad ibn-al-Wahhab started a reform movement to restore the basic practices of Islam as specified in the Koran. Al-Wahhab and his followers, the Wahhabis, denounced all innovations to Islam, including the celebration of Muhammad's birthday, and the worship of rocks, saints, and pictorial representations. They rejected Sufi practices and the clerical role assumed by Sufi mystics. They also banned the wearing of fine clothing or jewelry, shaving, swearing, smoking, music, and dancing. The stern Wahhabis preached that man's sole duty was to serve and obey Allah and accept what comes as his will. They dealt strict punishments for failure to comply with Islamic laws, and declared a holy war against anyone who did not share their beliefs.

After twenty years of failure, al-Wahhab formed

an alliance with Sheik Muhammad ibn-Saud, and began to win converts. Gradually, they established the Wahhabi practice of Islam as the official form of worship in Saudi Arabia; the practice is still followed today.

The practice of Islam consists of observing the Five Pillars which are the foundations of Islam.

Shahada, or recital of the creed, is the First Pillar. "There is no god but Allah, and Muhammed is the messenger of Allah" are the first words to greet the ears of a newborn Muslim, are frequently recited during life, and are the last to be uttered at his grave.

The Second Pillar is *salah,* or prayers. Saudis are required to face Mecca and pray five times each day at dawn, midday, mid-afternoon, sunset, and nightfall. The muezzin announce prayer times over public address systems from the mosques, and in many places, several different calls are heard simultaneously. Religious police, with reddish henna rubbed in their beards, urge compliance by slapping their camel sticks on tables and doors and shouting "salaat! salaat!" Stores close their doors, shops roll down their steel curtains, and Muslim office workers stop whatever they are doing to take fifteen-minute prayer breaks. Saudis either go to mosques or spread their rugs and pray wherever they happen to be: at the side of roads, on sidewalks, in building lobbies, hallways, alleyways and airport terminals.

When Muslims pray, they first spread a small prayer rug on the ground aligned so that they face the Grand Mosque in Mecca. Some prayer rugs have

built-in "Mecca meters" (compasses) to help the believers line up their rugs. King Khalid's personal
Boeing 747 had a gyro-controlled section of flooring
that always faced Mecca, no matter where his plane
was. Muslims begin the prayers by standing at the
foot of the rug, chanting aloud. Then they place their
hands on their knees, kneel and place their forehead
on the rug with their arms extended toward Mecca.
They lie prostrate and then stand again at the edge of
the rug.

The daily prayers consist of testimonies to God
specified by time of day. They chant: "I testify that
there is no god besides Allah; I testify that Muhammad is the messenger of Allah. Come to prayer!
Come to salvation! Allah is most great, and there is
no god besides Allah." If Muslims want to pray for
aid or guidance, these prayers are made separately.

Men are supposed to pray together, under a
prayer leader, at the mosque whenever possible, but
are obligated to attend on Friday for noon prayers
which are accompanied by sermons from religious
scholars.

Prayer times change slightly every day and their
schedules are published in English-language newspapers. Western expatriates have to adjust to the delays
in work schedules, shopping, and errands caused by
prayer breaks.

Zakat, or alms giving, is the Third Pillar. Saudis
are expected to donate one-fortieth of their income to
the poor as a voluntary act of charity. The Koran says,
"We are only feeding you for God's sake. We want no

reward from you nor thanks."

Despite the kingdom's social welfare programs, old crippled men and women with babies beg in the suqs, on the streets, in shopping centers, and in office buildings. The Saudis respond generously but shoo them out of their offices.

Sawm, or fasting, is the Fourth Pillar. The Saudis fast for thirty days during the month of Ramadan to commemorate Allah's revelation of the Koran to Muhammad.

The obligation to fast begins when the new moon is sighted over Mecca, and the start of Ramadan is signalled by the firing of cannons at sunrise the next day. The end of fasting for the day is determined when a thread can no longer be seen in the natural light, or by the sunset call to prayer. Westerners in public places at sunset are astonished to see the Muslims spread rugs on the ground wherever they happen to be and begin feasting on a variety of items which they whip out from under the folds of their garments.

Fasting includes complete denial of food, drink, tobacco, and sex from dawn to sunset. It applies to everyone in the kingdom, and is enforced by the Religious Police. Foreigners caught eating, drinking, or smoking during daylight hours are arrested. During Ramadan in the past, English notices were posted in the suqs even warning foreigners against wearing immodest dress, wearing Christian crosses, or holding hands in public. In 1981, the Saudis banned the sale of baby dolls because of their objection to human likenesses.

Unless foreigners want to observe the fast, they must smuggle bags of food and water to their work sites and find a place to hide while they take a drink of water, eat a sandwich, or smoke a cigarette. Many Saudis are tolerant of Westerners and invite them to smoke or drink coffee in the privacy of their offices. But, there is always the fear that someone less tolerant may report them to the Religious Police.

A Saudi tradition evolved of staying awake late at night and sleeping late in the day to minimize the impact of the fast. It has developed to such an extent that normal day and night routines are almost reversed during Ramadan. In the early 1980s, Ramadan occurred during June or July when nightfall was at about 8:00 P.M. During this period, streets normally crowded at 10:00 A.M. were deserted. Shops and banks were open from 11:00 A.M. until noon. They opened again at 8:00 P.M. and remained open until 2:00 A.M. Hordes of people crowded the market places at midnight. Traffic jams occurred around 1:30 A.M. as the Saudis returned home. Around 2:00 A.M. they ate large meals before turning in, and slept until mid-morning.

Saudi Arabia is cut off from the rest of the world during Ramadan. Business with Western governments almost comes to a stop and contract negotiations are suspended for several months because outsiders cannot reach the Saudis. Muslims are only required to work six hours per day during Ramadan, and everybody sets their own hours. Some organizations work during the day, others work at night, and some work a little of both. It is not uncommon for meetings to be scheduled at 10:00 A.M. and 10:00 P.M. the same day. In 1981, stonemasons rebuilt the wall surrounding the United States Embassy and several high-rise buildings were erected all in the darkness of night.

Productivity comes to a screeching halt. There is an initial productivity drop of 30 to 50 percent which rapidly increases to 75 or 80 percent by months end. It is extremely difficult for expatriates to get anything done. They cannot reach people by telephone and do not know which businesses are open. Many Saudi government officials and business managers leave the country during Ramadan, and half their employ- ees do not bother to report to work. Those who show up are not very cooperative and only work for a few hours. The postal service stops at the beginning of the month and does not resume until the next. Soon, everyone is irritable and short-tempered.

The month of fasting is followed by a three-day period of visiting, feasting, and gift-giving called Eid al Fitr. It is a festive time for Saudis but essentially closed to non-Muslims.

Ramadan is a shocking experience for Westerners. It is unlike anything that they have ever encountered before. Most of them regard it as an experience to be avoided if at all possible, and schedule out-of-coun- try business trips or vacations from the middle of Ramadan until the end of Eid al-Fitr. Consequently, it is extremely difficult to get bookings on flights in and out of the kingdom during this period unless reservations are made many months in advance.

The Fifth Pillar is the *hajj* (pilgrimage). It is the responsibility of every Muslim who can afford it, and is fit enough, to make the journey to Mecca at least once in his lifetime, during the twelfth month of the Muslim calendar. They can make the pilgrimage at any time, but it is holier during the hajj period.

Hajjis (pilgrims) enter the sacred area of Mecca wearing clothes that equalize all people. The men are bareheaded and wear two large, seamless, white cloths, one wrapped around their waist and hips, the other draped over their shoulders. The women wear white abayas without veils.

When they arrive, they walk around the Kaaba in the center of the Grand Mosque seven times, while praying. If they can get close enough, they kiss the black stone. Next, they walk back and forth seven times inside a long hallway attached to the mosque that runs between the small hills of Safa and Marwah. This symbolizes Hagar's search for water for her son Ishmael. They then wash themselves or drink water at the Zimzam well, the spring Hagar found. On the eighth day of the month, the hajjis hike four miles to the valley of Mina where they stop for noon prayers. Then they walk another six miles to the plain of Arafat where they camp in a tent city. On the ninth day, they stand bareheaded from noon until sunset at the foot of Mount Mercy and pray at the site of Muhammad's farewell address. After the spiritual climax at sunset, the pilgrims walk to Muzdalifah, spend the night, and return to Mina on the tenth day. There, they throw stones at three rock pillars representing Satan while shouting, "Allah is most great," and later sacrifice a sheep or goat. After that is done, the women cut off a lock of hair and men shave their heads. Then they discard their seamless garments and change into their normal clothes. After spending three days at Mina they return to Mecca. At Mecca, the pilgrims end the hajj by again circling the Kaaba before beginning their trip home.

The three-day period starting on the return to Mina is called Eid al-Adha and is a worldwide period of sacrifice during which multitudes of sheep and goats are publicly slaughtered and the meat given to the poor. Several years ago, the Islamic Development Bank funded the creation of a computerized system for distribution of the meat.

Pilgrims have been making the hajj for centuries. The annual hajj is a momentous occasion for all Muslims and is televised via satellite to forty-seven countries with the prayers broadcast over the radio in seven languages.

During the peak period of hajj, almost three million Muslims from all over the world converge on Jeddah, Mecca, and Medina. Jumbo jets are chartered from every conceivable airline to convey the pilgrims to Jeddah and frequently arrive at a rate of one plane per minute. Crowds of people wearing a wide variety of sandals, head coverings, shirts, skirts, and rags can be seen in and between the cities. Many of the pilgrims are incredibly poor and have saved all their lives to make a single pilgrimage to Saudi Arabia. Some are unbelievably filthy and foul smelling. During past hajjs, these people have carried highly contagious diseases to Saudi Arabia and caused fatal epidemics of smallpox, cholera, and malaria.

The pilgrims come to Jeddah by plane and ship bringing rolled up sleeping pallets and spending money. They leave carrying huge, cheap, vinyl suitcases, twice the size of steamer trunks, filled with purchases from the kingdom. They sleep with their stacks of baggage on sidewalks around the seaports and airports as they wait for transportation home.

The Saudi government has spent hundreds of millions of dollars on pilgrim welfare. It has built quarantine hospitals and special barracks for pilgrims at the seaport of Jeddah. It has constructed a special hajj terminal, several barracks, and a half-mile-square area of fiberglass tent panels suspended from giant concrete pylons at the new Jeddah airport. Pilgrims are provided with guides who speak their language and with a fleet of buses to carry them over an eight-lane expressway to Mecca. In the plain of Arafat, a several-square-mile tent city has been provided with sanitation systems, health care facilities, and fire-fighting equipment.

Despite these diligent efforts, the country's infrastructure is totally overloaded during hajj. The pilgrims usually stay in Mecca for about two weeks. Many start their preparations immediately after Ramadan and come to Saudi Arabia before hajj begins. Others stay in the kingdom after hajj ends. So, the effect is felt for about two months. During this period, the populations of Jeddah and Mecca are tripled or quadrupled. The population of the entire kingdom is almost doubled. Hotels are overbooked, and flights in and out of Saudi Arabia to points as distant as London and Jakarta are sold out months in advance. The passenger load ruins airline schedules throughout the Middle East, southern Europe and south central Asia. The roads between Mecca, Jeddah, and Medina are clogged with buses and trucks carrying pilgrims. Telephone circuits are overloaded.

Since the Ayatollah Khomeni came to power in Iran, the hajj has also become a major security problem as Iranian Shiites stage demonstrations and cause riots.

During the extended hajj period, Saudi productivity is reduced because of the strain on the infrastructure and the absence of workers making the pilgrimage. Consequently, many expatriate managers schedule personal vacations out of the kingdom to coincide with the period just preceding the public holiday of Eid al-Adha.

Islam is the single most influential factor of the Saudi culture, and influences absolutely everything else. Saudi religious convictions are so strongly reinforced that they are almost unchangeable. The beliefs and practices are totally alien to anything experienced by most Westerners, who are awed by them. It is difficult for many foreigners to imagine the experience of complete and continual submission to religious beliefs. Most expatriates admire the strength of conviction of the Saudis, but would prefer not to submit themselves. But they do not have a choice. The religion is the law and the law is upheld and enforced by the royal Saud family.

Chapter 5

DESERT DYNASTY

The al-Saud family is Saudi Arabia. They decide who can enter or leave the country, who will become rich or poor, and who lives or dies. An inner circle of sixty Saud family members can cripple entire nations by calling holy wars, by cutting off their oil, or by moving their own money. The country is named after the Sauds. They are the government. They make the laws and control the country's society, economy, foreign affairs, education, business, and religion. Their history is the country's history.

Their history began in the tiny Nadj village of Diriyah outside of Riyadh during the eighteenth century. It was there that the ibn-Saud family joined forces with the religious reformer, al-Wahhab, and his family, the al-Shaykh.

The eighteenth century found Ottoman Turkish garrisons along the coasts of the Arabian peninsula, with British ships patrolling offshore. The English East Indian Company set up shop in the Persian Gulf around 1600 and began a trade war with the Portuguese, who had controlled the area for a hundred years. After the British drove the Portuguese out of Oman, the Omani sultan joined the war and captured the Portuguese colonies in Bahrain, Zanzibar, and east Africa. The British captured Bombay in 1661 and began colonizing India. By 1745, they had defeated the Arab pirates and controlled the Persian Gulf.

On the peninsula, Mecca subsisted on taxes paid by Muslim pilgrims, and Jeddah prospered as a transshipment port between India and Egypt, collecting duties paid on cargo and the pilgrim trade. In the isolated central part of the peninsula, Nadj remained free of invasion or foreign occupation because it did not have anything to plunder. It was utterly destitute and only occasional pilgrim caravans crossed its interior. It had been out of the mainstream of cultural developments since 661 when the Islamic caliphate moved to Damascus, and it became a stagnant backwater in 750 when the caliphate moved to Baghdad. The loss of caravan trade finished the Nadj economy.

The Bedouin remained wretchedly poor and continued their tradition of hit-and-run raids to steal from neighboring tribes and villages. For over a thousand years there was almost constant feuding, village against village, tribe against tribe, and tribes against villages. The continuous fighting spoiled any chance for unity. There was no strong authority to make or enforce any kind of laws and the practice of Islam totally deteriorated.

A religious scholar, Muhammad ibn-al-Wahhab, tried to get people to return to the practice of Islam. Around 1745, he gained the support of Sheik Muhammad ibn-Saud of the Rwala tribe in Diriyah. Ibn-Saud led his tribe in raids against other nearby tribes. He gave them the choice of doing things al-Wahhab's way or dying, and soon converted them to the strict practice of Wahhabism. As the movement spread under the leadership of Muhammad ibn-Saud, he became known as the *emir* (ruler). Muhammad's son, Abdul Aziz ibn-Saud, married al-Wahhab's daughter and became the second emir when his father died in 1765. Old al-Wahhab vested the title imam on Abdul Aziz ibn-Saud and made him the spiritual leader as well as the political leader of the Wahhabi movement. Al-Wahhab's family then adopted the name al-Shaykh (family of the teacher). Abdul Aziz ibn-Saud led raids to the south and gained control over nearby Riyadh in 1773.

Some of the Nadj tribes fled from the Sauds to the Persian Gulf, where they formed new countries. The al-Sabah and al-Khalifah families migrated northward and camped by a large bay in what is now Kuwait. The al-Sabah settled there, became pearl fishers, and ran caravans between Riyadh and Mesopotamia. The al-Khalifah left and joined with the al-Jalahimah in 1766 to settle in the peninsula of Qatar. After they took over Qatar, they captured the Persian-ruled island of Bahrain. By 1783, the al-Sabah were the rulers of Kuwait, the al-Khalifah had become the rulers of Bahrain, and the al-Jalahimah continued as the rulers of Qatar.

By the start of the nineteenth century, the Saudis ruled Nadj, the Qasim area to the northwest, and the al-Hasa area next to the Persian Gulf. Then they began raids south into Oman and north into Mesopotamia.

In the south, the Saudis seized the large al-Buraimi oases and raided towns along the Persian Gulf and Oman. The Omani sultan retaliated in 1800 by seizing Bahrain. The Saudis helped the al-Khalifah recapture Bahrain and forced them to join the Saudi emirate. The Saudis also continued to occupy al-Buraimi at will until 1869 when they were driven out by tribes from Oman and Abu Dhabi.

In the north, the Saudis fought their way through Ottoman tribes to the town of Karbala near Baghdad. In 1802, they rode into town, slaughtered thousands of people and destroyed the tomb of Ali's son, Hussain, revered by the Shiites. The sack of Karbala angered the entire Muslim world and Abdul Aziz ibn-Saud was slain in revenge by a Shiite.

He was succeeded by his son Saud, who became the third emir. Saud ibn-Saud avenged his father by leading the Saudis east into Hejaz. In 1803, they pillaged Mecca and two years later they took Medina.

By 1810, the Saudis controlled most of the Arabian peninsula. But not for long, because the Saudis again infuriated the Muslim world by robbing the tomb of the prophet Muhammad to end worship of the site.

The Ottoman sultan was angered by the desecration of Islamic holy places and ordered Muhammad Ali, the governor of Egypt, to end the Saudi reign. In 1814, Saud ibn-Saud was killed when the Egyptian army liberated Medina and Mecca. His son, Abdullah ibn-Saud became the fourth emir and led the Saudis in retreat to Nadj. In 1818, Muhammad Ali's army leveled the Saud homeland of Diriyah after capturing Nadj and al-Hasa. Emir Abdullah ibn-Saud was beheaded, his oldest son Khalid ibn-Saud was imprisoned in Cairo, and Saud's second son, Mishari, became the fifth emir.

While the Saudis were making forays into the south, the British entered into defense treaties with Oman, Bahrain, and the sheikdoms of the Persian Gulf. The sultan of Oman promised to end his piracy and slave trading and to prevent other foreign powers from moving into the area. In return, the British put a garrison of Indian troops in Muscat and promised to protect Oman. Bahrain agreed to a similar treaty. The British then persuaded the gulf sheikdoms to sign five-year truce treaties in return for military assistance if they followed the guidelines set in Oman. The little sheikdoms of Abu Dhabi, Dubai, Sharjah, Ajman, Ras al-Khayman and Umm al-Qaywayn were thereafter known as the Trucial States.

During the same period, the Russians started a

series of drives to gain access to the Persian Gulf. The czarists began their southern expansion by warring on Persia between 1804 and 1828 and capturing the northern third of the Persian Empire.

On the Arabian peninsula, Turki ibn-Saud, the grandson of the first emir, recaptured Riyadh from the Egyptians in 1824 and became the sixth emir. When Turki was killed by one of his cousins in 1834 during a Saud family power struggle, his son Faisal ibn-Saud avenged his father to become the seventh emir. The governor of Egypt learned of the reemergence of the Saudis in 1838, and sent his army back to Arabia. The Egyptians took Faisal prisoner and left his cousin, and son of the third emir, Khalid ibn-Saud, in charge as the eighth emir. Faisal ibn-Saud was held prisoner in Cairo for five years until the Turkish sultan released him and ordered that Arabia be restored to Ottoman rule. Faisal swore allegiance to the Ottomans, was reinstated as the tenth emir, and paid annual tribute to the Ottoman governor of Mecca. During his twenty-five-year reign, Faisal reconquered most of Nadj.

As the Saudis regained control of Nadj, the British captured the island fortress of Aden, off southern Arabia, and set up a trading center in Jeddah. In 1858, Jeddah and Mecca rebelled against the Ottoman edict to halt their slave trading and threatened the safety of the British consulate in Jeddah until the British Navy ended the rebellion. In 1875, the British bought the newly opened Suez Canal from Egypt and took control of the Red Sea. Later, they strengthened their control by taking Egypt and Sudan from the Ottomans.

The British also extended their influence over the Persian Gulf. Between 1853 and 1868, they entered into permanent treaties with the Trucial States, Bahrain, and Qatar to end slave trading and arms smuggling in the gulf in return for British recognition of their sovereignty. By the end of the nineteenth century, the British controlled all the seas surrounding the Arabian peninsula.

Far to the north, Russia continued its southern expansion in quest of a warm water port in wars with Persia and Turkey, pushing its border to within six hundred miles of the Persian Gulf.

In 1896, the new emir of Kuwait began negotiating with Russia to build a railroad to the Mediterranean Sea. When the British learned of the negotiations, they made a counter proposal to prevent Russian access to the Persian Gulf, and later entered into a secret treaty with Kuwait.

Meanwhile in the desert, bad times fell on the Saudis. After Faisal ibn-Saud had regained Nadj, he tangled with the British in vain attempts to take Bahrain, the Trucial States, and Oman.

Abdullah succeeded his father as eleventh emir after Faisal died in 1865, only to be deposed by his younger brother Saud ibn-Saud who became the twelfth emir. When Abdullah exposed the Saudi weakness by asking the Ottomans to help him regain his power, the Ottomans grabbed the eastern Saudi territory of al-Hasa. After Saud ibn-Saud died in

1875, Abdullah was reinstated and made the thirteenth emir. Nine years later, the sons of Saud ibn-Saud put their uncle Abdullah in prison. The Hail-based Rashid clan, of the huge Shammar tribe, observed the dissension in the house of Saud and took swift action. Muhammad ibn-Rashid ran the Saudis out of Riyadh and became emir. Within six years, the Rashids had gained control over all of Nadj. In 1891, Abdur Rahman ibn-Saud, the younger brother of Emirs Abdullah and Saud, declared himself the fourteenth emir but was chased out of Nadj by the Rashids. The Sauds fled to Kuwait where the Ottomans gave them a monthly allowance and permitted them to settle.

Abdul Aziz ibn-Abdul-Rahman al-Saud, the oldest son of Abdur Rahman and future king of Saudi Arabia, started his career by avenging his father. In January 1902, twenty-one-year-old Abdul Aziz slipped into Nadj, scaled the walls of the Riyadh palace at night and killed the Rashid governor as he entered the next morning. Abdul Aziz then climbed to the roof, threw the governor's head to the crowd below and announced the return of the Saudis to Nadj. When he gained recognition as the ruler of Riyadh, his father passed him the responsibility of imam, and Abdul Aziz ibn-Saud became the fourteenth emir and imam of the Wahhabis.

With control of Riyadh, Abdul Aziz began a series of raids into Rashid territory. By 1905, he had recaptured most of Nadj and part of Qasim. The Saudis continued their skirmishes until 1906 when they killed ibn-Rashid, accepted the allegiance of his tribe, and gained control of most of east central Arabia.

Western Arabia, though, was under the control of Hussein, the emir of Mecca and sheikh of the Hashmite tribe. The Hashmites were *sharifs* (direct descendants of the Prophet's daughter Fatima) and had been the emirs of Mecca since the time of Muhammad. When the Ottomans took over Mecca, they let the Hashmites continue to rule as Ottoman governors under orders from the sultan in Constantinople.

As Abdul Aziz and Sharif Hussein expanded their emirates, the superpowers were jockeying for territorial control of the Middle East in a power struggle that would involve them both.

By 1900, the Ottoman Empire had been eroded by European conquests until it controlled only Arabia, the Sinai, Palestine, Syria, Mesopotamia, Turkey, and the southern Balkans. After they lost Egypt and Sudan to the British, the Ottomans turned to Germany for help. Kaiser Wilhelm sent military advisors to the sultan and began building a railroad from Damascus to Hejaz to carry troops to the Islamic holy cities. As the German presence grew stronger, a group of army officers, called the Young Turks, gained power and forced the sultan to implement a Western-type constitution.

During the same period, Shiite leaders gained control of Persia and formed a new government. Soon afterwards, Russia moved troops into northern Persia to within two hundred miles of the Persian Gulf to "protect its border." Britain then moved troops into southeastern Persia and Afghanistan to defend its Indian colony against the Russians.

As the Persian and Ottoman governments changed, automobiles and oil-fired steam engines were gaining wide acceptance, and petroleum gained value as fuel. In 1908, oil was discovered in Persia. The British bought their concession and formed the Anglo-Persian Oil Company to assure a source of fuel for their new, steam-powered navy. Soon afterwards, the Ottomans sold their oil rights in Mesopotamia to German, Dutch, and British interests.

In Arabia, Sharif Hussein of Mecca kidnapped Emir Abdul Aziz's favorite brother and held him for ransom. After Abdul Aziz had obtained his brother's release by paying tribute and swearing allegiance to Hussein and the Ottomans, he renounced his allegiance and vowed to get even with Hussein.

Emir Abdul Aziz continued his attacks on other tribes and by 1911 had won control over a large portion of central Arabia. The young emir spared the life of many of his enemies if they swore allegiance and joined his army. He also took as his wife a daughter from each sheikh he defeated, and thus became a family member of all the tribes in the area.

Abdul Aziz's Bedouin warriors liked to make swift raids, but were unreliable because they would quit fighting if they became bored, and left if they got the opportunity to take enemy loot back to their camps. So, he created an army of Wahhabi religious zealots called the *Ikhwan*. The Ikhwan were taught to show no mercy because they were the mujahdun who would go to paradise if they died in battle. They were incited to spread Islam and Saud power by conquest. Eventually, Abdul Aziz set up sixty villages at the frontiers of his captured territories with seventy thousand Ikhwan who were sworn to protect the areas with their lives.

In 1913, Abdul Aziz ran out of growing room. When he captured al-Hasa, he took on the Ottoman garrison and forced it to retreat. However, he was worried about the Ottoman retaliation and so in May 1914, he agreed to accept Turkish rule in return for being made Ottoman governor of Nadj. Abdul Aziz could not expand his emirate further south or east because these lands were under British protection. If he expanded to the north or west, he risked retaliation from the Turks. Since the probability of war in Europe was becoming obvious, and the German influence on the Ottoman Empire was well known, Abdul Aziz approached the British to obtain their support in a rebellion against the Turks.

Abdul Aziz contacted Sir Percy Cox of the Colonial Office's Indian government, which controlled the British forces in eastern Arabia. At the same time, Sharif Hussein contacted the British high commissioner of Egypt, an agent of the British Foreign Office.

On 2 August, Turkey signed a secret alliance with Germany as war broke out in Europe. The Ottoman sultan declared a holy war against the allies and called for all Arabs to drive the unbelievers from their lands. Neither Sharif Hussein nor Abdul Aziz was drawn into the jihad because they did not trust the

Turks and wanted them out of Arabia.

The following month, the British pledged to protect Sharif Hussein if he joined the war against the
Turks. Turkey entered the war on 30 November 1914,
but Sharif Hussein took no action. In April 1915, the
British governor general of Sudan tried to force
Hussein into action by promising that the Arabian
peninsula would be made an independent nation
when the Turks were defeated. Three months later,
Hussein asked the new high commissioner in Egypt,
Sir Henry McMahon, to appoint him king of Arabia
and caliph of Islam.

Meanwhile, the British Foreign Office entered into
the secret Sykes-Picot Agreement with France and
Russia to divide the Arab area of the Ottoman Empire
into European colonies and to form an allied-occu-
pied, independent Arab state after the war.

In eastern Arabia, Abdul Aziz made an agreement
with the British government in India to fight the
Turks for five thousand pounds sterling per month.
In December 1915, Sir Percy Cox signed the Anglo-
Saudi Treaty which recognized Abdul Aziz as the
king of Nadj and al-Hasa. The treaty promised King
Abdul Aziz protection from other countries if he re-
frained from entering into treaties with other foreign
powers and from attacking other British protectorates.

In western Arabia, Sharif Hussein made a better
deal six months later with the British in Cairo.
Hussein agreed to stage a revolt against the Ottomans
for eleven million pounds sterling in gold. On 9 June

1916, the British Navy began bombarding Jeddah and Hussein's army attacked the Turkish garrison in Mecca. A week later, the Ottomans surrendered Jeddah and several weeks later, Mecca fell.

Flushed with victory, Hussein persuaded the people of Mecca to proclaim him king of the Arabs and demanded tribute from Abdul Aziz. Abdul Aziz threatened to invade Hejaz and put an end to the Sharif until the British talked him out of it.

The British Middle East commander-in-chief was disappointed with Sharif Hussein's progress. His tribes managed to take the small port villages of Rabeigh and Yanbu but could not even get near Medina. So, Captain T.E.Lawrence was sent to Jeddah as military liaison. Lawrence, soon to become the legendary Lawrence of Arabia, led raids against the Damascus-Hejaz railroad and helped Hussein's sons, Faisal and Zehd, capture the northern port villages of Wejh and Aqaba.

In 1917, the Arabs learned of the British double-dealing. During the Russian Revolution, the Bolsheviks withdrew from the European war and made details of the Sykes-Picot Agreement public. About the same time, the British issued the Balfour Declaration, pledging to create a national home for Jews in Palestine after the war. The Arabs felt that they had been betrayed but kept fighting.

Faisal and Lawrence continued to gather Bedouin tribes and fought their way through Amman into Damascus where Faisal, who had broken with his father, expected to be made king of Arabia for his heroism. Abdul Aziz and the Ikhwan continued to fight the large Shammar tribe of northern Arabia which had remained loyal to the Ottomans.

On 30 October 1918, the surrender of Turkey triggered an explosion of nationalistic rebellion in the former Ottoman Empire. Armenia, Azerbaijan, Georgia and Yemen became independent states.

The Arabs expected Britain to keep the promises of independence made in the McMahon correspondence, the Sykes-Picot Agreement, the Anglo-Saudi Treaty and the governor of Sudan's letter. But each party made contradictory promises and suggested borders that did not coincide with the historical claims of the peoples involved. The first two documents stated there would be an international zone in Palestine, a British zone in Mesopotamia called Iraq, a French zone in Syria, and an independent Arab state between the zones called Transjordan. The Anglo-Saudi treaty gave Abdul Aziz ibn-Saud independence in the interior of Arabia while Sharif Hussein thought the governor of Sudan had promised that he would be king of all Arabia. The Balfour Declaration stated that "His Majesty's Government views with favor the establishment in Palestine of a national home for the Jewish people."

The problems raised by the conflicting promises were not resolved in the peace conference in Versailles at the end of World War I, and were intensified in 1919 when Persia and Afghanistan were granted independence.

While the British were occupied in the north, Abdul Aziz and Sharif Hussein took matters into their own hands and tried to consolidate their positions. In May 1919, Sharif Hussein sent his son Abdullah and four thousand men to secure the oasis town of Khurma in eastern Hejaz. A few nights later, a thousand Ikhwan sneaked into their camp at midnight, as the Sharif's men were sleeping, and murdered everyone except Abdullah and a few of his friends. When the British learned of the slaughter, they threatened to intervene if Abdul Aziz attacked nearby Mecca.

Hussein tried to protect his flank by persuading the Idrisi tribe of Jizan to join him. The Idrisi attacked the Aidh tribe of Abha to try to force them to fight the Saudis. Instead, the Aidh asked the Saudis for help. Abdul Aziz's son Faisal and the Ikhwan raced to Abha, overwhelmed the Idrisi and captured all the lands in Asir south of Mecca.

In Egypt and Mesopotamia, the Arabs rebelled against British occupation. In March 1920, they convened an Arab congress in Damascus and proclaimed Sharif Hussein's son Faisal the king of Syria, and Hussein's son Abdullah the king of Iraq.

During the conference of World War I victors held the following month, Britain was given the mandate to rule Iraq, Transjordan, and Palestine "with the obligation to carry out the policy of the Balfour Declaration." France was given the mandate to rule Syria and Lebanon. The French regarded Faisal as a troublemaker and kicked him out of Syria. The British, who felt they owed Faisal something for his wartime service, made him king of Iraq and made his brother

Abdullah the king of Transjordan. The San Remo conference later confirmed the appointments of Abdullah and Faisal and supported Hussein's claim as king of Hejaz.

Abdul Aziz was enraged at the appointment of his Hashmite enemies as kings of the neighboring kingdoms to his north and northeast and refused to recognize the authority of Hussein. So, he started a campaign of propaganda and violence against his neighbors and renewed his assault on the Rashids. After he reconquered the Rashids in 1921, he annexed the Shammar tribe and brought all of central Arabia under his control.

After repeated Ikhwan attacks on Iraq, Kuwait, and the Trucial States, the British told Abdul Aziz to stop the raids and began a series of meetings at the village of Uqayr to define Saudi boundaries. During the discussions, the Ikhwan raided Transjordan and massacred the entire population of a village outside Amman. The British air force decimated the Ikhwan raiders and spurred on the discussions of Saudi boundaries.

Since both sides claimed the territory, the British high commissioner, Percy Cox, set the borders as he saw fit. Cox took the opportunity to connect the borders of the British protectorates of Palestine, Transjordan, and Iraq to give Britain an overland route between them without crossing the French protectorates of Syria and Lebanon. He drew a series of straight lines on a map of Arabia to establish the borders with little regard for topography, natural boundaries, or the claims of the inhabitants. In the process, he gave thousands of square miles claimed by Abdul Aziz to Iraq and Transjordan. To compensate for the loss of those lands, Abdul Aziz was given a tiny area claimed by Kuwait, that was later discovered to be floating on oil. In November 1922, the parties signed the Protocol of Uqayr which defined the borders of Iraq, Kuwait, and Nadj.

In the course of World War I, the demand for fuel caused the price of oil to triple and forced governments to recognize its strategic value. Britain immediately grabbed the oil concessions offered by Bahrain, Oman, and the Gulf States. When they took over Iraq, they gave Germany's former oil shares to France and formed the Iraq Petroleum Company (IPC). But they did not have the concessions on the Arabian mainland. During the meetings at Uqayr, a New Zealand businessman finessed Percy Cox and obtained Abdul Aziz's oil concession.

During that same period, the British withdrew their troops from Egypt which, in 1922, also became an independent kingdom.

In March 1924, the Turkish Grand National Assembly adopted the Western alphabet, established secular law, separated the state from religion, and abolished the Ottoman caliphate. Sharif Hussein then proclaimed himself the new caliph of Islam and forbade the Ikhwan from making the pilgrimage to Mecca. That same month, Abdul Aziz became a free agent when he received the last payment for his wartime alliance with the British.

Three months later, Abdul Aziz struck. Large bands of Bedouin raced into Transjordan and Iraq, raided villages, harassed Hussein's sons and diverted their attention from the south. Meanwhile, tens of thousands of Ikhwan moved westward to Hejaz. In September, three thousand wild-eyed Ikhwan warriors raided Taif. Prince Ali and his Hashmite army deserted their outpost and Taif fell without a shot. As the Ikhwan set up camp they were fired upon. They retaliated by shooting and slashing three hundred people to death before their leaders could stop them. When the people of Mecca learned of the massacre in Taif they panicked. In October 1924, Sharif Hussein, the king of the Hejaz, abdicated in favor of his son Ali, and went into exile. Ali then retreated to Jeddah.

The Ikhwan rode into Mecca, destroyed the idols and shrines in the Kaaba and treated the Meccans as inferiors. In the second week of October, Abdul Aziz entered Mecca dressed as a pilgrim and told the Meccans that he would let an Islamic congress decide their fate.

Ali and the people of Jeddah prepared their defense inside the ancient walled city, but Abdul Aziz did not attack. Instead, he kept the city under siege for a year until thirst, hunger, and disease ruined their resolve. In December 1925, Ali surrendered Jeddah after he learned that the Ikhwan had captured Yanbu and Medina. On 8 January 1926, the leaders of Mecca proclaimed Abdul Aziz king of the Hejaz.

Abdul Aziz accepted his new title as a mandate to rule Hejaz. He promised to create a consultative council and national constitution and appointed the most trusted members of his family to rule his conquered territories. King Abdul Aziz made his oldest son, Saud, the governor of Nadj and his next oldest son, Faisal, the governor of Hejaz. His half brother, Abdullah ibn-Julwi, was made governor of Hail in the north, and another half brother, Abdul Aziz ibn-Musaid, was named governor of al-Hasa in the east. He then appointed the Alireza family as advisors and lenders to the court.

The British recognized Abdul Aziz as the king of Hejaz, Nadj and its dependencies in the Treaty of Jeddah on 20 May 1927, in return for his renewed promise to stop attacking Kuwait, Bahrain, Qatar, and the Trucial States.

After two hundred years of fighting, the Saudis had won uncontested control of most of Arabia, and for the first time in one thousand years, the interior of Arabia was under one rule.

In the meantime, the Shiites lost control of Persia. In 1921, Colonel Reza Khan overthrew the Shiite shah. Four years later, he proclaimed himself shah and adopted the ancient Persian name of Pahlavi to identify himself with the former Sassanid Empire.

Reza Khan rekindled the age-old frontier dispute between the Persians and the Iraqi Arabs by refusing to pay transit fees for crossing Iraqi territory. The British-Russian 1847 Treaty of Erzurum set the boundaries of the Ottoman and Persian empires on the Persian bank of the last sixty miles of the Shatt al-Arab river that flows into the Persian Gulf. Consequently, ships tied to Persian piers at the oil port of Abadan or the southern terminal of the Persian railroad at Khorramshahr were in Iraqi waters and were required to pay transit fees to Iraq to travel to the Persian Gulf.

Far to the north, the Soviet Union absorbed the countries of Georgia and Azerbaijan as it continued its southern expansion under its new Bolshevik leadership.

In Arabia, the fanatical Ikhwan spurned the Treaty of Jeddah and continued raiding tribes in Iraq and Kuwait in the hope of converting them to Wahhabism. The Ikhwan continued the strict Wahhabi rejection of modern ideas and forbade the use of innovations such as radios and cars. When Abdul Aziz began to use telephones and permitted the sale of tobacco to generate tax revenues, the Ikhwan felt betrayed and in 1927, they revolted.

Sheikh ibn-Bijad led the Utaibah, Mutayr, Ajman, and other Ikhwan tribes in a series of murderous raids into Iraq and provoked British retaliation. In February 1929, ibn-Bijad aborted an attack into Iraq because of a suspected British ambush, and raided tribes in Nadj instead. King Abdul Aziz responded to the challenge of his authority by raising an army of forty thousand Nadj townsmen and crushing ibn-Bijad and most of the Ikhwan. The following year, the rest of the Ikhwan were captured by the British during a raid into Kuwait.

Abdul Aziz disbanded the Ikhwan, imprisoned its leaders, banned tribal warfare, and began efforts to suppress tribal identification. When the Beni Harb tribe in Hejaz broke his ban and raided another tribe, Abdul Aziz swooped into the area with loyal tribes and killed two hundred Harb tribesmen.

After the Ikhwan raids into Iraq ended in 1930, King Abdul Aziz signed a peace treaty with his former Hashmite enemy, King Faisal of Iraq. Two years later, Iraq became an independent state.

On 18 September 1932, the dual kingdoms of Hejaz and Nadj were officially united as the kingdom of Saudi Arabia. The symbol of the new kingdom was the green flag of the Sauds which portrays a white horizontal sword under the Islamic creed, "There is no god but Allah, and Muhammad is the messenger of Allah."

King Abdul Aziz ibn-Abdul Rahman al-Saud became the first king of Saudi Arabia. He was the king of a totally barren land, with less than half a million subjects who did not trust each other and spent their time wandering in search of grazing lands.

In 1933, King Abdul Aziz sold Standard Oil Company of California (Socal) the previously lapsed oil concession in the "eastern portion of the kingdom." Six months later, Kuwait awarded its oil concession to the British Anglo-Persian Oil Company and Gulf Oil which together formed the Kuwait Oil Company. The next year, Qatar granted its oil concession to the British-controlled IPC, with no southern boundary defined. The race was on.

Socal began exploration in the coastal areas closest to Bahrain near Qatar and the Trucial States.

When IPC found a promising oil-bearing geological structure located in the southern Qatar peninsula, Abdul Aziz claimed that it was in Saudi territory. The British rejected his claim and Socal and IPC found themselves in contention for the same oil rights.

Britain claimed that the 1913 Anglo-Ottoman convention set the eastern Saudi border as a line starting at the Saudi coast west of Qatar and running straight into the Rub al-Khali desert. King Abdul Aziz was fed up with British lines drawn on maps and pointed out that he was not bound by that treaty because he had rebelled against the Ottomans prior to its enactment. He then claimed two hundred thousand square miles of suspected oil-bearing lands also claimed by Qatar, the Trucial States, and Oman, based on his family's historical occupation of the area, the Anglo-Saudi Treaty, and the Treaty of Jeddah.

Sixteen years later, King Abdul Aziz repeated his claim when Qatar exported its first oil. In October 1949, he claimed four-fifths of the Abu Dhabi sheikdom and all the oil concessions granted to the IPC. When the British objected, Abdul Aziz agreed to arbitration by international tribunal, but began secretly paying the tribal leaders of the al-Buraimi oases to claim Saudi citizenship.

Old King Abdul Aziz became seriously ill and had to depend on his son Crown Prince Saud to run the country.

Saud escalated the border dispute in August 1952 by sending an armed column of Aramco vehicles into al-Buraimi and capturing some Omani villages. The sultan of Oman counterattacked with several hundred tribesmen until the British government forced him to stop. The United States and Britain told both sides to sit tight until the dispute was decided by the international tribunal. During the subsequent two-year occupation, Prince Saud gave the local sheikhs millions of dollars and large supplies of arms to rebel and claim they were Saudis.

After leading his people for over half a century, King Abdul Aziz ibn-Abdul Rahman al-Saud died on 9 November 1953. He was succeeded by the oldest of his forty-seven living sons, Crown Prince Saud ibn-Abdul Aziz. His next oldest son, Faisal ibn Abdul Aziz, was named the new crown prince.

The second king of Saudi Arabia, King Saud, lacked the poise, wisdom, and discipline of his father. He jeopardized the kingdom through his rash acts and spent money on himself like it was going out of style.

When Saud became king, he built himself ten palaces, some costing over $25 million. He had the old palace in Riyadh torn down and built a new mile-square palace where he lived with hundreds of wives. The new royal complex included rows of fine villas, mosques, schools, shops and manicured gardens and was surrounded by a fifteen-foot high wall, seven miles long. It consumed more water than the entire city of Riyadh.

In August 1954, King Saud tried to win the border dispute by offering $140 million in bribes to the brother of the Abu Dhabi sultan and the imam of

Oman, Talib ibn-Ali. The next year, he tried to bribe two members of the international tribunal. In disgust, the Trucial States and Oman gave up, accepted the boundary claimed by Abdul Aziz in 1935, and evicted the Saudis from the oasis.

King Saud lost face by having his men kicked out of al-Buraimi and he sought revenge against the Omani sultan. After the sultan of Oman learned of his treachery, Talib ibn-Ali fled to Saudi Arabia. King Saud welcomed Talib and gave him weapons to attack the sultan. The following year, Talib ibn-Ali slipped back into Oman, declared that he was still imam and started a revolt which lasted eighteen months before the British army chased him out of the country.

The Saudi people became disgusted with King Saud. They painted anti-Saud slogans on the beautiful palace walls and started mutinies in the army. The unrest was so widespread by April 1955 that Saud's hot-tempered younger brother, Muhammad, started plans to depose him.

By that time, Saud had become a fan of Egypt's Gamel Nasser and supported his anti-West activities. President Eisenhower, alarmed by Russian involvement in Egypt, asked to meet with the Saudi king. Saud leapt at the chance for more American money and traveled to Washington. During the meeting, Eisenhower gave Saud a $250 million loan to support the West.

When King Saud made a few feeble, tactless attempts to support the West, he insulted Nasser. The Egyptian president retaliated by unleashing a humiliating campaign of radio broadcasts throughout the Middle East which described Saud's alcoholism, drug abuse, sexual depravity with young Bedouin girls, and other perversions. Several months later, the Saudi people tried to assassinate King Saud. Saud soon retaliated by paying $10 million to Gamel Nasser's personal pilot to put a bomb aboard his plane.

Saud's leadership was not any better than his diplomatic skills. The king and his corrupt staff ran the government with no regard for the needs of the kingdom, squandered its oil revenues and American loans, and amassed huge debts.

The ulama could not take any more of Saud's embarrassing behavior, incompetence, and wild spending. Afraid that the royal family would be overthrown, they ordered Saud to let his brother, Crown Prince Faisal, run the country.

In May 1958, King Saud issued a royal decree which made Faisal the prime minister, responsible for running the government. Faisal set up a Council of Ministers to supervise functions and approve expenditures, and made the Ministry of Finance responsible for creating budgets and collecting revenues. Faisal then started straightening out the kingdom's finances and planning the course of its development.

The kingdom was starting to get its act together, but King Saud could not leave well enough alone. He was irritated with the financial restrictions on his life-style so he began to manipulate his power to regain control. Saud promised his brother Prince Talal and four other princes that he would form a constitutional government if they gave him their support. In December 1961, King Saud used their leverage to force Faisal to resign. Saud then assumed the role of prime minister, and made Talal minister of finance.

But King Saud never had any intention of implementing a constitution. In February 1962, he refused to consider Prince Talal's draft of a constitution. When Talal persisted, Saud issued a royal decree specifying prison sentences for any ministers guilty of lying in attempts to "alter the royal order." King Saud finally fired Talal when he continued to push for the constitution. Talal and the other frustrated young princes left the kingdom in July and went to Beirut. There, they publicly criticized King Saud for not keeping his promise and demonstrated their interest in democracy by freeing their slaves and concubines. King Saud retaliated by voiding their passports. So, the young princes went to Cairo and joined forces with President Nasser.

Two months later, a group of army officers overthrew the North Yemeni imam and declared the country a republic. The following week, Nasser sent a large Egyptian expeditionary force to assist the Yemeni rebels. King Saud sent arms and supplies to support the deposed imam. In Cairo, Prince Talal broadcast that King Saud was a backward tyrant and called on the Saudi people to revolt and form a democratic republic. Several Saudi air force pilots ferrying supplies to Yemen heard the broadcast and changed course to Egypt. The next day, two more pilots defected to Cairo with their aircraft.

The desert dynasty was furious. On 17 October they forced King Saud to reappoint Prince Faisal as prime minister. Faisal, who was in the United States, met with President Kennedy and discussed his planned reforms. Before Faisal left, he got President Kennedy's approval of the reforms and assurance that the United States would support Saudi Arabia if attacked by Egypt.

With this encouragement, Crown Prince Faisal issued a ten-point reform program on 6 November 1962. The program abolished slavery. It promised to issue a constitution and set up local governments. It created a Ministry of Justice and a twenty-member Judicial Council. The program promised to reduce the influence of the Religious Police by strengthening Islamic propaganda. It pledged to provide public education and social welfare programs. The program vowed to provide water, agriculture, and roads. It also pledged to regulate commercial activities and develop the country's resources.

The implementation of reforms, however, was delayed by Saudi involvement in North Yemen. The Yemeni rebels quickly gained control of the cities and coastal plain but could not defeat the loyalist tribes in the rugged mountains. President Nasser sent additional Russian equipment and seventy thousand Egyptian troops to help the Yemeni rebels. The Saudis continued to give money and munitions to the royalists.

Nasser decided to end the Saudi support of royalist forces by launching air raids and ground assaults into Saudi Arabia. President Kennedy sent a squadron of United States fighter planes to Dhahran and the Egyptians ended their air strikes. Things cooled down in 1963, when both sides agreed to a United Nations-monitored cease-fire and non-intervention plan. Saudi Arabia stopped supplying the royalists, but Egyptian participation continued despite Nasser's promises to withdraw his troops.

Prince Faisal's reform program was blocked for two years by King Saud's struggle to exert power. King Saud just hid in his Riyadh palace under the protection of one thousand national guardsmen. In March 1964, the leading princes and the Council of Ministers declared Saud unfit to govern, stripped him of all powers, and transferred them to Prince Faisal. In spite of this declaration, King Saud challenged Faisal's authority and tried to regain control of the government. Finally on 2 November 1964, Saud was deposed by a joint resolution of the royal family, the Council of Ministers, and the ulama, which proclaimed fifty-nine-year old Faisal as the third king of Saudi Arabia.

King Faisal ibn-Abdul Aziz passed over his brother, Muhammad, and selected the next oldest half brother, Khalid, as crown prince.

Faisal was extremely pious and feared Zionism and communism as threats to Islam. Because of his deep religious convictions, Faisal was able to overcome the ulama's concerns regarding modernization.

In a major break from Wahhabi principles, King

Faisal convinced the ulama that television could be used to reinforce Islamic values and decreed that it could be shown in the kingdom. Other devout members of the royal family objected. When the new station began broadcasting, one of the princes led a large armed mob in an attempt to stop it. The prince and many of his followers were killed in a gun battle as they stormed the building, but television broadcasting continued.

The eastern frontier dispute continued as Faisal kept up the pressure. In 1965, Qatar's new emir ceded his claim on the Khaur al-Udaid creek to the Saudis. The concession of the bay ended the border dispute and gave the Saudis access to the Persian Gulf southeast of Qatar.

After former King Saud moved to Cairo, he switched his allegiance by supporting Nasser's attempt to gain control of all southern Arabia. King Faisal tried to negotiate with Nasser to stop his meddling in Arabia. After diplomacy failed, Faisal met with President Johnson in June 1966 to assure continued United States backing and lined up support from Morocco, Pakistan, Somalia, and Iran. Faisal then bought American planes and British armaments to defend the kingdom's southern frontier.

The following December, the Saudi National Liberation Front and the Popular Front for the Liberation of the Arabian Peninsula tried to kill the king by planting bombs in his Riyadh and Dammam palaces.

During the June 1967 Arab-Israeli war, King Faisal sent an army brigade to Jordan and cut off oil shipments to the West to force them to stop supplying ammunition to Israel. Faisal was enraged by the overwhelming Israeli victory. When he learned that the Israelis had captured Jerusalem, he appeared before a crowd in Riyadh and called for a holy war to return all of Arabia to the Muslims. The next day, on 7 June, Saudis set off bombs at the walls of the United States embassy in Jeddah. In Dhahran, anti-American riots erupted and mobs stormed the United States consulate, the airfield, and Aramco where they tore down American flags, destroyed houses, and disrupted work for a week.

The closure of the Suez Canal during the Israeli blitzkrieg halted the payment of transit fees to the Egyptians. Egypt's shattered economy finally forced Nasser to withdraw his troops from North Yemen. In pan-Islamic spirit, King Faisal met with Arab leaders in September 1967 at the postwar summit conference in Khartoum. During the meetings, Faisal smoothed his relations with Egypt and Jordan by pledging them annual subsidies of $140 million to help restore their war-torn economies.

While the surrounding countries were being devastated by civil wars, King Faisal tried to hold his kingdom together by compromising to satisfy the needs of Wahhabi religious extremists, Arab nationalists, and the young Saudis who wanted rapid modernization; but he was not successful.

In June 1969, a massive revolutionary conspiracy, which involved the Popular Democratic Front, the Saudi National Liberation Front, the Federation of

Democratic Forces, and the Islamic Revolutionary Organization, was discovered and crushed. Thousands of Saudis implicated in the conspiracy were arrested, including many military personnel based in Jeddah, Dhahran, and Riyadh—clerks, teachers, and government employees, hundreds of Shiites in the al-Hasa province, and individuals from prominent Hejaz families. Among those arrested were the dean of the University of Petroleum and Minerals, the commandant of the Military Staff College, the director of the Institute of Public Administration, the assistant director of the National Police Academy, and the commander of the Dhahran air base. During the purge, many ringleaders were tortured to death and air force officers were thrown to their death from airplanes. Over 130 military personnel were executed, 305 were imprisoned for life and another 750 were sentenced to fifteen years imprisonment.

After the Saud Dynasty realized how close they had come to being toppled, they divided the military into a regular army and a National Guard and put each under the direction of a trusted senior prince. The National Guard was made up of Nadj townsmen and Bedouin tribesmen with unquestioned loyalty to the king, and wore white turbans in the Ikhwan tradition. They were made responsible for internal security and counterinsurgency. The army was composed of townsmen from other parts of the kingdom and made responsible for protecting the kingdom against external attack. To further assure stability, the army was widely dispersed.

In August 1970, King Faisal approved a five-year development plan which allocated 25 percent of the budget for strengthening the kingdom's defense capabilities. It provided the balance of the budget for creating a basic infrastructure without disrupting religious and social values.

Three years later, Faisal warned the West that he was planning to use his oil as a weapon in the Arab conflict with Israel. In February 1973, Saudi oil minister, Ahmad Zaki al-Yamani, announced that, "Europe should watch out for the catastrophe which lies in wait for it....I have made my preparations, as have other Arabs, to deprive Europe completely of oil. We shall ruin your industries as well as your trade with the Arab world." Late in May, after meeting with President Sadat in Egypt, King Faisal told key oil company executives, "Time is running out with respect to United States' interests in the Middle East." He warned the executives that they " would lose everything" if the United States did not stop supporting Israel.

That fall, Israel was attacked by Egypt and Syria in a lightning offensive which destroyed many Israeli weapons. Israel desperately requested replacements from the United States and mounted a counteroffensive.

Faisal sent an ultimatum to President Nixon that he would cut off oil to the United States if he honored Israel's plea for weapons. When Nixon refused to submit to the threat, King Faisal stopped oil shipments to the United States and the American forces in

Vietnam.

On 20 October Faisal doubled his oil prices and persuaded the other Arab countries to join in a jihad against Zionism by suspending oil shipments to countries that supported Israel. Faisal told the Japanese that if they wanted oil, they would have to convince the United States to stop supporting Israel.

In November, the Saudis threatened to ruin the world economy if military action was taken to break the embargo. Secretary of State Henry Kissinger announced that the United States would have to consider countermeasures if the Arab boycott continued too long. Soon afterwards, Saudi oil minister al-Yamani appeared on Danish television, denounced the United States, and said that the Arabs would respond by reducing oil production 80 percent and raising the prices to $20 per barrel. Zaki al-Yamani also stated, "I don't know to what extent Europe and Japan will get together to join the Americans in any kind of measures, because your economy will definitely collapse all of a sudden. If the Americans are thinking of a military action, this is a possibility, but it is suicide. There are sensitive areas in the oil fields in Saudi Arabia which will be blown up."

The Arab members of OPEC met on 23 December 1973 and more than doubled oil prices again. They explained that the new prices were derived "on the basis of generosity and kindness." One Arab official announced that "it is our revenge for Poitiers!" in reference to the Christian defeat of the Arabs in 732.

By March 1974, King Faisal was the leading figure

in the Arab world. He lifted the oil embargo to the United States after he realized he had gotten away with quadrupling the price of oil during the last two months of 1973.

Faisal then negotiated a partial settlement to the ongoing eastern border dispute. He had previously demanded that Abu Dhabi stop oil production in his oil fields. When the United Arab Emirates gained their independence in 1971, the Saudis refused to recognize the new states or their common frontiers. In August 1974, King Faisal agreed to recognize the sovereign rights of the United Arab Emirates and renounce his claim to al-Buraimi oasis. In return, Abu Dhabi gave Saudi Arabia the western part of the emirate which included a large part of its Zarrara oil field and a narrow corridor between Qatar and the emirates.

On 25 March 1975, King Faisal's reign ended abruptly when he was shot by his nephew, Prince Faisal bin-Musaid, the brother of the prince killed by police at the opening of the first Saudi television station. After an extensive investigation concluded that there was no conspiracy involved, the American-educated prince was publicly beheaded before a cheering crowd of twenty thousand in Riyadh.

King Faisal was named "1975 Man of the Year" by *Time* magazine in recognition of all he had done for Saudi Arabia. He had organized its government, started a number of development programs, and improved his people's standard of living. Faisal helped the kingdom regain the respect of other Arab countries and took it from bankruptcy to great wealth. He also came close to destroying the world's economy and made a lot of bitter enemies. The *Washington Post's* editorial comment on King Faisal's death was that "Faisal probably did more damage to the West than any other single man since Adolf Hitler."

Faisal was succeeded by sixty-two-year-old Crown Prince Khalid as the fourth king of Saudi Arabia. King Khalid ibn-Abdul Aziz then selected his third youngest brother, Fahd, as crown prince over the strenuous objections of his fifth youngest brother, Abdullah.

King Khalid had over thirty years of administrative experience. However, his condition was so unstable, following previous open-heart surgery, that he traveled in a Boeing 747 equipped with an operating room and medical team. Thus, he immediately appointed Crown Prince Fahd as prime minister.

One of King Khalid's first official acts was to approve a second five-year development plan, over twenty times larger than the first, and expand the Council of Ministers to carry out the plan. It was drastically expanded at the last minute to buy as much Western technology as possible and allocated 26 percent of the budget to modernize the kingdom's defense capability while the bonanza oil revenues lasted.

King Khalid loaned Oman over $350 million to finance its civil war and arranged for Saudi mediation of discussions between South Yemen and Oman. The discussions resulted in a cease-fire in March 1976 and the withdrawal of South Yemeni forces from Dhofar. Several months later, the sultan's forces subdued the rebels and restored peace to Oman.

When the fighting stopped, Khalid cancelled Oman's debt in return for a fifty-mile-wide strip of the western Oman desert frontier. The settlement placed the Oman-Saudi Arabian border close to the fifty-sixth meridian originally claimed by King Abdul Aziz, and gave the Saudis undisputed ownership of more suspected oil-bearing land.

After resolving the border dispute with Oman, King Khalid resumed negotiations with Abu Dhabi. Abu Dhabi finally gave in and ceded Saudi Arabia another forty miles of its northern, twenty miles of its western, and ten miles of its southern frontiers. The concession gave the Saudis more of the Abu Dhabi oil fields. It also gave them a forty-mile-wide corridor to Khaur al-Duwahin bay on the Persian Gulf and provided the Saudis a location for an oil port and naval base.

Meanwhile, the Saud family was shaken by another conspiracy. Plans for a revolt of Saudi air force and army units at Tabuk, Hail, Dhahran, and Taif were discovered by Jordanian military intelligence. Jordan's King Hussein saved the day by sending his Desert Legion to suppress the rebellion.

The Saud dynasty again realized how shaky its power was and entered into a new agreement with the United States "to maintain the independence and integrity of Saudi Arabia under its present rulers." The Saudis promised to increase daily oil production to

10.4 million barrels per day and to sell the United States 2 million barrels per day to create a strategic reserve. In return, the United States guaranteed full political, economic, and military support to King Khalid.

On 20 November 1979, the first day of the Islamic year 1400, a band of religious fanatics seized the huge Grand Mosque in Mecca and threatened 50,000 pilgrims. The Koran, which says that whoever enters the mosque "shall be safe," was violated by 350 heavily armed Saudis and other Arabs led by a descendent of the former Ikhwan leader. He claimed that his partner was the mahdi who had appeared to deliver the country from the misconduct of the Saudi rulers. When the imam refused to recognize him, the group shot up the place and took hostages. They demanded that women's education, television, and soccer be banned from the kingdom, and that Shiites be forbidden to enter the sacred mosque. The demands caused riots in Shiite villages near Dhahran where the Followers of Ali broke into a police station, stole guns, and killed 15 people. Meanwhile, the National Guard fought their way into the mosque, and after many casualties, ousted its captors from the catacombs on 4 December. During the fighting, 75 rebels were killed. A month later, 63 more were brought to eight different towns throughout the kingdom and publicly beheaded before angry screaming mobs. The capture of the mosque outraged the entire Muslim world and caused massive loss of face for the Saud family. In the ensuing repercussions, many key Saudi officials were replaced, including the prince responsible for governing Mecca.

In May 1980, King Khalid approved a third five-year development plan that was double the size of the second plan and allocated 27 percent of the budget for continued expansion of the kingdom's defense capabilities.

Khalid died on 12 June 1982 and was mourned as a quiet, gentle man who guided his country along a moderate path. King Khalid was succeeded by sixty-two-year old Crown Prince Fahd as the fifth king of Saudi Arabia.

King Fahd ibn-Abdul Aziz al-Saud wanted to select his younger full brother Sultan as his heir apparent and make him prime minister. But the Saud family elders overruled him and forced him to select Abdullah, his despised half brother and next oldest living son of the first king, as crown prince. Thus, King Fahd retained the prime minister's office himself.

Fahd is the oldest of seven sons of King Abdul Aziz and his favorite wife, Hasa bint-Sudairi. He and his influential al-Sudairi brothers are known as the al-Fahd and have a long-standing blood feud with their half brother, Abdullah. The Saud family selected sixty-year-old Prince Abdullah, despite his mutual dislike of Fahd, to provide a balance that satisfied all interest groups in the kingdom. The Sauds, well aware of the results of religious discontent in Iran, were afraid that they would lose support of the Wahhabis if they did not appoint Abdullah.

During his twenty years in top government positions, Fahd was deeply involved in creating all three development plans and had served as the kingdom's senior ambassador in the mediation of peace discussions with warring neighbors. He was respected as a brilliant administrator, had traveled widely, and spoke fluent English. But he lacked the common touch and the father image the Saudi people have come to expect of their leader.

King Fahd is a pro-Western moderate with a prior reputation as a playboy who enjoyed drinking, gambling and womanizing. He is also extremely ostentatious. He built a billion-dollar palace overlooking Jeddah atop a 150-foot high island dredged from the Red Sea, and owns one of the largest yachts in the world. Fahd's son also caused tongues to wag by clearing a half-billion-dollar profit by acting as an agent in the award of one of the country's major contracts. These things did not sit well with the ulama.

Crown Prince Abdullah is very conservative. He has the support of the Wahhabi ulama, is closely associated with Bedouin tribal leaders and has the loyalty of the National Guard. Abdullah gives priority to Arabic and Islamic causes, is pro-Syrian, and favors holding oil production to a minimum.

Despite the Saud policy of presenting a united front to the world and keeping their potential enemies divided, it is widely rumored that Fahd and Abdullah have had violent clashes. One rumor has it that Abdullah tried an unsuccessful coup in Medina;

another suggests that Abdullah threatened to shoot Fahd. There have been so many rumors that the government has had to deny them officially.

The desert dynasty is in about its fifth generation, but that is difficult to define by Western standards. Instead of a family tree with clearly visible branches, the Saud dynasty is like a vine-entangled jungle. Many prominent sections of the family date back to the early emirs of Nadj and have taken different family names such as Jiluwis, al-Kabirs, the Abdullah al-Turki, and al-Shayk. The lineages became intertwined, as cousins married cousins, and broad, as the ancestors had many wives and many children by each wife. The first king, Abdul Aziz, had over three hundred wives, about fifty sons and countless daughters. Most of his sons also had many wives and children. About five hundred princes are direct descendents from King Abdul Aziz ibn-Saud. There are over four thousand adult princes in the extended Saud family which has intermarried with every family in the kingdom. The entire family is estimated to number over twenty thousand members.

Most key positions in the government are filled by members of the Saud family. King Fahd is prime minister. The second in line of succession, first deputy prime minister and commander of the National Guard, is Crown Prince Abdullah. Third in line of succession, second deputy prime minister, minister of defense and aviation and commander of the army, is King Fahd's full brother Prince Sultan. Prince Saud al-Faisal, a thirty-nine-year old Princeton graduate and leader of the Young Nephews, is minister of foreign affairs. The minister of the interior is Prince Naif. Prince Mutaib is minister of public works and housing and the minister of agriculture and water is Prince Abdul-Rahman.

Many of the princes are governors of parts of the kingdom. Prince Muhammad ibn-Fahd is in charge of the eastern province. Prince Khalid rules Asir province, and Qasim is run by Prince Abdulellah. Medina is run by Prince Abdul al-Majid, Prince Majid is in charge of Mecca, and Riyadh is under Prince Salman. Hail is governed by Prince Muqrin and Prince Abdulmujeed rules Tabuk.

Hundreds of other senior positions are held by members of the royal family. Prince Faisal is president of youth welfare. Prince Bandar is the ambassador to the United States. Prince Ahmad is deputy minister of the interior. Prince Badr is deputy commander of the National Guard, and about twenty-five other princes are senior officers in the National Guard, army, and air force.

The Wahhabi al-Shayk family, related to the Sauds for over two hundred years, holds key positions that enforce religious values such as minister of justice, minister of pilgrimage affairs, minister of higher education, director general of public security forces and head of military intelligence. Other key spots and sensitive positions in government are given to natives of Nadj that the royal family feels it can trust.

Saud family members receive financial allowances from the government based on lineage, generation, and age. King Abdul Aziz's sons receive payments of about $180,000 per year and junior members receive annual payments of roughly $36,000. That is over $150 million per year just for allowances, but the Saudi economy can handle it.

Chapter 6

RAGS TO RICHES

Saudi Arabia soared from bankruptcy to the world's twentieth richest country in twenty years. By 1980, its gross national product of $100 billion was higher than the long-established countries of Czechoslovakia, South Africa, and Argentina and slightly less than Switzerland at $106 billion, and Sweden at $111 billion. In terms of per capita income, Saudi Arabia ranked fourth out of 171 countries, with an average of $18,344 for every man, woman and child in the kingdom, ten places ahead of the United States, which had $11,360.

It is the largest oil-exporting country in the world

and its proven oil reserves exceed the combined total of those of the United States, Russia, Venezuela, Mexico, and Canada. Saudi Arabia's reserves are estimated to comprise 150 trillion barrels of oil and 85,000 trillion cubic feet of natural gas; enough to last almost one hundred years at current production rates.

With no national debt and with reserves of about $50 billion worth of gold, United States treasury bills and investments in Western banks, Saudi Arabia is one of the most solvent countries in the world. It alone can single-handedly boost the world's economy or cripple leading industrial countries by varying its oil production rates.

But in 1932 it had nothing. When the kingdom was founded, it had no roads, railroads, ports, or airfields. It had no known natural resources and almost no agricultural production. Its revenues came from taxes paid by pilgrims visiting Mecca and it was a million dollars in debt. As soon as King Abdul Aziz got the tax money, he spent it and kept no record of his expenditures. The king's treasurer, Abdullah Sulayman, had to suspend payment of debts, commandeer gasoline from merchants, and borrow $500,000 from Britain to survive.

The next year, Saudi Arabia got a break when Socal asked King Abdul Aziz for drilling rights in the kingdom. Socal had discovered oil in Bahrain and felt there could be major oil deposits on the mainland. It outbid the British and paid an advance of $250,000 and $25,000 per year for a sixty-year tax-free concession for oil rights over 361,000 square miles. Socal also agreed to pay royalties for any oil produced.

In 1936, Socal sold half its concession to the Texas Oil Company (Texaco). Together they formed two new companies called the California Arabian Oil Company (Casoc) and the California Texas Oil Company (Caltex). Casoc's mandate was to locate oil and begin its production; Caltex was responsible for marketing and distributing the oil.

Socal's investment paid off in March 1938 when Casoc struck oil in Dhahran. In 1939, Casoc produced four million barrels of oil and paid the king revenues of $1.9 million. In return, King Abdul Aziz granted Casoc another concession of 77,000 square miles in the neutral zone between Saudi Arabia and Kuwait.

Italian planes bombed the oil terminal at Dhahran in October 1940 and forced Casoc to scale down its efforts. World War II material shortages delayed expansion and limited oil production to twenty thousand barrels per day. The war also prevented pilgrims from visiting Mecca. The financial situation in Saudi Arabia became critical and King Abdul Aziz asked Casoc and the Allies for loans against future oil revenues. Casoc loaned the king $3 million and Britain loaned him almost $2 million per year. Executives of Socal and Texaco appealed to the United States government to finance the kingdom. They argued that Casoc could not afford to loan more money to the Saudis because its oil production was too low and they were convinced that the British would try to get Casoc's oil concessions in return for aid. The United States government shared the concern and considered buying out Casoc to keep the oil as an American strategic reserve. Instead, it loaned Abdul Aziz $81 million. The following year, Casoc changed its name to the Arabian American Oil Company (Aramco), to more effectively express its American interests.

As the war left the Middle East, Aramco and the "Seven Sisters"—Socal, Texaco, Gulf, Shell, the Standard Oil Company of New Jersey (Exxon), the Standard Oil Company of New York (Mobil), and British Petroleum (BP)—resumed oil exploration and production. Aramco started building a refinery at Ras Tunurah and hired Bechtel to lay two pipelines. One was to run twenty miles under the Persian Gulf to a refinery in Bahrain. The other, called the Trans-Arabian pipeline (TAPline), was to run one thousand miles to the Mediterranean Sea to shorten the distance for transporting oil to Europe and the United States.

When World War II ended, the kingdom's economy was still a mess. Riyadh consisted of mud huts; most of Jeddah's water was rain stored in underground cisterns; the government payroll was four months in arrears; and the kingdom had only fifty miles of paved road. In 1947, the king's treasurer tried to control spending and built a budget based on revenues of $103 million per year, but Saudi's actual revenue was less than $40 million. The Saudi economy was out of control and Abdul Aziz depended on Aramco loans to survive.

Aramco loans to Saudi Arabia tied up the assets of Socal and Texaco so that in 1948, they reduced the drain on their cash by selling 40 percent of Aramco

ownership and relinquishing their northern concessions. Aramco then sold 30 percent of its shares to
Exxon and 10 percent to Mobil. The following year,
the king sold the former Aramco neutral zone oil
concessions to Getty Oil for a $4 million down pay-
ment and fifty cents per barrel in royalties.

The Saudis reached several developmental milestones in 1950 with the opening of the TAPline, a $50
million railroad from Dammam to Riyadh, and a
paved road from Dhahran to the Jordanian border.
The $250 million TAPline was designed to carry half
a million barrels of oil per day from Dhahran to Lebanon's Mediterranean port of Sidon. Construction of
the TAPline included a road to haul material and
heavy equipment, and nine large pumping stations at
one hundred-mile intervals to maintain the flow of
oil. Each of the stations was provided with a deep
well to supply water and a small village of houses,
schools and infirmaries. When the TAPline was finished, the government resettled Bedouin tribes at the
stations to operate the pumps.

The year 1950 also marked a financial turning
point. Aramco's daily oil production had reached
almost a half-million barrels. For each barrel, the
Saudis received twenty-one cents in royalties and
Aramco earned $1.10 profit—an annual revenue for
the kingdom of $39 million, and profits for Aramco of
$221 million. But King Abdul Aziz was not satisfied.
He learned that the Venezuelan government had recently forced the oil industry to pay it half its profits.
Since Abdul Aziz was spending $83 million a year on

"state palaces, princes and royal establishments," he demanded half of Aramco's profits to finance the royal family's extravagant life-style. Aramco asked the United States government for help as the demand was a breach of contract. Since the United States government was concerned about the spread of communism in the Middle East, it decided to placate the king. It told Aramco to give him $50 million per year which would be deducted from the company's United States income tax. Thus, Saudi revenues climbed to $56 million by year-end.

An underground sea of oil, over 150 miles long by 30 miles wide, was found by Aramco in 1953. The discovery of the Ghawar oil field, the largest oil field ever, meant that a lot of oil was going to come out of Saudi Arabia. It also meant that the Saudis were going to have to learn how to manage their money.

The Saudis only used coins for currency—Saudi Arabian silver riyals, Austrian Maria Theresa silver dollars, and British gold sovereigns. Their value fluctuated so widely in the world market that it was impossible to control expenses. The United States government sent a financial expert to the kingdom, and he persuaded Abdul Aziz to create the Saudi Arabian Monetary Agency (SAMA). In 1953, SAMA issued gold Saudi coins to replace the British coins and distributed the kingdom's first paper money, called Pilgrims' Receipts, for use by the hajjis. The Pilgrims' Receipts were readily accepted by merchants and were soon used throughout the country. King Abdul Aziz then authorized the use of regular state budgets which separated the state treasury from the king's personal funds.

Unfortunately, the old warrior did not live long enough to set his financial controls in place. By 1956, King Saud was spending three times the annual revenues of $250 million and had brought the kingdom to the brink of bankruptcy.

When Crown Prince Faisal took over as prime minister in 1958, he set up a Supreme Planning Board, joined the International Monetary Fund, and revamped SAMA. He made Pakistani financier Dr. Anwar Ali head of SAMA and hired a group of Egyptian and Pakistani financial experts. Faisal also required commercial banks to keep a reserve of 15 percent of their deposits in SAMA. SAMA then used these deposits and $186 million in gold to fully back the riyal. It devalued the currency and tied its value to that of the United States at 4.5 riyals to the dollar, making the riyal worth about twenty-two cents. Then, SAMA started a strict austerity program with rigid controls. It balanced the budget by restricting royal family expenditure and monitoring the kingdom's income. SAMA paid off all the debts within two years.

While SAMA was getting a handle on expenses, Faisal came up with a gimmick to stabilize and increase Saudi revenues. The Saudis had previously decreed that Aramco sell its oil at a publicly fixed or posted price upon which its taxes were based. But Aramco and the other oil companies changed their posted prices at will in response to changing market conditions. Faisal fixed the posted price of oil above the selling price to prevent fluctuations, which also forced Aramco to pay a higher tax and shifted the risk to the oil distribution companies. He changed the basis of taxation from income on oil sold by the companies to a flat charge on oil produced.

In 1959, a number of new oil deposits were discovered in the Persian Gulf area. Oil was found offshore of Abu Dhabi and Dubai in 1959. In January 1960, the Japanese-owned Arabian Oil Company struck oil in the neutral zone offshore concessions it had bought from Saudi Arabia three years earlier. Later in the year, oil was found in the Mukban oil field located in the disputed Abu Dhabi-Saudi Arabian frontier region.

About that time, the Saudis decided that they wanted a bigger slice of the pie. Abdullah Tariki, the Saudi director general of petroleum and mineral resources, declared it was unfair for the kingdom to receive less than 20 percent of the profits made on the sale of its only resource. He argued that the countries that owned the oil should set its prices rather than the companies that bought it, and that the oil-producing countries should receive an equal share of the profits. Soon afterwards, Saudi Arabia, Kuwait, Iran, Iraq, and Venezuela formed the Organization of Petroleum Exporting Countries (OPEC). In November 1962, Crown Prince Faisal created the General Petroleum and Minerals Organization (Petromin), as the state oil corporation and a vehicle to facilitate industrialization.

When Faisal was made king in 1964, he dissolved

the Supreme Planning Board because its members were incapable of getting things done, and instead formed the Central Planning Organization. He staffed it with decisive men, engaged the Stanford Research Institute, retained several Harvard and MIT economists as consultants and directed the group to prepare a long-range development plan.

King Faisal next brought in Western contractors to construct a basic infrastructure. American companies began building roads and modernizing the telephone service. Engineers designed new water and electricity systems. Contractors started erecting a power generation/desalination plant to convert sea water to drinking water, and a refinery in Jeddah. Experts laid out new airports in Jeddah and Riyadh. TransWorld Airlines took over operation of the national airline. Surveyors and geologists searched for more water and mineral deposits. Then Faisal sent young Saudis to Western universities and the new College of Petroleum and Minerals to learn how to operate oil fields and refineries.

Almost seven thousand miles of road had been paved by 1967, including a highway from the Red Sea to the Persian Gulf which connected the major cities. Revenues had risen to over $600 million per year. The closure of the Suez Canal during the Arab-Israeli war increased the demand for oil shipped through the TAPline, so Faisal slapped a surcharge on its passage and increased the kingdom's revenues again.

The Saudis started an ambitious series of programs in 1970 to turn the kingdom into a leading

153

industrial nation. King Faisal approved a five-year development plan to strengthen Saudi defensive capabilities, increase the gross national product by 10 percent per year, diversify the industrial base, and develop the kingdom's human resources. The first five-year development plan allotted 25 percent of the budget for defense; 25 percent for education and health; 30 percent for public utilities, housing, and transportation; and the remainder for agriculture and industrial development. The $9 billion plan was based on 1970 oil prices of $1.80 per barrel and expected revenues of $2 billion in 1971 and $2.7 billion in 1972. However, revenues soon exceeded these projections.

In the opening months of 1971, the Saudis and their OPEC partners gained the upper hand over the oil companies. During the December 1970 OPEC meeting, its members had decided to end separate negotiations between oil companies and oil-producing countries and charge a 55-percent tax on oil production. In January, twenty-three oil companies got together and sent a message to OPEC requesting that they negotiate with a joint oil company committee to work out a five-year oil contract. In February, the Arab members of OPEC rejected the request. They threatened to stop oil production unless the companies agreed that OPEC alone would set the prices using Arabian light crude as the bench mark for pricing. The oil companies gave up without much of a fight and signed a five-year contract to pay a 55-percent tax to the oil-producing countries based on a posted price of $2.18 per barrel. The oil companies also agreed to an annual increase of five cents per barrel plus 2.5 percent.

Saudi daily oil production rose like mercury in a hot thermometer from 3.5 million barrels in 1970, to almost 5 million barrels in 1971 and to 5.7 million barrels in 1972.

During the fall of 1972, Saudi Arabia became the leading Middle East oil producer and began to use its unchallenged power of ownership. In September, the kingdom announced its intention to acquire "participative ownership" in Aramco. When the parent companies balked, the new Saudi minister of petroleum and minerals, Ahmad Zaki al-Yamani, warned them that the kingdom would "nationalize 100 percent of Aramco if they did not cooperate." The oil companies knew that al-Yamani was not bluffing. Prior to his appointment in 1963, Zaki al-Yamani had served as an Aramco director after graduating from New York University and the Harvard Law School. They knew that al-Yamani took his orders from the royal family. In December 1972, the Saudis took their "participative ownership" of 25 percent of the assets of Aramco and gave the charter for marketing their share of oil to Petromin. In 1973, Saudi oil production rose to 7.2 million barrels per day.

The Saudis placed embargoes on oil shipments to countries supporting Israel during the Yom Kippur War in October 1973 and raised their posted price to $5.12 per barrel. Two months later, the Arab members of OPEC raised the price again to $11.65 per barrel.

In the spring of 1974, King Faisal declared "participative ownership" of another 35 percent of Aramco assets to give the Saudis 60 percent ownership. By this time, the kingdom was producing over 8 million barrels of oil per day. It was also refining almost 750,000 barrels per day into gasoline and other products at Aramco's refinery at Ras Tunurah, the Petromin refineries in Riyadh and Jeddah, the Arabian Oil Company refinery at Ras al-Khajfi, and the Getty Oil refinery.

The 1973 compound price increases of oil had a disabling impact on the West and triggered the most dramatic transfer of wealth in history. Oil accounted for over 5 percent of the expenditures of industrial countries and its price increase had a domino effect on the prices of other goods and services. The increases were passed on by the oil companies bringing them unprecedented profits but drastically affecting their customers. Gasoline prices quadrupled, electricity prices doubled and tripled, and air fares and long distance transportation costs doubled. Other prices increased significantly as manufacturers, distributors and retailers passed along their increased costs to consumers. Producers, builders, utilities, and other industries suddenly had to borrow funds to meet unplanned expenses. The banks in turn seized the opportunity for quick profits by raising their loan rates and lending to the hilt. The central banks raised their interest rates to control the flow of funds and suddenly, inflation rates soared into double digits.

The inflation added to government debts and caused them to borrow more money at higher rates, thus fueling the inflation. The United States government's borrowing reduced the value of the dollar and increased the price of gold.

The inflationary spiral was intensified in non-oil-producing countries, which found themselves paying more for imported oil than they were receiving for the sale of their own exported products. Soon, many countries had to resort to deficit spending to obtain their oil. Many countries bought their oil on credit and had to pay interest to the oil-producing countries as well. By 1974, the world's monetary system was totally upset. The Yom Kippur tandem oil price hikes had transferred about 3 percent of gross world product from oil consumers to a few oil-exporting countries and almost destroyed the international economy.

Money poured into the kingdom. Many of the banks in Saudi Arabia, a country that had no word for "million" forty years earlier, had so many billion-dollar deposits that they stopped taking new deposits! The Saudis went on such a spending spree that the Japanese could not ship Sony TVs and Toyotas fast enough to meet the demand.

By mid-1974, Saudi Arabia's oil revenues had increased to over $30 billion. The Saudi riyal increased in value to 3.55 to the United States dollar, or about 28 cents. Its gross national product was growing at 16 percent. Its per capita income was twice that of the United States and its gold and currency reserves were greater than the combined reserves of the United States and Japan.

The Saudis pumped their new wealth into domestic development projects and doubled the amount of spending on the five-year plan. The government had improved the standard of living for many Saudis, for the death rate declined and the birth rate increased. It provided jobs or paid training programs for those who wanted to work, and welfare programs for those who could not. It built water desalination plants in Jeddah, al-Wajh, Dhaba, al-Khafji, and al-Khobar and a dozen dams to collect rainwater in wadis. It also dug a thousand-mile network of irrigation canals in the central province to provide water to two towns and forty-eight villages. Its geologists discovered what could be one of the richest mining areas of the world, with veins estimated to contain over thirty million tons of iron ore as well as copper, silver, gold, chromium, lead, and zinc.

But few of Faisal's development projects were on schedule. The construction of communication systems, road networks, and health services had fallen behind. Agricultural production was less than expected. The Bedouin homestead farm project failed, so the government paid them to raise sheep. Almost three hundred small manufacturing companies had been started, but were operating at less than two-thirds of their capacity because the kingdom did not have markets for their products nor the manpower to run them. Over 70 percent of the population was still illiterate and had no industrial skills. As Sheikh

Hisham of the Central Planning Organization complained, "We are a nation of only six or seven million and it is people, not money, that is the crucial factor in our plans."

The Saudis again turned to the United States for help. Prince Fahd; the ministers of petroleum and minerals, of foreign affairs, of finance, of commerce, and of industry; senior managers of the Central Planning Organization and senior military officers went to Washington in June 1974. They met with President Nixon; the secretaries of state, of defense, of commerce, and of the treasury; and the head of the National Science Foundation. During the meetings, a plan was hammered out for Saudi Arabia to buy enormous quantities of technological and military goods from the United States to reduce the American balance of payments deficit. In return, the United States-Saudi Arabian Joint Commission for Economic Cooperation was set up to provide American managerial and technical expertise to the Saudis through the formation of joint venture companies. In addition, the Saudi Military Modernization Program was formed to develop a modern defence force.

Inflation spurred by oil prices came back to haunt the Saudis in the form of increased prices for imported foods, goods, services, and labor. Even though the kingdom's farms produced almost a million tons of wheat, dates, tomatoes, melons, grapes, figs, oranges, lamb, beef, and milk, it had to import huge quantities of food. By 1975, the Saudi inflation rate had risen to 50 percent. Food costs doubled, wage rates jumped, and land prices soared out of sight. The Saudi people were hurt and they complained that the rate of economic and social changes was too rapid to be absorbed. The government began subsidizing food costs to take the strain off the people. Then it learned that the gigantic cash reserve was losing purchasing power faster than it was gaining interest on investments. The royal family became furious and blamed the West for the inflation which they regarded as a plot to extort their money.

The Saudis had so much money lying in banks in 1975 at interest rates lower than the inflation rate, that they came up with a grandiose $193 billion second five-year development plan to spend the money as fast as they got it. The minister of planning described it as "an experiment in social transformation." The plan allocated $142 billion to continue improvement of the infrastructure and exploit natural resources, and $51 billion for military modernization.

Its most significant program was a $70 billion effort to build two major industrial cities, Yanbu and Jubail, from empty desert under the direction of a royal commission. The plan provided $13 billion to start up its 75 major and 130 minor projects. It consisted of laying two huge, thousand-mile-long pipelines to carry oil and natural gas to Yanbu so that oil could be shipped from the Red Sea if the Persian Gulf was blockaded, and to enable industrialization of the West Coast. It also provided for a cement plant, an oil refinery, a lubricating oil plant, and several petrochemical plants to be built at Yanbu. At Jubail, on the

Persian Gulf, it provided for two oil refineries, three petrochemical plants, a steel plant, and an aluminum smelter to be erected. It also included building airports, deep water seaports, combination power generation/desalination plants, and enough houses, schools, mosques, hospitals, and stores to support populations of 100,000 at both locations.

The plan provided for construction of a cement plant and a lubricating oil refinery in Jeddah and adding a cement plant, two ammonia fertilizer plants, and grain silos in Dammam. Over $5 billion was earmarked to erect a network of plants to create liquefied natural gas from the four billion cubic feet of gas being burned off each day. Another $5 billion was provided to construct a complex of buildings and campus for King Saud University in Riyadh. It budgeted $10 billion to build two hundred thousand housing units in the cities to accommodate the influx of Bedouin and villagers. The plan authorized funds to the national airline, Saudia, to expand domestic service to twenty locations, and monies to install coaxial cables to link the cities together with telephone, radio, and television, as well as construction of roads to all neighboring countries. It also funded a study to determine how to exploit the newly discovered iron, gold, silver, and copper deposits in the Arabian Shield.

Development efforts mushroomed to an unprecedented scale and the kingdom experienced a boom-town immigration of almost two million foreign workers.

As enthusiasm grew for the new development plan, Saudi economic policy appeared to moderate. Saudi oil minister al-Yamani even acknowledged the effects of Saudi price increases on the West's economy by saying, "We know that if your economy falls, we fall with you." The Saudis appeared to demonstrate their concern in December 1976 by limiting their price increase to 5 percent when the rest of OPEC raised prices by 10 percent. However, six months later, Saudi Arabia raised its prices by another 5 percent to $12.70 per barrel to offset cost overruns on the five-year development plan.

By 1977, the Saudis were producing twice as much oil as they had done five years earlier, but they needed the money. They were also spending twice as much for the five-year plan as had been budgeted because of inflation, bureaucratic incompetence, and unforeseen problems that plagued Western contractors. So, they cancelled construction of the aluminum smelter in Jubail, an automobile assembly plant, and five power generation/desalination plants. They also scaled down the size of the planned steel plant and extended the schedule for completion of the gas liquefaction plants. But the second five-year development plan was successful in creating most of the basic infrastructure required for a modern industrial country.

When the Iranians walked off their oil fields in October 1978, the loss of their oil to world market increased demand on other producers. Some Arab members of OPEC wanted to make hay while the sun was shining and immediately jacked up the prices, but the Saudis convinced them to hold the price increase down to a modest 15 percent for the coming year. The kingdom then stepped up production to ten million barrels per day from its forty oil fields to "prevent shortage and maintain prices." When the shah of Iran abdicated in January 1979, the Saudis raised their price to $14.34 per barrel. The Iranian oil fields still lay idle in April under the leadership of Khomeini, and the Saudis raised their price again to $15.64 per barrel. When the demand continued in June, they raised the price to $18 per barrel. On 30 January 1980, they went for broke and boosted their price another 40 percent to $26 per barrel; a combined increase of 100 percent during one year!

The multiple price increases clobbered the world's economy again and delayed its recovery from the 1973 escalation. The oil companies paid the prices and passed them on to the oil-consuming nations. The foreign trade deficits of the oil-consuming countries doubled again, and another 3 percent of the world's gross product spilled into the Middle East.

The new windfall provided the Saudis with a gigantic boost for their lagging development programs. In May 1980, they unveiled the $391 billion third five-year development plan which had been based on revenues of $18 per barrel, and began pouring additional money into their projects. The third plan provided $106 billion for defense and $285 billion to complete development of the infrastructure. It overlapped the second plan and contained more than one hundred programs to complete unfinished infrastructure development projects and begin creation of new industries.

Extensive funding was provided for the petroleum industry to complete the east-west pipeline and the natural gas gathering facilities in the eastern province and to accelerate Yanbu's development by constructing an oil terminal, two refineries, a lubricating oil plant and a grease plant.

Transportation programs were funded to pave 2,500 miles of roads; lay 320 miles of rail track; acquire 36 locomotives, 1,320 railroad cars, and 12 wide-bodied jet aircraft; install navigational aids and improve airports; and to construct 15 additional ship berths at the ports of Jeddah and Jizan.

Electrical and communication programs included provisions to add 7,600 megawatts of electrical generation capacity and 3,800 miles of electrical distribution lines. Funds were included to erect 15,000 telex lines, string 480,000 telephone lines, add 16,000 mobile telephones, and extend the microwave system to the Persian Gulf countries. The plan also included funds to establish a satellite television and telegraph broadcasting system, and to add a second television channel and a fourth radio station, and build twenty-seven radio transmission stations.

The housing program was given a budget to build 10,000 public housing units, and connect 720,000 houses to water systems and 473,000 houses to sewage systems.

Water resource programs were included to erect

14 dual-purpose power generation/desalination and two solar-powered desalination plants. Funds were allocated to drill 700 wells and modernize 540 water supply systems. A budget was also provided to build 37 flood control dams, construct 100 miles of storm drains, reclaim and irrigate 10,730 acres of land, and build new sewage treatment systems.

The health care program earmarked monies to build 36 hospitals to provide 10,700 beds, build 320 health care centers, expand specialized medical units, and create a nationwide computerized health records system.

Agricultural programs were included to construct two flour and feed mill complexes, grain storage facilities, animal disease laboratories, and a vaccine manufacturing plant.

In the commercial, financial, and social sectors, the plan included funds to establish new chambers of commerce in eight towns. It included provisions to standardize reporting procedures of commercial banks to SAMA, to offer shares in public industry to private investors, and study the need for a local stock exchange. Funds were also included to upgrade the Institute for Applied Social Research, set up a computerized social data base, and double the provision of social security to cover the entire Saudi labor force.

Educational programs were budgeted to build sixteen thousand additional classrooms, two health training institutes, five female nursing schools, three farmer training centers, an electrical energy training center, and ten private industry vocational training centers. Funds were also given to the Institute of Public Administration to train government employees.

An ecological program set up marine meteorological observation and air pollution monitoring networks. Funds were given to develop standards for air and water quality, marine ecology, and solid waste disposal, and establish specifications for four hundred products used in the kingdom. The program also included funds to develop an emergency oil spill response capability.

Over a third of the development budget, $105 billion, was dedicated to the industrialization program. Funds were allocated for the creation of private companies in glass, metallurgy, automotive parts, and animal feed.

Two government holding companies, the Saudi Arabian Basic Industries Corporation (SABIC) and Petromin, were charged with funding projects too large for the private sector to handle: SABIC was assigned responsibility for petrochemical and heavy industries, and Petromin continued to be responsible for oil-related industries. Each company was authorized to invest $11 billion in equal partnership joint ventures with Western firms which would use Saudi oil and gas to produce other products. The petrochemical plants were to create xylenes used to manufacture plastics, synthetic fibers, and paints. The new refineries were to create solvents, gasolines, jet and diesel fuel, and heating and lubricating oils. It was expected that these products would multiply the kingdom's revenues and allow the Saudis to better control demand for oil production.

The third five-year development plan was so ambitious that the Saudis needed Western companies to provide the managerial and technical skills to build and operate the plants, market the products, and share the financial risk. To lure Western firms, the Saudis offered fifty-fifty joint venture partnerships which provided guaranteed oil supplies, low interest loans, and cheap feed stocks. The oil guarantee offered five hundred barrels per day per $1 million of investment. The credit arrangement required the partners to pay an advance of 15 percent of the project's cost, which would be matched by SABIC or Petromin. The Saudi Public Investment Fund offered to loan 60 percent of the cost for a 3 to 6 percent carrying charge, with a five-year grace period on repayment. The ethane gas feed stock was to be provided at 50 to 85 percent below the world market price.

For a $2 billion joint venture project, a potential partner liable for $1 billion had to come up with $300 million cash and borrow $600 million from the Saudi Public Investment Fund and $100 million from commercial banks. These were high stakes for anybody! They represented a large front-end cash drain, with interest payments on commercial loans throughout the multi-year construction period and the need to earn annual project profits of about $150 million after becoming operational. Yet the projects also carried very high risks.

Their success was dictated by long-term profitability which depended on a continuous supply of cheap gas and a ready market for the products. There was the risk that the Saudis would increase gas prices as they had done with oil. Another risk was a reduced supply of raw feed stock if crude oil production dropped. A third risk was that there would not be a ready market. A fourth risk was that the products would be boycotted by the Western countries whose higher production costs would cause them to be displaced from the international market. A fifth risk was that the Saudis would nationalize the assets under the guise of "participative ownership" as they had done with Aramco. A sixth risk was being stuck with the need to take, and pay for, guaranteed oil supplies during periods of oil surplus. But these risks seemed insignificant at the time!

By 1980, Saudi Arabia was importing its products and services primarily from the United States, followed by Japan, Germany, Italy, Britain, and France. Japan was its leading oil customer, followed by the United States, France, Holland, Italy, and Singapore. Saudi Arabia was the United States' sixth-ranked trading partner. The United States had over 50 percent of the service contracts, 20 percent of product sales, and 10 percent of the Saudi Arabian construction contracts. In return, the United States imported about 15 percent of its oil, 1.5 million barrels per day, from Saudi Arabia.

The Saudis ended 1980 in outstanding financial condition. After raising their oil prices to $34 per barrel, they raked in $90 billion during the year. The riyal rose to 3.38 to the dollar and was worth about 30 cents. In December, the kingdom became the sole owner of Aramco when it declared "participative ownership" of its remaining assets. At year end, Saudi Arabia had over $90 billion surplus invested in the West, which earned $7 billion in interest. The private sector also prospered. Over 450 private companies had been started using low interest Saudi Industrial Development Fund loans, and individuals had stashed another $90 billion in the West.

During the summer of 1981, King Khalid and Crown Prince Fahd celebrated the opening of the new King Abdul Aziz International Airport in Jeddah, and gas and oil started flowing through Petroline, the new east-west pipeline to Yanbu.

That year, the Saudi economy continued to improve. The Saudis produced oil at an average of 10 million barrels per day. Their oil revenues were over $100 billion, their foreign investments earned another $6 billion, and they had a surplus of $45 billion after funding all their development programs and foreign aid.

Saudi Arabia did not need the revenues from sustained high oil production rates, but it needed the five hundred cubic feet of ethane gas released with each barrel of oil that it produced. The Saudis had completed their computer-controlled master gas collection system and needed the gas to fuel their power generation/desalination plants and to satisfy contractual requirements for delivering liquid petroleum gas to Western companies. They also needed over a billion cubic feet of gas per day to supply the new petrochemical plants which were the key to their industrial diversification. The Saudis needed daily oil production of about 1.6 million barrels to meet domestic gas fuel requirements, 2 million barrels to satisfy gas export requirements, and 2.4 million barrels to provide gas feedstock to the petrochemical plants: a total of about 6 million barrels per day.

The boom peaked out in 1982 when the Iranians undercut the market. Selling of oil at 25 percent under OPEC prices enabled Iran to increase its market share at the expense of the Saudis. By midyear, Saudi Arabia's share of the market dropped from 40 to 30 percent. As demand fell off, the Saudis cut back their oil production to about 5 million barrels per day. By year-end, Saudi revenues dropped to $90 billion and their surplus for the year was only $4 billion.

When their income fell, the Saudis cut $20 billion out of their 1982-83 budget to reduce it to $70.4 billion. They postponed some multibillion dollar contracts and rescheduled others to accelerate development of the petrochemical plants. The Saudi government also gave subsidized loans to stimulate personal investment and shape the growth of private agriculture and industry. By year-end, small gains were made in agricultural development and private sector revenues rose to provide about 18 percent of the kingdom's total revenue.

Despite the deteriorating economy and risks to the partners, by 1983 SABIC had entered into contracts for petrochemical plant development with Shell for $3 billion, with Mobil for $2 billion, with Dow for $1.6 billion, and the Celanese Corporation for $400 million. Petromin entered refinery plant development deals with Mobil for $1.5 billion, Shell for $1.4 billion, and with Socal-Texaco for $1 billion.

In March 1983, OPEC threw in the towel. After the embargo in 1973 and the price hikes of 1973 and 1979, most countries had implemented strict oil conservation measures, started building strategic reserves, developed alternative oil fields, or began exploring other energy sources. By 1981, these measures had begun to take effect, and combined with the global recession to reduce the total demand for OPEC oil. OPEC's production dropped to half of its 1973 level, but the excess Iranian oil flooded the market and created a surplus. OPEC regarded the glut as temporary, but could not predict when the demand would strengthen since this depended on world economic recovery and on the actions of individual OPEC members. Iran was determined to continue its high level of production and sell its oil at any price. Venezuela, Nigeria, Egypt, and Iraq wanted to increase production and hold the prices up. Saudi Arabia and the gulf states thought it was better to cut back production and lower prices to maintain reasonable revenues while conserving the supply. Finally, OPEC agreed to reduce total member production to 17.5 million barrels per day and drop the posted price to $29 per barrel until demand strengthened.

Saudi's production quota was set at 5 million barrels per day. Since the kingdom needed to produce about 6.5 million barrels per day to pay for its development programs without drawing from its cash reserves, King Fahd put a freeze on government hiring and new contract awards, and tightened controls on spending. The Council of Ministers compelled Western contractors to lower costs and deferred payments to overseas companies. The council then reevaluated their domestic priorities, rescheduled critical development projects, and eliminated less important projects such as housing construction. These actions reduced the 1983-84 development expenditures from $100 to $75.5 billion.

In 1984, SABIC's joint venture partners grew restless. Mobil, Texaco, Socal, and Exxon took a combined loss of $7 billion during the year by having to buy Aramco oil at Saudi posted prices, and they demanded lower prices and better credit terms. Mobil was forced to cut back its European petrochemical production and Dow withdrew from the deal because of its debt level. SABIC then sold 30 percent of its stock to private investors.

The kingdom further emphasized the importance of the private sector by authorizing a group of private investors to form the National Industries Company (NIC) for use by private individuals.

As the oil glut continued, the kingdom ended its fiscal year with revenues of only $65 billion and had to draw on its huge cash reserves. In the meantime, the dollar continued to gain strength and the Saudis were forced to begin devaluing the riyal.

They then started cheating on OPEC. They increased their daily oil production to 5.8 million barrels and sold about 10 percent of it on the spot market to increase their purchasing power without technically exceeding their OPEC quota. They also started bartering and Prince Sultan arranged a deal to trade 34 million barrels of oil through third parties to acquire ten new Boeing 747 jumbo jet airplanes.

In October 1984, the North Sea oil producers lowered their prices by almost $2 per barrel. Within days, Nigeria broke ranks with OPEC and dropped its prices. OPEC convened in Geneva, decided to reduce its production again to hold the oil prices at $29 per barrel, and cut the Saudi production quota to 4.3 million barrels per day.

By year-end, Saudi Arabia had been forced to devalue the riyal seven times to a low of 3.57 riyals to the dollar. Its imports were down 11 percent from the previous year and it began selling light Saudi crude oil on the spot market for one dollar under its official price. As Saudi Arabia's oil revenues dropped, its growing non-oil private sector revenues rose and contributed about 50 percent of the gross domestic product.

The third five-year plan had achieved about half its goals. The industrialization program was accomplished when the refinery and petrochemical plants at Jubail and Yanbu started operations, and the kingdom accounted for 5 percent of world petrochemical production. The agricultural program was less successful. After so much had been spent on drilling wells to irrigate the desert, it was learned that the water level was dropping in the subterranean aquifer and more desalinated water would have to be used for irrigation.

The kingdom launched its $277 billion fourth five-year plan in March 1985. The plan was designed as a series of options to allow the Saudis to meet their highest priority goals within available revenues. Half of the budget was allocated to expand defense capabilities in light of the growing threat of the gulf war. The other half of the budget was allocated to consolidate past civilian sector growth by improving operational efficiency, further developing agriculture and financial services industries, stimulating private-sector investment, and further integrating the kingdom's economy with those of the other members of the Gulf Cooperation Council. Considerable emphasis was given to increasing power generation/water desalination capacity, expanding irrigation facilities, developing new industrial estates, expanding health services, and achieving a 23 percent reduction in the use of expatriate labor.

The last item had become a major issue. Despite the kingdom's massive efforts to train the Saudi work force, the expatriate work force had grown by 12 percent per year to 4,563,000 and comprised 60 percent of the total. Consequently, a royal decree was issued that restricted the freedom of foreign workers to change jobs without leaving the kingdom.

Saudi oil production dropped to 2.2 million barrels per day and drastically curtailed revenues. The

kingdom stopped acting as an OPEC "swing producer" and increased its production so that, by the
last quarter of 1985, its oil exports rose to their highest
level in two years. Then, OPEC dropped its production quotas to offset falling prices and by July 1986,
oil prices had dropped to less than $10 a barrel.

As oil revenues bottomed out, the much-delayed
$1 billion causeway linking Saudi Arabia to Bahrain
was finally completed. Other Saudi construction projects wound down or went bankrupt and about one
million foreign workers left the kingdom.

After the price of oil dropped to $10 a barrel,
production levels and prices fluctuated wildly. King
Fahd dismissed Ahmad Zaki al-Yamani as minister of
petroleum and mineral resources and replaced him
with Sheikh Hisham Nazer who was formerly minister of planning. The kingdom then began efforts to
increase both production levels and prices. In December, OPEC set a target price of $18 per barrel and
allotted Saudi Arabia a production quota of 4.1 million barrels per day.

About that time, the Saudi government shifted
from using the Hegira calendar to something closer
to the Gregorian calendar for budget purposes, leaving a ten-month gap in statistics. Hence, data for that
period is variously classed for 1986 or 1987 depending on the source, and is full of distortions. For example, the real gross domestic product growth
percentages were variously reported at -8.7 for 1985,
up to 8.5 for 1986, and back down to 0.19 for 1987. In
June 1987, oil prices rose to $18 per barrel and OPEC

increased the Saudi production quota to 4.3 million barrels per day.

The kingdom almost lost its foreign work force in January 1988, when it announced that all expatriates would have to pay tax on personal income. The response was immediate and overwhelming as expatriates from all nations quit their jobs and applied for exit visas. The business community was appalled at the thought of losing this vital source of expertise and prevailed upon the king to withdraw the tax.

The following month, Saudi Arabia used part of its defense budget to purchase $3 billion worth of ballistic missiles from China and in July it overran its budget by doubling the value of its contract with the United Kingdom to purchase aircraft, tanks, and ships, and construct two huge air bases.

It was recognized in 1988 that the fourth five-year plan would not achieve its goals. The steep decline in oil revenues caused postponement of many civilian projects and a larger than-expected share of the budget was diverted for defense. The multibillion-dollar agricultural plan to become self-sufficient in food was successful, but it cost the kingdom over $1 billion to produce wheat that could have been imported for $120 million. By mid-1989, Saudi oil revenues had fallen 80 percent from the 1981 peak, and the kingdom was forced to use its cash reserves to sustain a budget which was half that of 1981.

Saudi Arabia is still in transition. It spent most of its revenues during the last two decades on creating a modern infrastructure and establishing an effective defense capability. Now that most of the infrastructure is completed, Saudi Arabia has no need for additional international airports, major harbors, or new cities. As it strives for security and self-sufficiency, the kingdom is concentrating on expanding its defense and agricultural capabilities, completing Yanbu and Jubail, diversifying its industry, and training its citizens.

Saudi goals remain unchanged: to create a diversified, multistaged economy that will optimize and conserve the country's oil while providing sufficient revenues to take care of the long-term needs of the people. The delay of the development plans caused by the reduced demand for oil and lowered prices has not discouraged the Saudis; they do not think a two-year delay of most projects is critical.

Without taxing its citizens, the Saudis can still finish building their petrochemical plants and refineries; build a few more air bases; add a couple of hundred more miles of electrical distribution lines, paved roads, and railroad tracks; erect some new mosques; get more 747s; build more power generation/desalination plants; install a few more computers; build another dozen hospitals and schools; acquire a few squadrons of the latest aircraft; get several hundred ballistic and surface-to-air missiles; buy a few more warships; pay the Saud family allowances; educate all their children; and provide free medical care for all their people.

Chapter 7

*D*ELICATE BALANCE

*S*audi Arabia is trying to maintain its security in the middle of the most unstable area of the world—an area where every country has been at war against one of its neighbors during the past twenty five years. Saudi Arabia is an attractive, rich prize trying to survive in an area plagued with religious hatred, dynastic rivalries, and greedy expansionism.

The huge kingdom is strategically important because it sits astride two of the world's most vital waterways, and is economically rich because of its tremendous oil reserves. It is extremely vulnerable because of its long borders, large population of immigrant workers, and constant influx of pilgrims. It is also vulnerable because it is not militarily strong enough to defend itself. Saudi's population is a sixth that of Egypt, a fifth that of Iran, and a little over half that of Iraq. Because of its small population, its 110,000-man military organization is greatly outnumbered by its neighbors: Iraq has 1,000,000 troops; Egypt has 895,000; Syria has 565,000; and Iran has 475,000.

To survive in this environment, despite being such a tempting target, Saudi Arabia delicately balances its foreign affairs while keeping a low profile. The kingdom's foreign policies are based on its need for security, devotion to Islam, and identification with other Arab nations as well as its interest in maintaining favorable oil prices, selling its oil, developing its economy, and keeping peace in the area. It carries out its foreign policies through backstage diplomacy and a series of, at times, conflicting alliances. It has set itself up as a champion of the third world by not declaring allegiance to any superpower, yet it is largely dependent on the United States. It is the leader of the Islamic world and promotes solidarity among Islamic governments. It shares the struggle against Zionism with other Arab nations and helps them in time of need. It cooperates with oil-producing countries to get the best prices and maximize its earnings, but tries to maintain friendly relations with industrial countries to have the broadest markets for its oil.

Saudi Arabia's foreign policies also reflect the

past actions and anticipated intentions of neighboring countries and superpowers. When the kingdom was formed, Egypt and Persia were its strongest independent neighbors and many of the surrounding countries were European colonies. Britain was the dominant superpower and kept peace in the area.

Saudi Arabia was a country without clearly defined borders. Within months of its formation, it established part of its southern border after a war with Yemen. During a civil war between clans of the Idrisi tribe, Imam Yahya of Yemen gave support to the southern clans. King Abdul Aziz retaliated by sending armies under his sons Faisal and Saud in a two-pronged southern attack. Prince Saud captured the oases town of Najran. Prince Faisal overran half of Yemen's Red Sea coast and captured the main port city of Hodeida. The assaults cut off supplies to the Yemen capital and forced the imam to surrender. In the 1934 Treaty of Taif, the imam ceded several hundred miles of productive farming land to Saudi Arabia.

Across the Persian Gulf, Iran came into being in 1935 when Shah Reza Khan came into power, named himself the country's religious leader, and changed the country's name from Persia.

Less than six hundred miles to the north, the Soviet Union announced its intention to continue its southern expansion. In November 1940, the Axis powers of Germany, Italy, and Japan made a pact defining their areas of geographic interest and asked what their Russian partner wanted. The Soviet minister told them that "the general direction of the Persian Gulf is the center of aspirations of the Soviet Union."

After the Germans invaded Russia in 1941, the Russians switched sides and joined the Allies. Russia claimed to be concerned about its southern flank because of suspected German agents in neutral Iran. When the shah refused to get rid of the Germans, the British and Russians invaded Iran to protect their oil supplies and secure an overland route to ship war material to Russia. After Allied planes bombed Tehran, British paratroopers seized Iranian oil fields, and the BBC denounced the shah as a dictator, Reza Khan abdicated in favor of his son Muhammad Reza Khan.

As the war moved out of the Middle East into Europe, Arab nationalism reemerged. In October 1944, King Abdul Aziz and King Farouk of Egypt laid plans to form a coalition of Arab states to end British rule in the Middle East and halt the migration of Jews to Palestine. Several months later, the two countries formed the Arab League.

On St. Valentine's day in 1945, King Abdul Aziz and his entourage of armed body guards, goats, and sheep boarded a spotless United States Navy cruiser in the Suez Canal to meet with President Roosevelt. Roosevelt tried to persuade the king to support the United States plan for large-scale resettlement of European Jewish refugees in Palestine. King Abdul Aziz refused and said, "If the Germans took away their homes, why don't you give the Jews the Rhine Valley?" After President Roosevelt learned the degree of Arab concern about the Jewish state, he agreed to postpone implementation of the plan until after extensive discussions with both sides. Several months later, President Roosevelt died and was succeeded by Harry Truman.

Give-'em-hell-Harry said he had more Jewish constituents than Arabs and persuaded the British to admit 100,000 Jewish war refugees into Palestine. The refugees swarmed out of Europe into their national homeland, displaced Arabs who lived in cities, and set up farming communes on Arab grazing lands. The settlements moved inland toward the Sea of Galilee and Jerusalem as the Jewish population swelled to over 600,000.

Just prior to the end of World War II, King Abdul Aziz declared war on the Axis powers so that the kingdom could qualify as a founding member of the United Nations. In October 1945, Foreign Minister Prince Faisal signed the UN charter.

When the war ended, Russian troops refused to leave Iran and tried to persuade Iran's northwestern provinces to revolt and declare themselves separate republics. After the UN censured the Soviet Union and the United States threatened to provide military support to Iran, the Soviets reconsidered, withdrawing their troops in May 1946. As Iran regained its independence, the French ended their colonization in the Middle East, and Lebanon and Syria became sovereign nations.

Two years later, Israel and Jordan were formed. In the spring of 1947, because of its poor post-war economy and local nationalistic pressures, Britain decided to withdraw from Palestine and India. In November, the UN voted to make Palestine an independent state and divided the country into three parts. The Jews were given the land along the Mediterranean Sea; the Arabs were given the inland area; and Jerusalem, in between, was to be shared by both the Jews and the Arabs. The defined boundaries provided no territorial integrity or security for the Jewish state in view of the armed Arab resistance to its formation.

On 15 May 1948, the kingdom of Jordan was formed by adding part of Palestine to Transjordan, and Israel was created from the remaining land. As the British moved their troops out of Israel, Jordanian, Syrian, and Lebanese troops moved in. The fighting escalated as Saudi Arabia, Iraq, and Egypt sent troops to help the Palestinian Arabs.

At the urging of their political leaders, Arab civilians left their homes and fled from the combat zone. The Jews had no place to retreat and were forced to fight with their backs against the sea. By the end of 1948, Jewish Israelis had captured three-quarters of Palestine. When a cease-fire was arranged in 1949, the Israelis held all the Mediterranean coast and lands to the Sea of Galilee. Jordan had annexed Jerusalem and the west bank of the river Jordan.

By the end of the war, Israel had 879,000 Jews and 140,000 Arabs. Another 600,000 Arabs had fled to Lebanon, Jordan, and Syria. Many returned to the Israeli-occupied lands after the fighting stopped.

Those who did not were interned in twenty UN-supervised refugee camps on the Jordanian-controlled west bank and in other nearby countries. The Jews saved their homeland, but that did not bring peace. The Arabs bitterly resented their humiliating defeat and the displacement of the Palestinians.

In 1951, Saudi Arabia agreed to lease its air base in Dhahran to the United States in return for military training assistance. The following year, leftist Colonel Gamel Nasser overthrew King Farouk of Egypt and began a cancerous campaign to dominate the Middle East. Nasser used anti-Israeli and anti-Western propaganda in radio broadcasts to fan the discontent of ignorant peasants in surrounding Arab countries, and called for the use of oil as a weapon against their enemies.

Prime Minister Mussaddiq of Iran responded to Nasser's broadcasts by nationalizing the Anglo-Iranian Oil Company and leading a National Front that forced Shah Muhammad Reza into exile in August 1953. A coup by his former army officers quickly restored the shah to power, and he promptly executed the leaders of the National Front and outlawed the Communist party.

Saudi Arabia's new king, Saud, also fell under the influence of Nasser. In 1955, Gamel Nasser made an arms deal with the Soviet Union and imported thousands of Russian military and technical advisors. With Soviet backing, he pressured other Arab countries to unite and rid themselves of Western domination. King Saud publicly supported Nasser and paid

Syria $20 million to reject the pro-West Baghdad Pact which was being formed to stabilize the Middle East.

In July 1956, Nasser nationalized the British and French-owned Suez Canal and immediately banned Israeli ships from the waterway. The ban continued Arab exploitation of the strategic weaknesses of the territory occupied by Israel after the 1948 war. In the northeast, Arab terrorist organizations used the Golan Heights of Syria as a base for artillery and rocket bombardment into Israel. In the east, Jordan occupied territory less than fifteen miles from Tel Aviv and the Mediterranean Sea. In the south, the Egyptian coastal area of Gaza extended into the heart of Israel.

When Nasser started receiving arms from the Soviet Union, he began a series of offensive moves against Israel. He built fortifications in the Gaza strip and sponsored Fedayeen terrorist raids into Israel. He also put artillery batteries in fortifications at Sharm el-Sheikh in Sinai at the entrance to the Gulf of Aqaba and prevented Israeli ships from sailing to the Israeli port of Elat. The Egyptian navigation restrictions in the Suez Canal and the Gulf of Aqaba impacted Israel's trade and hurt its economy.

On 29 October 1956, Israel struck back by invading Gaza and Sinai to destroy the Egyptian fortifications. The next day, the British and French governments warned Egypt that they would intervene in twelve hours if the Egyptian army did not stop fighting. On 5 November, Israel accomplished its objectives by capturing the southern part of the Sinai peninsula and the Gaza strip. On the same day, British and French forces bombed Egyptian air bases in Cairo and seized the Suez Canal.

Repercussions were immediate. The Egyptians sank ships in the canal to prevent its use. The Saudis broke off diplomatic relations with Britain, blew up a French joint venture munitions plant in the kingdom, and closed the pipeline to the refinery in Bahrain to prevent oil from reaching British ships. The Syrians severed the Iraq Petroleum Company's pipeline to the Mediterranean to deny oil to the Anglo-French forces. The Soviet Union reacted by threatening to fire a salvo of nuclear missiles at Israel, Britain, and France if they did not stop the war.

The United States, shocked by the Soviet threat, led the United Nations in persuading the British and French forces to withdraw from the canal, and Israeli forces to relinquish Sinai and the Gaza Strip. The UN action made Nasser a hero in the Arab world.

The Soviet Union then tried to expand its toehold in the Middle East by giving a large loan to Syria. In February 1958, Egypt joined with Syria and formed a new country called the United Arab Republic (UAR). The Syrian portion of the UAR immediately helped Muslim extremists to try to overthrow the Lebanese government. The United States thwarted the attempt by landing United States Marines in Beirut. The Syrians gave up and three years later, disbanded the UAR.

In July 1958, the Soviets gained more influence in the Middle East when Iraqi King Faisal and the royal family were murdered by rebels who installed a leftist regime and declared Iraq a republic.

Kuwait proclaimed its independence in June 1961. Two weeks later, Iraq, with less than ten miles of coastline, announced its intention to take over the new country and build a naval base on the Kuwait island of Bubiyan. The British forestalled the Iraqi invasion by deploying troops in Kuwait.

On the other side of the Persian Gulf, the shah of Iran started a "white revolution." In 1962, he implemented secular laws, emancipated women, gave crown lands to the people, and redistributed millions of acres of land to the farmers. The Shiite religious leaders challenged the shah's modern ideas and protested the government's requisition of their property. In the holy city of Qum, a Shiite teacher named Ruhollah Khomeini was arrested for leading riots against the shah. In return for past favors, the secret police classified Khomeini as an ayatollah, or religious leader, and banished him from Iran to allow him to escape imprisonment.

To the north, the Palestine Liberation Organization (PLO) was formed during the 1964 Arab summit meeting to deal with the refugee problem. The PLO immediately called for the dissolution of Israel and the creation of a separate Palestinian state.

In May 1967, Syria and Jordan moved their armies to Israel's borders and threatened an invasion. On June first, Israel lashed out against its antagonists, and by the fifth day, had succeeded in destroying Egypt's air force and severely crippling the air forces of Syria, Jordan, and Iraq. On the sixth day, Israel captured the Sinai peninsula and pushed the Egyptian army across the Suez Canal, drove the Syrian army out of the Golan Heights, captured Jerusalem, and forced the Jordanian army across the river Jordan.

About a quarter of a million Palestinians fled the west bank of the river Jordan during the war and increased the number of displaced Palestinians to 850,000. The Arab countries were furious about their predicament, but only Jordan welcomed the refugees and granted them citizenship. The PLO was so angry that it broke away from its sponsors and became a renegade organization, heavily financed by Saudi Arabia and supported by the Soviet Union.

Meanwhile, in southern Arabia, communist guerillas supported by Egyptian president Nasser were trying to take over North Yemen, South Yemen, and Oman. The terrorists gained ground in Aden, and fanned out to the north and east. Then they gained control of the sultanates in Hadramaut and raided the Saudi frontier. In November 1967, Britain was forced to abandon Aden. The following month, Hadramaut fell and became known as the People's Republic of South Yemen.

After the loss of Aden, the British government decided to withdraw from the lands "east of Suez" and announced their intention to pull out of the Persian Gulf, despite offers by the emirs of Bahrain and the Trucial States to pay the operating costs of British troops. This regrettable decision marked the end of

British maintenance of stability in the Persian Gulf.

By 1969, the PLO had increased in strength to almost 15,000 Palestinian, Syrian, Iraqi, and Libyan members who had committed acts of terrorism throughout the Middle East. That year, its warring factions chose Yassir Arafat as their leader.

In southern Arabia, fighting continued to escalate. Unrest prevailed in the Republic of North Yemen after the royalists surrendered. In Oman, the South Yemeni Communists gained control of the guerillas and launched a drive on the provincial capital of Dhohfar.

Sparks of rebellion fanned by Gamel Nasser burst into flames of revolution throughout the Middle East. Colonel Muammar Qaddafi overthrew pro-Western King Idris in Libya. A radical army group took over the government of Sudan. Iraq agreed to trade oil with the Soviet Union for modern weapons. Then the PLO started a civil war in Jordan which ended when King Hussein's army chased the guerillas into Lebanon.

The effects of the revolution spread into Saudi Arabia when its TAPline became a target for terrorists. In 1969, the Popular Front for the Liberation of Palestine blew up the pipeline and closed it for four months. This lost the Saudis $40 million in revenues. TAPline was knocked out again in May 1970 by a bulldozer in Syria. The broken pipeline cost the Saudis $200,000 per day, but Saudi technicians were refused permission to enter Syria to make repairs. The Saudis retaliated by refusing to let Syrian goods or vehicles enter the kingdom. The Syrians responded by refusing to allow cargo destined for Saudi Arabia to enter their country. The stalemate continued, at a loss of over $50 million, until January 1971 when a new regime came to power in Syria.

Gamel Nasser died in September 1970 and was succeeded by Anwar Sadat as president of Egypt. The Saudis breathed a sigh of relief and gave a large loan to Sadat to encourage him to get rid of his Russian advisors and stay away from Qaddafi in Libya.

It was too late to undo Nasser's deeds. South Yemen had turned into a Communist colony called the People's Democratic Republic of Yemen, which bristled with Russian weapons and aircraft. Russian officers ran its army, Cuban pilots flew its jet fighters, red Chinese technicians were building its roads, and East German secret police were creating the national police force.

In neighboring Oman, South Yemeni Communists and Omani rebels had gained control of the Dhofar region and began attacking government garrisons in the center of the country. The old sultan abdicated in favor of his son, Qabus, who was a graduate of the British military academy. Big Q, as he was called, immediately started social reforms, declared amnesty for the Dhofar rebels, bought more weapons, and mounted an all-out campaign against the South Yemeni guerillas.

King Faisal watched in horror as the surrounding Islamic countries turned to the atheistic Communist nations for support. He went to Washington and pleaded with President Nixon to help the Arab nations and tried to convince him that the United States' preoccupation with Israel could lose the Arab countries to the Soviet Union. But Faisal did not accomplish very much.

On 15 August 1971, Bahrain became an independent country; on 1 September, Qatar became independent and on 2 December, the Trucial States became an independent nation called the United Arab Emirates.

During the last day of British responsibility for their protection, the Trucial States' islands of Tunbs and Abu Musa were invaded by Iranian troops.

Because they did not intervene and stop the Iranians from evicting the Arab residents, the British were accused of arranging the invasion with the shah of Iran. Iraq retaliated by breaking off diplomatic relations with the United Kingdom and Iran, and deporting 60,000 Iranian immigrants. Libya retaliated by nationalizing the assets of the British Petroleum company.

The power vacuum created in the Persian Gulf by the withdrawal of Britain was immediately filled with United States and Soviet forces. In December 1971, Bahrain invited the United States to station a squadron of U.S. destroyers at its former British naval base.

In April 1972, Iraq agreed to provide the Soviet Union with military and naval facilities. Two months later, Iraq nationalized the Iraq Petroleum Company, and in December, it demanded a large loan from Kuwait. After Kuwait refused to grant the loan, Iraq massed troops along Kuwait's border and demanded the right to build a port and refineries on Bubiyan Island. When this demand was rejected, Iraq invaded Kuwait and tried to take the island. The Iraqis withdrew in April 1973 after King Faisal sent Saudi troops to help the Kuwaitis. As the Soviet Union gained influence in Iraq, Anwar Sadat kicked the Russian advisors out of Egypt.

During the Jewish atonement period of Yom Kippur in 1973, Egypt and Syria attacked Israel to regain their lands lost in the 1967 war, and to restore their dignity. On 8 October, the Egyptian army swarmed across the Suez Canal and overran Israeli emplacements. The Israeli army counterattacked across the Suez Canal on the night of 16 October, and surrounded most of the Egyptian army. On the eastern front, Israeli forces advanced to within twenty-five miles of the Syrian capital of Damascus. The next day, Saudi Arabia sent an infantry brigade to Jordan and cut off oil shipments to the United States for helping Israel.

The effects of the oil embargo were immediately felt throughout the world and caused traditional American allies to submit to the Arab demands. Fuel shortages forced hardship on Americans at home. In Vietnam, the fuel shortage reduced the mobility of American and South Vietnamese troops and enabled the North Vietnamese army to overrun and capture large areas of South Vietnam.

The 1973 war was celebrated as a victory by the Arabs because of the heroism of its soldiers and the gains made during the first few days of combat. It appeared to the West that Israel had won the war. However, the Egyptians claimed that allowing the Israeli army to completely encircle the Egyptian army in Sinai was a clever trap which the Egyptians would have sprung if the United States and the Soviet Union had not arranged a cease-fire. Consequently, the Arabs felt that they restored their honor.

Lebanon, the Switzerland of the Middle East, turned into a battleground in 1975. During the previous year, Arab leaders made the PLO the sole representative of the Palestinians and the organization used Lebanon as its base for increased attacks on Israel. Lebanon's mixed population of Maronite Christians, Sunni, Shiite, and Druze Muslims disagreed over their support of PLO guerilla activity. The Maronite Christian president condemned the PLO's sneak raids into Israel to bomb airports and schools, and the hiding of PLO guerillas in innocent refugee camps to escape retaliation. The Muslim extremists supported these activities. Soon a civil war erupted. Libya and Iraq gave arms to the PLO guerillas and Israel gave arms to the Christian guerillas. Saudi Arabia tried to end the fighting by giving money to the Christian government.

In January 1976, the Palestine Liberation Army invaded Lebanon from Syria and attacked the Christian Lebanese government army in the south. In March, Muslims in the Lebanese army mutinied and joined the Palestinian guerillas in attacking the Christian Lebanese government in Beirut. The Syrian government tried to stop the fighting and found itself in conflict with Lebanese Muslim guerillas. Saudi Arabia gave the Syrian government financial assistance to end the civil war and Iraq brought pressure against Saudi Arabia to undermine Syria. In May, Syria sent 250 tanks into Lebanon to relieve the beleaguered Christian villages. Saudi Crown Prince Fahd negotiated a partial cease-fire with the Syrian and Lebanese governments and in October, King Khalid met with Arab leaders to end the war. Soon afterwards, a 30,000-man Arab peace-keeping force from Saudi Arabia, Syria, Sudan, and Egypt moved into Lebanon.

In the meantime, Saudi Arabia began to fear the armada that the shah was assembling in the Persian Gulf. The Iranian navy had grown to three destroyers, four frigates, four corvettes, twenty patrol boats, fifteen hovercraft, and three squadrons of American F-14 jet fighters. The Iranian navy was supported by a naval base at Bandar Abbas and was building a $2.5-billion naval base and airfield at Chah Bandar outside the Strait of Hormuz. The shah of Iran claimed that the large navy was being developed to protect Iran's daily shipments of five million barrels of oil. The Saudis were afraid that the Iranian navy would be used to capture their offshore oil fields or interfere with international tanker traffic to Ras Tunurah.

The following year, Saudi Arabia grew concerned about Communist incursions west of the Red Sea. A non-Muslim leftist regime had ousted Emperor Haile Selassie and gained control of Ethiopia. In January 1977, the Soviet Union gave the junta $386 million in military aid. The next month, Ethiopian government forces attacked the Muslim Arab secessionist province of Eritrea on the Red Sea and started a campaign against the Somalian Arabs in the east. In March, Fidel Castro sent Cuban troops to the country. The following month, Ethiopia expelled the United States military mission and cancelled its permission for the United States to use the air base at Asmara. By summer, the Ethiopian army and thousands of Soviet and Cuban advisors were in an undeclared state of war with Somalia. The Saudis then shipped arms to Somalia.

Saudi Arabia was very vulnerable to the surrounding threats. High performance Mig-21s were being flown by Communists in South Yemen and Ethiopia and F-14 fighters were based in Iran, all within easy striking distance of Saudi Arabia. The Israelis frequently sent their F-16 fighters on simulated bombing runs and touch-and-go landings at the Saudi air base in Tabuk. The Saudis were irritated by the violations of their airspace and alarmed because they did not have any planes that could counter F-14s, F-16s, or Mig-21s.

In May 1977, Saudi Arabia asked the United States for permission to buy American F-15 fighters. The request was hotly debated in the United States Congress. The Jewish lobby tried to block the sale to prevent the F-15s from being used against Israel. A bloc of sixty-two senators sent President Carter a letter urging him not to sell the planes because Saudi Arabia had not honored its previous commitments.

The Treasury Department warned Congress that the Saudi government could wreak financial havoc by suddenly withdrawing the $50 billion it had invested in the United States. After a year of bitter debate and thinly veiled threats, the United States government agreed to sell Saudi Arabia the advanced combat aircraft.

By that time, southern Arabia and the horn of Africa were seething with Communists. Russian and Cuban troops had driven the Somalians far into the horn of Africa and almost pushed the Eritreans into the Red Sea. South Yemen had Russian air bases and naval stations at Aden and Mukalla, and a communications base on the island of Socotra which supported Communist troops in Africa.

During February 1979, South Yemen moved a column of Russian tanks, under Mig-21 air cover, deep into North Yemen. The Saudis thought the thrust was aimed at their southern border and put their forces on alert. But the North Yemeni army held and stalled the Communist drive. The Saudis rushed American F-5 fighter bombers, M-60 tanks, and armored personnel carriers to North Yemen and gave them loans to fight the South Yemenis.

While the Saudis helped their Arab brothers in Somalia and North Yemen, they abandoned their Arab brothers in Egypt. Egyptian president Anwar Sadat initiated a series of meetings with Israel president Menachim Begin and President Carter to end Israel's control of the Suez Canal and the oil fields in Sinai. In February 1979, the discussions resulted in an Egyptian-Israeli peace treaty and a troop withdrawal plan. King Faisal was angered by Egypt's abandonment of the united Arab war against Israel. In retaliation, he broke off diplomatic relations and led other Arab countries in an economic boycott of Egypt.

To the east in Iran, internal pressures boiled up against the shah. The Communists accused him of investing billions of dollars of oil revenues in his personal real estate, industrial, and bank holdings. Merchants complained that half the country's development programs were failures. Shiite religious leaders resented the land redistribution and rebelled against the secularization of laws. The exiled Ayatollah Khomeini added to the pressure by stirring up the Shiites through underground guerilla organizations.

Iranian workers started striking in 1977, and within a year were rioting against the shah. The pressure caused the shah to take increasingly stronger measures to protect his regime. In September 1978, resentment mushroomed when several hundred demonstrators were shot. In October, Khomeini was deported by Iraq and went to Paris from where he arranged a strike by the Iranian oil workers. The strike stopped oil production and halted the flow of revenue to the country. In November, the riots increased in intensity as the economy slowed down. The shah was forced to leave Iran on 25 January 1979. The following month, Khomeini and his Shiite followers assumed power.

The ascension to power of the fanatical Shiites had

disastrous consequences for Americans. The Iranians denounced the United States for its support of the shah and the chaotic new government stopped honoring its contracts with American firms. Commercial airlines suspended operations to Iran and the United States government had to fly American expatriates back home. On 4 November 1979, Iranian students seized the United States embassy in Tehran and took the remaining Americans as hostages.

A month later on 27 December, the Soviet Union helped to overthrow the government of Afghanistan. When Afghani Muslims revolted against the new puppet government, thousands of Russian troops were sent in to put down the rebellion.

By 1980, almost one-third of all the oil produced in the world was being shipped through the Persian Gulf and the narrow Strait of Hormuz. Each day, almost eighteen million barrels of oil worth $300 million was being carried by ships within 350 miles of Afghanistan.

The sudden deterioration of political stability and blatant Soviet encroachment in the Middle East caused extreme concern in the United States. On 23 January 1980, during the State of the Union address, President Carter stated that the Russian presence in Afghanistan "poses a great threat to the free movement of Middle East oil." He warned, "An attempt by any outside force to gain control of the Persian Gulf region will be regarded as an assault of the vital interests of the United States of America and such an assault will be repelled by any means necessary, including military force."

A Rapid Deployment Force (RDF) was established by the United States government to protect Saudi oil fields against attack. It stationed seventeen ships loaded with enough military material to support a twelve-thousand-man combat brigade at the Indian Ocean island of Diego Garcia, set up a unified RDF headquarters command, and designated the military units needed to respond to a threat.

Meanwhile, Ayatollah Khomeini began making radio broadcasts to Shiites in other countries, inciting them to become better Muslims by rebelling against their governments. Thus, in February 1980, on the first anniversary of the Khomeini regime, the Shiites in the Saudi refinery town of al-Qatif rioted, looted two banks, and burned dozens of cars.

In the north, Israel provoked the Arabs, who were frustrated by their inability to visit the holy city, by announcing that "Jerusalem is the undivided capital of the Jewish state." Saudi Prince Fahd retaliated in August by calling for another jihad against Israel. In September, Libya and Syria responded by announcing their intention to form a single country dedicated to regain the lands captured by Israel.

But in the northeast, Iraq's president Saddam Hussein decided to take the oil-rich, Arab-populated, province of Khuzestan from strife-torn Iran. Iraqi soldiers poured across the Shatt al-Arab River, shelled refineries in Abadan, and bombed the airport in Tehran. Khomeini despised Hussein for kicking him out of Iraq, detested Iraq's mistreatment of Iranian pilgrims visiting the Shiite holy city of Karbala, and resented the Iraqi ownership and control of Shatt al-Arab River. So, Khomeini retaliated with a passion by bombing the Iraqi oil refineries and Baghdad. Soon, both sides had armies totalling over two hundred thousand men, two thousand tanks and five hundred combat aircraft locked in conflict about 80 miles from the Saudi border.

Each side tried to destroy the other's economy to reduce its ability to fight. The Iranians prevented oil from being shipped from Iraq's main port at Basra down the Shatt al-Arab River to the gulf, and caused Iraq to lose most of its revenues. Iraq knocked out the Iranian oil terminal at Abadan, but Iran's Kharj Island terminal, 150 miles southeast of Abadan, remained intact. Iran then increased its revenues by producing more oil and selling it at eight dollars per barrel less than OPEC prices.

Soon after the war started, the Saudis tried to negotiate peace by offering Iran billions of dollars for reparations, but Khomeini refused. The Saudis then asked for American help. The United States sent four airborne early warning aircraft systems (AWACS) to the kingdom to provide early detection of belligerent fighter planes entering Saudi airspace. The United States also sent a contingent of the Rapid Deployment Force to Egypt to train with the Egyptian army in preparation for possible deployment.

Saudi Arabia started the year 1981 by strengthening its ties with other Islamic countries. In January, Saudi Arabia hosted the third Islamic conference at its new, $135 million conference center in Taif. During the meeting, King Khalid and forty other heads of state renewed their vow not to rest until Jerusalem was returned to Islam.

In February, the kingdom joined with Kuwait, Bahrain, Qatar, Oman, and the United Arab Emirates in forming the Gulf Cooperation Council to promote military and economic cooperation between the six member states. The council started efforts to ease the flow of money, goods, and labor between their countries and cooperate in regional development. Its members also started planning a common defense against Iranian attack.

As the Iraq-Iran war continued, strange alliances evolved. Israel bombed Iraq's new nuclear reactor to eliminate its capability to make nuclear weapons, and sold Iran spare parts for its American weapons. Iraq's enemies, Syria and Libya, allied themselves with Iran. Syria closed the main Iraqi pipeline to the Mediterranean Sea, leaving only a small Iraqi pipeline across Turkey. The Arab League condemned Iran. Saudi Arabia and the Gulf States gave Iraq millions of dollars in military aid. Saudi Arabia also agreed to let Iraq run a pipeline through its territory to the Red Sea. The Soviet Union helped both sides. It sold Russian tanks to Iraq which were delivered to Yanbu and transported across Saudi Arabia to the Iraqi border. The Soviets also sold planes to Iran, and drove convoys of trucks carrying American weapons spare parts that had been sold to Iran by Israel across Syria to the Iranian border.

Crown Prince Fahd tried to end the hostilities in the north in August 1981 by proposing an eight-point peace plan. His plan called for Israeli withdrawal from all Arab territory occupied since 1967, and the establishment of an independent Palestinian state with Jerusalem as its capital so that all states in the region could live in peace. Fahd's proposal caused great concern in the rest of the Arab world because of its implied recognition of the state of Israel. However, Israel was not interested in the plan.

Two months later, a wave of religious extremist violence rocked the Middle East. In October, Iranian Shiite pilgrims started riots in Saudi Arabia by carrying posters of Khomeini and distributing leaflets calling for the overthrow of King Khalid. On 6 October, Muslim fundamentalists assassinated Egyptian president Sadat. In December, Shiites caused riots in Bahrain and tried to overthrow the Sunni emir.

The Saudis were alarmed by the spread of Shiite terrorism and worried about outright Iranian attacks. After having the temporary use of American-owned-and-operated AWACS for the past year, the Saudis sought United States government permission to buy the planes. The Saudis pointed out that the flying time of a bomber, from takeoff in Iran to attack on Saudi oil fields, is twelve minutes; and that ground-based radar cannot pick up an attacking plane over the Persian Gulf until it is less than two minutes away from its target. The Saudis said they needed the AWACS to give them enough time to scramble their fighters to defend themselves.

The Saudi request caused another series of heated debates. The United States Congress pointed out that the Saudis failed to honor their 1977 agreement to supply the United States with the oil required to create a strategic reserve. American military planners, sorely aware that the Khomeini regime was using premier F-14 aircraft and Phoenix missile systems sold to the former shah of Iran, warned that the top secret AWACS systems could also fall into the wrong hands. The American Jewish lobby referred to the recent Saudi calls for holy wars against Israel and declared that the AWACS could be used to neutralize the Israeli air force. Mobil oil company ran full-page advertisements promoting the sale, emphasizing the United States special friendship with Saudi Arabia by listing the names of over eight hundred American companies doing business in the kingdom. The Saudis finally swung the deal by loaning the United States $25 billion at 5 percent interest and the sale was approved in November.

In the meantime, Israel had grown fed up with PLO raids across its borders from Lebanese refugee camps and launched a series of air raids against the guerilla bases. During the process, several Israeli planes were shot down by the Syrian army using sophisticated Russian anti-aircraft batteries and surface-to-air missiles. Thus, the Israelis found it necessary to use greater force to root the PLO from its strongholds. During the summer of 1982, Israel invaded Lebanon with several armored columns under heavy air cover. The Israelis annihilated the Syrian air force, pushed the Syrian army aside, and trapped eight thousand PLO guerillas in Beirut. But world pressure prevented the Israelis from devastating the capital city in the pursuit of their enemy.

While the Israelis held Beirut under siege, Saudi King Fahd mediated between Yassir Arafat and the United States to arrange a cease-fire and the evacuation of the guerillas. But none of the other Arab countries wanted to offer the PLO refuge. Finally, Syria and several other Arab countries agreed to provide temporary sanctuary for the guerillas and a cease-fire agreement was reached. That fall, American Marines, French Foreign Legionnaires, and Italian soldiers entered the city as a peace-keeping force and protected the PLO as it withdrew by sea.

Within days after the evacuation, the Lebanese civil war flared to life again. When the Israelis backed off, the Christian Phalange President-elect, Bashir Gemayel, was killed in a bomb attack by unknown assassins. Later, in apparent retaliation, Lebanese Christian militiamen entered a Palestinian refugee camp and massacred hundreds of suspected PLO men, women, and children. Wholesale fighting broke out. The Israelis refused to leave the country in a state of war and with the threat of take-over by the Syrians, and the Syrians would not leave the northern part of the country because of the Israeli presence. The United States government was reluctant to pull out the American Marines because all the belligerents were still present.

The United States government sent envoys to the

new Christian Phalangist president Amin Gemayel with a proposed Middle East peace plan, and Saudi Prince Bandar Sultan tried to negotiate a cease-fire. But the Soviet Union and its clients, the PLO, Syria, Libya, and South Yemen, rejected any peace plans that could weaken the Soviet position in the Middle East. Then, Soviet leader Yuri Andropov met with Yassir Arafat and Syrian president Hafiz Assad. Soon afterwards, five thousand Russian military advisors and new Russian surface-to-air and surface-to-surface missiles were sent to Syria.

President Reagan also tried, during the spring of 1983, to persuade Israel to allow the Palestinians to govern themselves on the West Bank under the administration of Jordan. He offered to discuss the plan with Jordan's King Hussein who formerly ruled the disputed area. But Hussein was politically bound by the Arab League's recognition of Yassir Arafat as Palestinian spokesman, to first obtain Arafat's approval. Arafat refused, and his military commander explained the refusal by asking, "What's in it for the PLO?" When Arafat later appeared to be ready to negotiate a peace settlement, his more militant factions rebelled against him. Syria supported the rebels and Arafat had to concentrate on his survival. The PLO became so divided that it ceased to be a major force.

In the east, the Persian Gulf became polluted as the Iraq-Iran war dragged on. In February 1983, the Iraqis bombed the Iranian offshore Now Roz oil field and released a torrent of oil into the gulf. The Iranians refused to stop fighting to allow neutral parties to contain the spill or stop the oil flow, unless Iraq surrendered. By May, over half a million barrels of oil had spilled into the water and formed a 5,000-square-mile, two-foot-thick oil slick. As the sludge drifted slowly toward the Strait of Hormuz, it polluted the coastlines of Saudi Arabia, Qatar and Bahrain. The thick goo killed fish and oysters, clogged the water inlets to desalination plants, and contaminated fresh water supplies. It also interfered with trade and navigation, and caught fire and threatened offshore oil rigs as it flowed toward the Indian Ocean.

Saudi Arabia and the other Gulf Cooperation Council members sent their newly formed multinational Rapid Defense Force to Oman in October 1983, to participate in a joint military exercise called Peninsula Shield in practice defense against the Iranian threat.

In the north, Lebanon was the scene of a free-for-all of warring armies. As peace talks were held in Switzerland, 30,000 Israelis, 40,000 Syrians, 3,000 Russians, 10,000 Palestinians, 25,000 Lebanese regulars, 15,000 Christian guerillas, 5,000 Lebanese Maronites, and 5,000 Druze and Shiite guerillas were fighting. Only 2,000 French, 1,500 Italian, 1,200 American, and 100 British troops were trying to keep the peace. The guerilla groups fought the Lebanese army; the Muslim groups fought the Christian groups and the Israeli army; the Syrians fought the Israelis and fired on the Americans; the Palestinians fought among themselves; the Druze shelled the Christians and Americans in Beirut; Shiite Muslims bombed the French and American Marine headquarters; and United States battleships pounded Druze and Syrian positions with heavy shellfire.

Saudi Crown Prince Abdullah supported the Syrian stand in Lebanon and called for the withdrawal of the American Marines from Beirut in February 1984. Shortly thereafter, the peace-keeping forces pulled out and let the locals kill themselves without Western intervention.

As world attention was focused on Lebanon, the Iran-Iraq war grew nastier and spread farther from the battle line. The grandfatherly eighty-four-year old ayatollah started sending unarmed, twelve-year old children walking across mine fields to blast paths for Iranian tanks. The Iraqis countered by spraying mustard and nerve gas over the Iranians. By early 1984, over 50,000 Iraqis and 200,000 Iranians had been killed. Iran bombed Kuwait to block shipments of supplies to Iraq and tried to sabotage convoys in Saudi Arabia. Ayatollah Khomeini also threatened to bomb Saudi oil fields and block the Strait of Hormuz if Iraq bombed its Kharj Island oil terminal. He further threatened to sink United States ships if they tried to stop Iran from blockading Hormuz.

Then the Iraqis received a shipment of French-made Super Etendard jet fighters and Exocet missiles. The Saudis feared the worst and ordered a $4.7 billion French air defense system of radar-guided surface-to-air missiles. A month later, the Persian Gulf turned into a shooting gallery. The Iraqis fired Exocet missiles into a Saudi tanker at Kharj Island and into a supply ship servicing one of Saudi Arabia's offshore oil rigs. The Iranians blasted a tanker near the Saudi Ras Tunurah oil terminal and on 24 May set another ablaze off the Saudi coast.

President Reagan assured Saudi Arabia that the United States was committed to keeping the Strait of Hormuz open and sent a United States aircraft carrier battle group to reinforce the guided missile destroyer squadron already in the gulf. The president also promised American support to King Fahd in a possible war against Iran and rushed two hundred shoulder-launched Stinger missiles to the kingdom.

The Saudis extended their air defense zone out into the gulf to what they called the "Fahd line" and went on full alert. American-manned KC-10 aerial tankers refueled Saudi fighters as they orbited over the coast and American AWACS crews scanned the Persian Gulf. On 5 June, two Saudi F-15 Eagles were vectored sixty miles northeast of Jubail where they picked up two attacking Iranian F-4 Phantoms. The F-15s intercepted the Iranians over a protected zone for shipping and blew them out of the air with a couple of American-made Sidewinder missiles.

Insurance rates doubled as attacks on shipping continued in the northern Persian Gulf. By August, over one hundred ships of all nationalities had been hit by Exocet missiles; fifty-seven ships were either sunk, run aground, or towed away for scrap. Neither side gave indications of stopping and each demanded more than the other would give. Hussein wanted

Iran to recognize Iraq's ownership of the Shatt al-Arab River, return the Abu Musa and Tunbs islands to the evicted Arabs, and give self-rule to the Arabs in Iran's Khuzestan province. Khomeini wanted Iraq to admit that it started the war, pay Iran's cost of waging the war, recognize Iran's right to use the river, and get rid of President Hussein.

In the meantime, the attacks on ships had spread to the Red Sea. During the summer, over twenty ships were damaged by mines in the Suez Canal, and in the Red Sea off North Yemen and the Saudi Arabian coast. Egyptian and Saudi mine sweepers were assisted by American, British, French, and Russian navy teams in removing the Russian-built mines. The mines were believed to have been laid by a Libyan ship to punish Egypt and Saudi Arabia for helping Iraq.

The United States was concerned about the escalation of the gulf war and offered to provide additional assistance. However, Saudi Arabia refused to allow American troops to be based in the kingdom.

Saudi Arabia wanted to defend itself. In early 1985, it engaged Boeing to build a computerized air-defense command, control, and communications system called Peace Shield. In February 1986, Saudi Arabia signed a $7.5 billion agreement with the United Kingdom to obtain seventy-two Tornado fighter-bombers, thirty Hawk trainers, thirty Orion surveillance aircraft, and an assortment of missiles and bombs in exchange for cash and petroleum. The kingdom also made arrangements to start drafting young Saudis for induction into the army.

As the gulf war escalated, an Iraqi-piloted Mirage F-1 fighter fired two Exocet missiles at the United States frigate *Stark* and killed thirty-seven American sailors. Iraq apologized for the error. In June, the United States then agreed to sell Saudi Arabia five AWACS for $8.6 billion despite the strong protests of the Jewish lobby in Washington.

The Iranian offensive grew stronger and in January 1987, Iraqi president Hussein offered a cease-fire when Iran's army approached Basra. Iran rejected the offer and kept on fighting.

Iranian forces also attacked merchant ships sailing to and from Kuwait and seized their cargo as punishment for Kuwait's assistance to Iraq. In July, Iran deployed Chinese-made Silkworm surface-to-surface missiles at the entrance to the Strait of Hormuz and the Faw Peninsula at the northern end of the gulf. Kuwait then registered most of its fleet of tankers under the flags of the United States, the United Kingdom, Liberia, and the Soviet Union to deter Iranian attacks.

However, the first Kuwaiti tanker registered under the American flag struck a mine while being escorted to Kuwait by the United States Navy. Saudi Arabia, the United States, the United Kingdom, France, Netherlands, Belgium, and Italy then deployed mine-sweeping vessels to clear Iranian mines from Persian Gulf shipping lanes.

The United Nations Security Council grew alarmed at the spread of the conflict and adopted

Resolution No. 598 on 20 July, urging an immediate cease-fire between Iraq and Iran. But both sides ignored the UN resolution and the war continued to escalate.

Meanwhile, during the hajj in Mecca, Saudi security forces clashed with Iranian pilgrims who were illegally demonstrating and caused a stampede which killed 402 people, including 275 Iranians. The ayatollah claimed that the Saudis had shot his people and vowed to avenge the pilgrims' deaths by overthrowing King Fahd. The Saudis responded by setting up a national quota system of one thousand pilgrims for every million of citizens which allowed Iran a quota of 45,000. Ayatollah Khomeini raged against the quota and insisted that 150,000 Iranians should be allowed to make the pilgrimage.

In September, the gulf war became even more heated when Iran fired three Silkworm missiles into Kuwait to punish it for continuing its support of Iraq, and a United States Navy helicopter strafed an Iranian boat caught laying mines in the gulf. The following month, four United States ships destroyed two Iranian oil platforms about sixty miles east of Qatar that were being used as a base from which to attack shipping.

During November, Saudi Arabia resumed full diplomatic relations with Egypt.

But tension in the Middle East increased following the American action in the Persian Gulf, and in November 1987, the Arab League condemned Iran for prolonging the war. Iran said it would observe a cease-fire only if the UN identified Iraq as the aggressor. The fighting continued and by year-end, Iraq and Iran had attacked 178 ships.

The year 1988 started with a bang as the Iraqis began bombarding Tehran with Russian-made Scud-B ballistic missiles and Iran responded by launching Chinese-made Silkworm missiles at Baghdad. In March, Iraq enraged world leaders by using outlawed mustard gas to kill four thousand of its own civilians in the town of Halabja for supporting a Kurdish uprising.

Saudi Arabia reacted by purchasing intermediate range ballistic missiles from China. The 1,700-mile range, 3,000-pound warhead DF-3 missiles posed a threat to the entire region. The Israelis threatened a preemptive strike to remove the Saudi threat. The United States warned Israel against the attack and warned Saudi Arabia not to use the new missiles. King Fahd then asked the United States to replace its ambassador.

The United States Senate responded in May by voting to ban arms sales to Saudi Arabia unless the United States president could certify that the kingdom had no biological, chemical, or nuclear warheads with which to equip the Chinese missiles.

The Saudis then signed one of the largest arms contracts in history with the United Kingdom to buy about $150 billion worth of Tornado fighters, Hawk training aircraft, and helicopters.

In the meantime, the American forces in the gulf went on full combat alert on 14 April after a United

States frigate was severely damaged by an Iranian mine. Four days later, the American navy sank six Iranian warships and destroyed two more Iranian oil platforms. On 3 July, in the belief that it was under attack by an Iranian F-14 fighter-bomber, the United States guided missile cruiser *Vicennes* shot down an Iranian airliner, killing 290 passengers and crew.

By that time, the Iranian government had lost popular support for the war and its army retreated back across the border into Iran for the first time in two years. Finally, on 18 July 1988, Iran agreed to United Nations Resolution No. 598 for a cease-fire. The Iraqi army continued fighting for another week despite the cease-fire and advanced one hundred miles into Iran before withdrawing. A cease-fire finally came into force on 20 August. Peace talks began, interrupted by artillery duels and other cease-fire violations.

President Hussein, however, continued his belligerence by turning on Kuwait, which had loaned Iraq $10 billion to conduct the gulf war. He accused Kuwait of stealing Iraq's oil and demanded that the debt be reduced by $2 billion.

To ease the concerns about Saddam Hussein's expansionist ideas, King Fahd signed a non-aggression pact with Iraq in March 1989. Fahd also announced that he would help pay for the rebuilding of Iraq's nuclear reactor if it were to be used for peaceful purposes. But just in case, during the following July, King Fahd bought three more French frigates and $77 million worth of Austrian howitzers.

That same month, a new era began when Hashemi Rafsanjani was elected as the new president of Iran to succeed Ayatollah Khomeini, who died on 3 June, 1989. However, Iran boycotted the hajj pilgrimage for the second time by refusing to submit to the Saudi quota system.

Saudi Arabia has a 45,000-man army, a 25,000-man National Guard, a 15,000-man air force, an 8,500-man frontier force and coast guard, a 7,500-man navy, and a 1,800-man special security force. The king also has an elite unit of 8,000 Pakistanis who guard the royal family and protect sensitive installations. The army units are stationed at major military bases near the Israeli and Jordanian borders at Tabuk, near the Iraqi and Kuwaiti borders at King Khalid Military City, near Yemen at Khamis Mushayt, at Taif, Kharj, and Hail. The air force squadrons are based in Riyadh, Kharj, Jeddah, Hail, Tabuk, and Dhahran and the naval units are based in Jeddah and Jubail.

Since Saudi Arabia is such a tempting target and its armed forces are so small, the government has spent almost $200 billion to make its forces effective. It sent its military personnel to the United States, the United Kingdom, France, and Pakistan for training. It hired American and British pilots to train its air force, Vinnell Corporation to train its National Guard and Basil Corporation to train its navy. It engaged the United States Army Corps of Engineers to build its military and naval bases. It also contracted Lockheed, Northrop, McDonnell-Douglas, and the British Aircraft corporations to train its air force. In addition, it hired Raytheon and Bendix corporations to teach the army how to use the American-made missiles and organize their logistical support.

It is estimated that the Saudi army and National Guard have over 1,000 tanks, 500 armored personnel carriers, 400 armored cars, 1,500 field guns, and 16 surface-to-air missile batteries. The air defense command has 33 Hawk and Crotale surface-to-air missile batteries and numerous anti-aircraft artillery batteries. The air force has 5 E-3A AWACS, 62 F-15 fighters, 114 F-5 fighters, 72 Tornado fighter-bombers, 41 Lightning fighters, 46 Strikemaster attack aircraft, 79 C-130 transport aircraft, 8 KC-707 and 4 C-130 mid-air refueling tankers, and 500 helicopters. It also has Hawk advanced trainer airplanes, Sidewinder air-to-air missiles, TV-guided missiles and laser-guided bombs. The navy and coast guard have 9 corvettes, 4 guided missile frigates, 2 replenishment ships, 2 fleets of oil tankers, 13 missile attack boats, 4 torpedo boats, 4 mine sweepers, 18 hovercraft, 160 coastal patrol craft, 300 inshore patrol cutters, surface-to-air and surface-to-surface missiles.

But the Saudi forces are no match for the long-standing threats seen from Iranian Shiite extremists, Iraqi Baathists, Israeli Zionists, and Russian Communists.

The Saudis fear Iran because its fanatical ayatollahs are trying to force their ideology on the Sunni Muslims of Saudi Arabia. The conflict dates back to A.D. 661 when the Shiites broke away from Sunni Islam. It intensified in A.D. 878 when the Shiites insisted that Muslims be under the religious leadership of an ayatollah, despite the Sunnis' belief that there can be no intermediary with Allah. The Saudi Sunnis accept their king as their religious leader. However, when the ayatollahs came to power, they continually called for the overthrow of the Saudi government and tried to create dissension between church and state in Saudi Arabia as in Iran.

Saudi Arabia fears Iraq because it has coveted their land since 1921 when the British government appointed the son of King Abdul Aziz's worst enemy as king of Iraq. Saudi fears were first realized in 1922 when the British gave thousands of square miles claimed by King Abdul Aziz to Iraq. They were renewed in June 1961, when Iraq's Baathist regime announced its intention to take over the new country of Kuwait, and again in April 1972, when Iraq invaded Kuwait.

However, during the gulf war, their fear of Iran was greater. So, the kingdom loaned Iraq $25 billion to buy arms, and built a pipeline from its northern border to the TAPline to enable Iraq to tranship its oil to Yanbu to be loaded on tankers. Saudi Arabia then signed a non-aggression pact with Iraq, seven months after the gulf war cease-fire, to preserve its territorial integrity.

The Saudis share their fellow Arab Muslims' conflict with Israel over Zionist control of Jerusalem and occupation of Palestinian lands. The conflict started when Joshua led the tribes of Israel into battle against the Canaanites around 1200 B.C. It intensified in A.D.

622 when Muhammad claimed to have ascended to heaven from King Solomon's temple in Jerusalem and tried to convert the Jews in Medina.

After the Jews were deported from Israel by the Romans in A.D. 135, they were without a national identity until the conferences of the victors of World War I made Palestine their national home. Since then, the Jews have vigorously defended their right to remain in their ancestral home and exist as a nation. As former Israeli president Golda Meir said, "We Jews just refuse to disappear. No matter how strong, brutal, and ruthless the forces against us may be, here we are."

The Arab Muslims believe that Muhammad was the last true prophet and their religion is the successor to Judaism. They hold the Dome of the Rock as their third most sacred place and feel betrayed by Western treaties which allow the Jews to resettle there. They do not recognize Israel as a country and have been in a technical state of war with it since 1948.

In 1967, the conflict intensified when the Arabs fled from the thirty-mile wide by seventy-five-mile long area on the west bank of the River Jordan, and from Jerusalem, just nineteen miles from Jordan, to be interned in crowded, unsanitary refugee camps. It is still raging as Israelis build permanent settlements in the West Bank and refuse to let the Palestinian refugees return home. To add fuel to the fire, Rabbi Meyer Kahane, the head of the Jewish Defense League and a member of the Israeli parliament, dedicated his life to trying to force Israel's government to evict the remaining 2.2 million Arabs from the country.

The Palestinians' claim to the West Bank is based on almost two thousand years of continuous occupation. Yassir Arafat said, "Our argument is not with the Jews. We are both Semites. They have lived with us for centuries. Our enemies are the Zionist colonizers and their backers who insist that Palestine belongs to them exclusively. We Arabs claim deep roots there, too."

Saudi Arabia has provided over $100 million per year to the PLO to help the Palestinians regain their lost lands. King Fahd, and King Faisal before him, said that Israel can live in peace after it returns Palestine, Jerusalem, and the lands captured during the 1967 war. King Fahd has proposed an eight-point peace plan with Israel based on making Palestine a separate state with east Jerusalem as its capital. Jordan's King Hussein has also offered to make a separate peace treaty with Israel if it gives the West Bank back to the Palestinians. But so far these offers have been rejected by Israel.

The Soviet threat is also of great concern. Russia and later the Soviet Union have tried for several centuries to get a warm water port with unrestricted access to the world's oceans. It moved steadily southward, annexing Persia and Turkey as vassal states, and trying to annex Afghanistan.

During the last decade, Soviet and Communist satellite forces have surrounded Saudi Arabia with over 100,000 Russian soldiers in Afghanistan, 5,000 troops in South Yemen, 5,000 in Syria, 3,000 in Iraq,

3,000 in Ethiopia, and 1,000 in Libya. The Soviets had four hundred combat planes in Afghanistan within twenty-eight minutes flying time from the Strait of Hormuz and fifty minutes from Saudi oil fields. Several squadrons of Russian planes were based in South Yemen within forty-five minutes flying time, and Cuban jets were in Ethiopia within thirty minutes flying time of Jeddah and Mecca.

The Saudis saw the ring of Communist bases around it as a strategy to capture their oil fields. Although the Soviet Union is the world's largest oil producer, its consumption exceeds production by almost three million barrels per day. The Soviet Union is dependent on imports of Middle Eastern oil in exchange for weapons and machinery, but it is doubtful if the Soviets can export enough products to pay for the oil. Therefore, the Soviet Union is very interested in securing a continuing source of oil in the region.

Saudi Arabia did not establish diplomatic relations with Communist countries until 1990 because it opposes their atheistic beliefs. Instead, it has aligned itself in conflicting agreements with the United States, the Arab world, the Islamic world, and the Gulf States.

Pacts between Arab countries are as fickle as pacts between Bedouin tribes. Saudi Arabia aligned itself with Iraq because Iraq opposed the Iranian Shiites, yet Saudi Arabia distrusts Iraq because of President Hussein's greed, instability, and Communist leanings. Saudi Arabia supported the Lebanese Christian government because it wants peace in the region. At the same time, Saudi Arabia finances the anti-Zionist PLO that breaches the peace. Saudi Arabia is a friend of Jordan, yet cannot offer material support because this will antagonize Syria. Saudi Arabia depends on Syria, but distrusts it because of its Alawite Muslim leaders and its alliance with the Soviet Union.

Saudi Arabian diplomacy consists largely of secret negotiations and financial gifts. It gave large grants to Egypt, Syria, and Jordan to improve relations and bought weapons for North Yemen, Somalia, and Iraq. It gave loans and conducted negotiations to end wars in Lebanon and Oman, and tried to do the same in Iran. Although it has close ties with Pakistan, Saudi Arabia's alignment with non-Arab Islamic countries, such as Indonesia, is mainly philosophical.

Its alignment with the Gulf States provides a surplus of money, but little else. Kuwait has an army of 26,000, the United Arab Emirates has 25,000, Oman 22,500, Qatar 4,700, and Bahrain 2,300: a total of 80,500 troops. With their money, they can buy the best weapons systems available. To this end, Saudi Arabia tried to promote the joint purchase of American F-20 fighter planes throughout the Gulf States.

Saudi Arabia's main ally is the United States. The Saudis have received continuous financial and military assistance from the United States since the kingdom was founded. Yet the alliance, like a marriage, has its ups and downs.

The Saudis say that Saudi Arabia has a very "special friendship" with the United States. The friendship is based on what they claim to be the shared responsibility to achieve a just peace settlement in the Middle East (including the return of occupied Arab lands and holy places) and the security of non-Communist nations, to help assure fair and reasonable oil prices, to stimulate the global economy without inflation, and to deepen their partnership to mutual economic benefit. The Saudis say the special friendship is also based on the annual sale of $15 billion worth of oil to the United States and annual purchase of $6 billion worth of American goods. The Saudis also say the friendship is based on the award of over a dozen billion-dollar development contracts to American companies and employment of over thirty thousand Americans to carry out the contracts. In addition, the Saudis say it is based on the attendance of over fifteen thousand Saudi students at American universities. Yet, the Saudis think the United States gets more than it gives. Crown Prince Abdullah even says that the United States is the most dangerous threat to the Middle East because of its alliance with Israel.

The United States' perception of the "special friendship" is slightly different. The Americans believe that it is based on Saudi Arabia's need to protect itself from other nations, and to produce oil, sell it, and build a non-oil-dependent economy; and the United States needs to ensure an uninterrupted flow of oil to sustain the free world's productivity and bring peace to the Middle East.

The views differ in that although the United States wants peace in the Middle East, it does not mandate that Israel surrender Jerusalem to the Arabs; it seeks an alternative solution. The United States also wants a stable economy and does not like major Saudi oil price hikes that cause inflation, or the use of Saudi petrodollar deposits to influence United States foreign policy. The United States does not like the fact that it had to spend $461 million on modernizing military bases in Oman, Somalia, and Kenya to defend the Saudis because Saudi Arabia refused to allow American troops to be based permanently in their country. The United States does not like the foreign trade inbalance between the countries which results in a constant flow of dollars to Saudi Arabia, a situation which could be rectified if the Saudis awarded more of their contracts to American firms and hired more Americans. The United States also dislikes the Saudi use of oil embargoes as a weapon in Islamic causes.

Nevertheless, in February 1986, President Reagan renewed the United States guarantee to help the Saud family stay in power. The Saudis have the most sophisticated weapons in the American arsenal, as well as the assurance of United States help against Iraqi interference with production or shipping of their oil. Saudi Arabia has a long-term commitment of support from the United States despite its entirely different culture and set of values.

Chapter 8

BENEVOLENT DICTATORSHIP

Saudi Arabia is not a democracy. It has no constitution defining the government, its powers, its processes, or the rights of its people. It has no elections or means for its people to have a say about what the government does. Political parties are illegal. Its people have no freedom of religion, of assembly, of speech, or of the press; no protection from search and seizure; and no right to a speedy trial. The Saudi government is called a theocratic monarchy, but it could also be called a benevolent dictatorship.

The country is ruled by a king who is its religious

leader, prime minister, and supreme commander of its armed forces. The king and his closest male relatives have absolute authority over the country and function similarly to a large Bedouin tribal council. The government, or the Saud family, controls almost every aspect of the country. It has total control of the kingdom's religion, military, education, oil, water, electricity, communications, airline, railroad, and most industries.

The king is selected by a consensus of senior members of the Saud family and ulama, who can also depose him if he is incompetent. The king selects a crown prince as his heir apparent, subject to family and ulama approval, who is the next oldest, capable, surviving descendent of the kingdom's founder. So far, succession has passed to the crown prince appointed by the prior king. The king's duty is to ensure that Islamic law, called Sharia, is observed. It is everybody's duty to obey his commands.

Weekly majlis sessions are held by the king, at which any citizen can personally give him a petition with a complaint or request for a favor from His Majesty. The king discusses the petitions with his assistants and delegates appropriate action.

Key religious and Bedouin leaders report directly to the king, including the secretary general of the Senior Ulama Committee, the head of Bedouin Affairs, the head of the Holy Mosque Committee, and the head of the Supreme Committee for Administrative Reform. Otherwise, the king rules through the Council of Ministers.

If he were so inclined, the king could appoint the crown prince as prime minister to administer the operation of the government. However, King Fahd has not delegated this authority to Crown Prince Abdullah.

In the past, the prime minister, with the king's approval, selected ministers to head sectors of the government and lead the Council of Ministers. Several agencies also reported directly to the prime minister, including the Royal Commission for Jubail and Yanbu, the Ports Authority, the Supreme Petroleum Council, the Agency for Technical Cooperation, the Experts Division, and the Military Section.

The Council of Ministers collectively proposes laws for the king's consideration. When the king agrees to a proposal, he reviews it with the Supreme Judicial Council to ensure that it is not in conflict with Sharia. If there is no objection, the king then issues the laws as royal decrees in a form which begins with, "Allah, in his infinite wisdom, has ordained that...."

Several organizations report to the full Council of Ministers, including the National Guard, the Civil Service Bureau, the Public Morality Committee, the Grievance Board, the Female Education Agency, and the Supreme Council for Education.

The twenty-one-member council consists of ministers of interior, health, communications, municipal and rural affairs, planning, transportation, finance and national economy, commerce, foreign affairs, industry and electricity, justice, defense and aviation, labor and social affairs, agriculture and water, public works and housing, education, higher education, pilgrimages and waqfs, information, posts and telephones, and petroleum and mineral resources.

Each of the ministries contains numerous departments and many have the responsibility for quasi-governmental organizations. SAMA, the Institute of Public Administration, the Real Estate Development Fund, the Saudi Industrial Development Fund, the Saudi Credit Bank, and the Agricultural Bank are all functions of the Ministry of Finance and National Economy. The National Security Council, the Frontier Forces, and the Departments of Immigration and Public Security are part of the Ministry of the Interior. The Department of Civil Aviation, Saudia Airlines and the Meteorological Agency are part of the Ministry of Defense and Aviation. The General Organization for Social Insurance is a part of the Ministry of Labor and Social Affairs. SABIC is part of the Ministry of Industry and Electricity and Petromin is part of the Ministry of Petroleum and Minerals. The Israel Boycott Office is part of the Ministry of Commerce. The Saudi News Agency is part of the Ministry of Information.

Western executives consider the government to be grossly inefficient. Confusion reigns because of the duplication and overlap of functions that were rapidly created when the government expanded to administer the spending of its sudden wealth. Foreign governments and corporations cannot determine which organization to deal with. Companies wishing to bid on government contracts must go through the costly process of pre-qualifying with all organizations that are likely to award contracts in their areas of expertise.

As the number of government organizations grew, the number of rules governing business increased. Often, different government organizations would issue *Catch 22*-type, conflicting rules that were impossible to follow. As the number of rules grew, so did the requirements for forms and documents. Then, the documents would get lost, misplaced, misfiled, and shuffled between departments and ministries.

As the functions of government grew, the size of its staff increased. Between 1966 and 1970, the number of government employees doubled. By 1980, 20 percent of the work force was government employees.

Although overstaffing has increased organizational complexity and compounded communication problems, the number of staff is still expanding. During the last decade, the government absorbed about 30,000 graduates of American universities who had to fulfill their obligatory terms of government employment. Although it probably has more new Ph.D.-holders on its staff than any other government, it also has thousands of semiliterate, untrained middle managers and thousands of total illiterates in lower level jobs, none of whom are skilled administrators.

Those administrators who are experienced refuse to delegate authority. They say that there would not be managers at lower levels who would take the initiative to make decisions or carry out actions. Consequently, many levels of approval are needed to arrive at final decisions. In 1981, even ministers could not make decisions on matters involving more than $30,000 without approval of the full council.

Government administrators did not spend much time in their offices, so in 1975, the Council of Ministers set official government working hours to "invigorate Saudi society and alter rigid, inefficient old habits." They made the official working hours 7:00 A.M. to 1:00 P.M. and 4:00 P.M. to 6:00 P.M., Saturday through Wednesday, except during Ramadan. However, many government employees did not return in the evening, so the working hours were changed to 7:30 A.M. to 2:30 P.M.

As the government bureaucracy grew, the number of people who had to deal with it grew, increasing the need for people to personally visit government officials. Government officials follow very formal personalized procedures and have little concern for time. The visitors are treated with cordial, ritualistic Saudi hospitality in which business is dragged out in slow motion. The relaxed pace of meetings results in backlogs of visitors whose meetings have to be postponed to another day, and the day after that. Bureaucratic inefficiency makes it very difficult for those dealing with the government to obtain approvals, decisions, or answers regarding matters such as contract awards, payments, visas, work permits, driver's licenses, and goods in customs.

Western governments complain about the corruption of Saudi officials. They do not understand that Saudi officials are traditionally expected to use their positions for personal gain. The Saudis consider bribery and family profiteering as normal business practices. What is considered in the West as conflict of interest is glorified by Saudis as "continuation of interest." Old Saudi hands, Thomas Barger and Frank Jungers, both former chairmen of Aramco, say that in the past "the corruption has been accepted and unquestioned."

The most effective method to expedite government business is through a friend of a friend, particularly if the friend is a senior prince. Government concessions or contracts are obtained by bribing the right official after paying a ranking member of the royal family to use his influence. The cost of the influence and the amount of the bribe are proportional to the size of the contract, and some contracts have been colossal. During the last fifteen years, dozens of princes and friends of the royal family have gotten incredibly rich by helping foreign companies to do business in the kingdom.

Prince Muhammed ibn-Fahd, the then twenty-five-year-old son of King Fahd, made more profit than most of the top American corporations by helping N.V. Philips corporation of Holland to get a $7 billion telecommunications contract. He was paid half a billion dollars for using his influence. King Faisal's son, Prince Abdullah al-Faisal, received $75 million for helping to get the Saudi Arabian National Guard modernization contract.

Adnan Khashoggi, a friend of the royal family, was paid $106 million by Lockheed to help get a C-130 aircraft contract, $45 million by the Sofna company of France to help get a $600 million tank contract, and $5.8 million by a British company to help get a helicopter contract. He also allegedly received $45 million from Northrop to assist them in getting an F-5 fighter plane contract by bribing two Saudi air force generals.

Several princes with insider knowledge of the five-year development plans purchased undeveloped property and resold it to the government for construction projects. A leading prince made a $2 billion profit on the resale of the property used as the site for the Jubail industrial complex and several others made $8 billion on the resale of land used for the new Riyadh airport. Informed United States officials claim that many unnecessary construction projects have been included in the development plans to guarantee a steady flow of profits to government insiders.

A handful of princes and their friends made a killing on oil export deals. During shortages, they reaped commission fees of $6 per barrel on tanker loads of oil by selling them on the spot market above the posted price, and then buying them for immediate delivery at the lower official Saudi price. An enterprising Petromin executive demanded a $120 million bribe to sell ninety million barrels of oil to the Italia Oil Company.

Many members of the middle and lower classes resent these practices. Some resent them because they cannot participate. Others, especially the technocrats, resent the scale of the corruption for the personal benefit of a privileged few.

In the early years the Saudis did not have to scheme to be corrupt as there are few laws in Sharia regulating government, business or commerce. So they ran their government the way the Ottomans had for the previous 650 years, and dealt with business as tribal leaders. They had very little control over these areas until the 1950s. Since then, the kings have issued numerous laws which deal with the operation of government, ways companies conduct business, and the behavior of the people.

Many of these laws significantly affect foreign companies. The companies are bound by laws specifying how they can form joint venture companies, invest money, deal with and enter into contracts with the government, acquire products, hire employees, and manage their staffs.

One of the first decrees made Saudi Arabia a member of the twenty-country Arab League, then based in Damascus, Syria. All member countries are bound to boycott products originating in, or made by, companies doing business with Israel. When companies are chosen to be boycotted or blacklisted, the information is sent to the member countries. In Saudi Arabia, the lists are maintained in computers by the central Ministry of Commerce and the local chambers. Over fifteen hundred American companies were listed on the 1980 boycott blacklist, including Ford, American Motors, RCA, Xerox, Sears-Roebuck, Monsanto Chemical, and Coca-Cola, as well as products made by or featuring Barbara Streisand.

Any company can be blacklisted for refusing to reply to a questionnaire from the boycott authorities. Manufacturing or trading firms are blacklisted for establishing headquarters, factories, plants, or agencies in Israel; owning shares in an Israeli firm; allowing an Israeli firm to use its name or manufacturing license; giving technical assistance to Israeli factories; being agents of Israeli firms or importers of Israeli products; prospecting for natural resources in Israel; belonging to foreign-based Israel chambers of commerce; and using parts or materials produced by a blacklisted firm.

Banks are blacklisted for making loans to major Israeli firms distributing or promoting the sale of Israeli bonds, establishing firms in Israel, and investing in firms anywhere which have Israeli capital.

Foreign companies in Saudi Arabia are restricted from using familiar products of their preference. They have to check with the local chamber of commerce before specifying or ordering any product whose status is unknown. Even previously acceptable products on order could be blacklisted prior to arrival in Saudi Arabia, thus forcing the companies to try to arrange for waivers, to make costly last-minute arrangements for substitute products, or to slip their schedules.

In July 1981, the company operating computers for the Saudi Meteorological Agency ordered an additional component from Control Data Corporation to expand their computing capability. The delivery time for the product was six months. Five months after it was ordered, the company was told that Control Data had been blacklisted in Kuwait. The time remaining to complete the expansion contract was not sufficient to obtain an alternative product. There was a significant penalty clause in the contract for failing to finish the expansion but no relief clause for boycott actions. The company just managed to break even by taking expensive actions to get the equipment delivered before Control Data's name could be added to the Arab League blacklist and sent to Saudi Arabia.

The Saudi government uses only fixed-price contracts which require companies submitting proposals to provide bank guarantees. A guarantee of 1 percent of the bid price is required at the time of submission and a guarantee of 5 percent must be paid if the contract is awarded. Shortly after contract award, the government pays the successful bidder 10 percent of the contract price as a mobilization fee to enable them to obtain the staff resources necessary to perform the work. If the contractor fails to perform, the government can immediately draw against the guaranteed funds.

The million-dollar bid fee a British company posted with the Saudi government in 1981 was lost after it failed to borrow the $5 million needed for the guarantee. Most foreign companies in Saudi Arabia run into severe cash flow problems. Mobilization incurs major front-end expenses of hiring, relocating, and housing expatriate employees, but the payments are not provided until well after the start of the contract and payments for work performed are held back several months.

King Saud issued a decree in 1956 regulating the union activities of workers. He banned labor unions and any other kind of pressure groups and made any form of group negotiation or strike subject to severe punishment.

A group of Saudi employees petitioned Aramco in May 1953 for higher wages and better housing. When the Saudi government learned about the petition, it imprisoned the whole group. The next day, the rest of the employees rioted, attacked the police station and stoned company vehicles. The government put down the riot with five thousand troops. That October, 17,000 Aramco workers went on strike to protest their treatment. The government ended the strike by exiling all its leaders to their home villages. In 1956, the workers struck again for better treatment. Three days later, government troops arrested 200 strike leaders and publicly beat three of them to death to discourage any more workers from striking.

When Turkish construction workers in Tabuk went on strike in 1977 in protest over harsh working conditions and rotten housing, the government sent in air force C-130 cargo planes, loaded the workers aboard, and flew them back to Turkey.

In 1957, while planning a small tanker deal, King Saud issued a decree to control foreign capital investments. It stated that Saudi nationals must have controlling interest of any company which invests in the kingdom. It stipulated that 75 percent of the staff of these companies should be Saudis who would receive a minimum of 45 percent of the salaries paid by the firms.

A decree was issued in 1961 which set stiff penalties for commercial fraud, and in 1963, another decree was issued which set up a special committee to review contract disputes between the government and Western companies.

In 1970, King Faisal issued a decree called the Work and Workmen's Regulation. The law stated that 75 percent of all company work forces should be Saudi nationals who would receive at least 51 percent of the company's total compensation. In most cases, notwithstanding the size of the companies, there were only one or two Saudis hired, but they still received 51 percent of the salaries. Sometimes these Saudis got paid for doing absolutely nothing. Since it would be extremely difficult to get anything done with an all-Saudi work force, the decree provided that permission could be obtained to hire expatriates after showing proof that no qualified Saudis were available. It specified that expatriates must complete a minimum three-month probationary period before they could be considered to be permanent employees. The decree also required employers to submit lists of expatriate employees to the labor office and to have expatriates undergo a complicated termination procedure to clear sponsorship, liquidate debts, and ensure their departure.

The work law went on to require new employees

to pass a pre-employment physical examination, and for employers to maintain medical records of their employees. It stipulated that employers provide medical coverage, thirty days sick leave at full pay, and sixty days sick leave at three-quarters pay. It also set the private sector workweek at forty-four hours from Saturday through Wednesday, and half-day on Thursday. It further provided for fourteen- to thirty-day vacations.

Two paid, 5-1/2-day, public holidays per year were provided by the work law: the Ramadan holiday of Eid al-Fitr and the hajj holiday of Eid al-Adha. It did not state when the holidays would occur because the exact dates of observance cannot be established until the first sighting of the new moon. It is up to each company to set its own holiday dates and hope that the days chosen are the same as the holidays of its suppliers and customers. Some companies also observe National Day, which commemorates the unification of the kingdom. National Day falls on the first day of Libra in the zodiac calendar, roughly 23 September.

Employers were made responsible under the work law if their employees brought illegal items, like beer or *Playboy* magazines, to a work site. The law defined disciplinary procedures for given offenses which consist of a series of warning letters, fines, and involuntary termination. The procedures also provide for managerial appeals, evidence, witnesses, and timing of disciplinary actions. The work law further provided an elaborate set of grievance procedures for employees which start at the Ministry of Labor and Social Affairs and can extend to a hearing by the king.

The work law made it an offense for a foreigner to insult a Saudi. It provided stiff penalties, fines, imprisonment, and/or deportation of any foreign national found to have offended a subject of the kingdom "either by hand or tongue, scoffing or any kind of offense, scorn, or contempt." The subjective terms like "offend" and "contempt" forced Western managers to be extremely careful to avoid doing anything that could be construed as offensive—to the extent of letting their Saudi employees do anything they pleased. In 1981, a British director at Saudia was released from his position after he "offended" two Saudis by not recommending them for promotion.

In 1973, King Faisal issued a decree establishing the Social Insurance Law. The law required that all employees in Saudi Arabia pay taxes, similar to United States social security taxes, to the General Organization for Social Insurance (GOSI). The amount paid was based on the employee's salary and housing allowance at the beginning of each year. The employer was required to contribute 8 percent and the employee had to contribute 5 percent through withholding. The actual amount the employee paid was about 6 percent of his salary. If an expatriate employee remained in Saudi Arabia long enough, he would theoretically have been eligible for retirement benefits. Expatriates who were in the kingdom for less than a year were exempt.

Saudi Arabia does not have tax treaties with the United States or with many other countries. Saudi employers do not issue income statements or withhold taxes from expatriates' salaries. It is the responsibility of foreign employees to take care of these things for themselves if their native country requires it.

In 1974, the king decreed that banks could charge service fees. Under Sharia, interest and usury are illegal and banks are not allowed to charge or pay interest. But by that time, so much money had begun flowing into the kingdom that it was realized that the country had to compete with foreign banks that were not bound by Sharia. So the decree enabled the Saudi National Commercial Bank and Riyadh Bank, the two major Saudi Arabian banks, to charge substantial "service fees" for loans, and pay "commissions" on deposited funds. After this law was enacted, foreigners began noticing references to service fees charged and commissions paid in financial transactions that were accrued and were calculated just like interest!

During the same year, King Faisal decreed that a 20-percent tax had to be paid on any imported products or services that could be supplied within the kingdom. The protective tariff was decreed to protect Saudi Industrial Development Fund investments in Saudi-owned building material companies. The law forced foreign corporations to either price their products 20-percent lower than those of the Saudis or else demonstrate that they were of much higher quality in order to remain competitive.

King Khalid dealt with the problem of royal family payoffs in 1978 by issuing a decree which became the Service Agents Law. This law formalized the need for foreign companies to use Saudi service agents to obtain government contracts. It limited the agent's fees to 5 percent of a contract price; but if a foreign company wanted the contract badly enough, or if the service agent squeezed a little harder, who was to know how much was paid?

The king also issued a related decree which required any foreign company that wanted to do business in the kingdom to have a joint venture Saudi partner who held a minimum equity of 25 percent. This law was a boon to wealthy or influential Saudis. Many foreign companies from all over the world courted Saudis for joint venture partners. Many foreign companies acquired legitimate partners; others wound up with Saudis who charged large fees to be partners and did not put up any capital. Some Saudis got involved in so many joint ventures that they could not keep track of their foreign partners. Many top-ranked Western companies failed in Saudi Arabia because of the lack of real influence or participation of their partners.

In 1982, King Fahd issued a decree establishing an import agent law: "Henceforth, foreign companies which enter into contracts with the state cannot import their requirements from abroad but must obtain them locally or through Saudi importers." However, American companies in partnership with the Saudi government were excluded from the decree. Large independent contractors were forced to use middle-men, who were not as familiar with sources of supply as their own purchasing personnel, to acquire products, or else pay a Saudi agent to be a non-functioning middleman. This decree added an importer's fee to the cost of acquiring materials and caused an additional delay in receiving them.

Royal decrees also restrict the individual freedoms of expatriates in the kingdom. The government does not tolerate freedom of speech. In 1984, former minister Ghazi al-Gosaibi was fired for publicly criticizing the royal family for awarding contracts to friends. The recruiting brochures of Saudi organizations state that, "all employment of foreign contract personnel is also contingent upon their strict avoidance of public discussion of, or participation in, religious or political matters of a controversial nature." Private discussion is also dangerous; telephone conversations are monitored; and occasionally, expatriate mail is opened and read by the secret police. Expatriates have to be careful what they do, say, and write. If they are disturbed by a "controversial matter," they should keep quiet about it and/or try to get out of the country.

There is very little freedom of the press. News is censored and propaganda is used so that people in the kingdom are told only what the government wants them to know. Newspaper and magazine editorial appointments are approved by the Saudi Ministry of Information and the news published must conform to that released by the Saudi News Agency. Neither of the two English language newspapers in the kingdom report controversial events, such as riots and demonstrations in which expatriates may be involved, or provide news of interest such as the status of wars in nearby countries.

The Saudis censor all kinds of things. They blank out the name of Israel on maps of the Middle East and show the Persian Gulf as the "Arabian Gulf." They tear off the front covers of American paperback books or magazines if they picture a woman in a low-cut dress or with exposed legs. They scribble with felt-tip pens over cigarette advertisements in magazines with pictures of women in bathing suits, and rip out pages with liquor advertisements or news they do not like.

It is difficult for Westerners to get accurate information from the government. They are bombarded with pro-Saudi propaganda from government agencies and organizations dependent on government support. Between the censorship and the propaganda, there is a lack of unbiased, factual, and complete information regarding the activities of Saudi Arabia. The kingdom has many worthy goals, has made many valuable contributions to its people, and has accomplished much in a short period. It has also acted to hurt the West or in ways which are considered repugnant to Westerners, like enforcing the oil embargoes and supporting the PLO, which have been reported by Western newspapers and are common knowledge. However, the censors omit these facts and always present Saudis in the most favorable light.

There is no freedom of movement. Nobody can enter or leave the kingdom without a Saudi visa stamped in his passport. There are no tourist visas. Entry visas are only granted for the hajj, to visit a blood relative, or for business. To obtain a visa for the hajj, the traveler must prove he is Muslim. A visa for a visiting relative must be obtained by the family member residing in the kingdom.

To obtain an entry visa for business, a foreigner must be sponsored by a Saudi employer or business partner who requests the visa from the Consular Affairs Department of the Ministry of the Interior. After the ministry approves the request, the visa number is sent by pouch to the appropriate Saudi Arabian embassy. The foreigner must then submit a multi-page visa application to the Consular Affairs Department for approval. If they suspect that the applicant is Jewish or if he has an Israeli visa in his passport, the visa will be denied. The process can take anywhere from two weeks to three months.

A resident visa is needed to be able to work in Saudi Arabia. It is obtained the same way as the entry visa, except that a copy of the job offer and a signed copy of the Arabic version of the contract must be submitted with the application.

The government is paranoid about non-Saudis and non-Muslims in the kingdom. It vigorously checks visas at entry points into Saudi Arabia, in spot checks of pedestrians in towns, and at both random and fixed road blocks. In 1979, fifty Africans stayed in the country illegally after the hajj to try to find work. They were eventually shot to death by the police.

Expatriate workers cannot apply for visas for their families until they have completed a probationary period. If they have a college degree, the expatriates may be allowed to get visas for their families after three months. Otherwise, they must wait for a year. Visas are only granted for wives and for children under seventeen years of age.

Foreigners must have an exit or exit/reentry visa to leave the kingdom. An exit visa can be held up by bureaucratic inertia or by the sponsor. The sponsor can demand a commission or percentage payment if the person he sponsors made any business deals with third parties during his stay in the kingdom. If the sponsor is not happy, he can complain under oath against the expatriate and prevent his departure until investigation of the complaint is completed. In some cases, the foreigner is put in jail until the matter is cleared up.

Because of claims against his business dealings, American businessman Donald Fox was detained by the Saudis against his will for several months until his release in March 1982. During the same period, a British executive of SACEM International was held in Saudi Arabia without trial for eleven months and tortured by the Riyadh police because of $1.6 million in unpaid claims against his company. A Houston businessman was denied an exit visa for six months after a dispute with members of the royal family, despite appeals to the United States ambassador and

King Khalid. He finally escaped from the kingdom by being packed into a crate and shipped overseas as air cargo.

Many expatriates have considered committing a minor crime to get themselves deported from the kingdom, but were afraid that they would be flogged or imprisoned instead. However, expatriates frequently leave the kingdom on vacations or business trips and never return.

Multiple exit/reentry visas, which enable a foreigner to leave the kingdom at will, are available. But Saudi sponsors are reluctant to apply for these visas; they are more expensive and their possession reduces the sponsor's power over the expatriates.

Visas are a major problem. They often do not get issued or are issued incorrectly, are sent to the wrong countries, are sent weeks late, or get lost. Visa processing problems have separated families for months, cancelled major business trips, and ruined personal vacations. One American family sold their house and had to live in hotels at their own expense for three months because they could not get entry visas. Another American family was stranded in London for five weeks for the same reason. A Briton who had been in Saudi Arabia for over two years married his fiancee during his home leave and had to wait for six months before he could get an entry visa for his new wife. A Canadian tried to make the best of the situation and had his family stay in nearby Bahrain until they could get their visas, but he could not get an exit/reentry visa to visit them.

The effect on expatriate morale is staggering. When family visas get held up, the husbands get angry, stop working, and threaten to commit rash acts. Western managers have to spend huge amounts of time trying to pacify their staff and expediting the issuance of visas. Managers have had to pay fines for staff who could not get their resident visas renewed on time. They have had to arrange business trips for their men to visit stranded families waiting for entry visas. They have even been forced to have employees work illegally on visitors' visas.

Expatriates also need permits to work in Saudi Arabia. The employee's sponsor must submit the expatriate's passport, an application, and photographs to the Ministry of Labor and Social Affairs. If the employee has previously worked in Saudi Arabia, he must also produce an endorsed "release letter" from his previous Saudi employer. Approximately ten days later, the expatriate is given his *iqama* (work permit) and must surrender his passport to be locked in his employer's safe. The passport is not returned until the expatriate has permission to leave the kingdom. Police frequently stop cars and pedestrians to check for passports and work permits. Foreigners without work permits or passports with visitor's visas are arrested on the spot.

The release letter gives Saudi employers great power over expatriates. An expatriate working in Saudi Arabia cannot accept an offer from another company of any nationality in the kingdom unless his current Saudi sponsor provides him a release letter.

Thousands of expatriate employees working in Saudi Arabia who were unhappy with their jobs and had opportunities to stay in the country with other employers could not get the required letter.

Foreign visitors can use their valid national drivers' licenses to drive in Saudi Arabia until they get their work permits. Then they must obtain a Saudi license. There is no test of laws or signs, no eye test, and no driving test. The process involves filling out an application, obtaining government approvals, having a blood test at a Saudi hospital, and getting finger- printed at a police station. If an American has a valid license from any state, and is helped by a knowledgeable Saudi, he can sometimes complete this process in one day. More often, it takes Americans and their Saudi guides two full days and visits to twenty or thirty offices to get their licenses.

Very few expatriates are ever told about, or given English-language booklets which explain, Saudi traffic laws. Most Americans just follow the same rules as they would in the United States, obey any posted English-language signs, and yield the right of way to all drivers who have cloth draped over their heads.

All parties to an accident, including witnesses, are normally arrested and held until the police complete their investigation. This can take up to a week.

Saudi authorities hold that all parties involved in accidents share guilt and penalties are apportioned according to their degree of blame. But the principles of causation are peculiar from a Western perspective. For example, a passenger in a taxicab can be held responsible for an accident because he caused the taxi to be where the accident happened. It is almost instinctive for Westerners to stop at the scene of an accident to give first aid to a victim or try to help in some way. In Saudi Arabia, this can be rewarded by a week in jail as a witness, so Westerners try not to look at the bleeding victims of car wrecks and sadly drive on.

If someone is involved in a personal injury accident, it is very difficult to get out of jail on bond. Bonding depends on the degree of blame, on whether the injured party is expected to recover in less than a month, or whether the injured party waives his rights.

Traffic accidents involve both government regulations and the Sharia. Injured parties may sue for damages and the government can prosecute for violating a regulatory law. In most minor accidents, damage claims of one driver against another are settled on the spot before the police arrive, although expatriates usually have to honor exorbitant claims.

The police determine guilt and judges set the punishments. A driver who injures or kills someone in an accident is obligated to pay blood money to the victim or his family. Third-party automobile insurance covers these claims. If the driver is not insured and cannot raise the money, he will be imprisoned for debt. But imprisonment does not discharge the debt. After this has been fulfilled, the punishment for the regulatory offense is considered. The Saudis often impose jail sentences on drivers found guilty in accidents involving personal injury, even if the injuries are minor and the injured parties do not file a claim.

A lot of time is spent by Western managers in trying to spring their employees out of Saudi Arabian jails. They cannot do it themselves, but have to obtain the assistance of an influential Saudi who has a friend in the right place, or knows whom to bribe. Western expatriates live in fear of being involved in traffic accidents. An often-repeated warning is, "If you get in an accident, drive away; if the car won't move, run away; if you're caught, deny everything."

Chapter 9

Sharia

*T*he Arabic word for citizen is *mukallaf* (one who has the responsibility for performing his religious duties and observing the Sharia, the pattern of communal order). Everyone in Saudi Arabia, citizen or not, is subject to the medieval Sharia. It is derived from the Koran and Hadith as interpreted through the 800-year old Hanbali school of legal reasoning. Ahmad Hanbal deduced that all human actions fall into five categories: what Allah had commanded, had recommended, had left indifferent, had condemned, and had specifically forbidden. The Hanbalis say that the only area in which man can legislate is that which

Allah had left indifferent. Everything else is bound by the Sharia, including personal actions, social relations, community life, and the functioning of the state.

Sharia functions very simply. If a complaint is made to the police, the accused is arrested and jailed. No one is notified. It is up to the family or employer to ask the police if they know the whereabouts of someone who is missing. While the investigation continues, the accused may be forbidden to have outside contact with family, friend, employer, lawyer, or diplomat. Foreign embassies cannot do a thing to help the accused other than to offer advice. The accused is usually held for a long time before he is charged with a specific crime. There are no jury trials. Once charged, the defendant is required to make a statement to a Muslim judge who will determine if he has committed a crime.

Those charged with a crime are expected to strongly deny it and are encouraged to try to avoid punishment. The Sharia considers punishment as purification from sin. The Koran says that when a man came to Muhammad and said, "Purify me" (punish me), the Prophet said, "Allah will forgive the sins of every believer except when the sinner himself makes them known; Allah loves those of his servants that cover their sins." So, Sharia directs the guilty party not to confess, but lie and hide his guilt as much as possible! If he does confess, he should later deny his previous confession. Judges are directed to show the accused persons all extenuating circumstances and the advantages of revoking their confessions. More-over, in major crimes, the criminal act must be wit-nessed by three adult Muslim males to prove guilt, and witnesses are recommended not to testify against accused persons.

If the accused is found guilty, he is held in custody until he is sentenced to punishment by the judge. Sentence sometimes is not announced for several months since it must be ratified by the provincial governor or the Ministry of the Interior. Punishments are the same for foreigners as for Saudis. The judges follow Sharia in determining the kind of punishment except in cases of personal injury or death, when punishment is the private "right of man." The judge can even remit punishment unless the "right of man" is involved and the victim or his family demand the punishment of the guilty party.

The "right of man" allows the injured party or his relatives to demand either retaliation or blood money. If retaliation is chosen, the victim or his family can kill, wound, or mutilate the guilty party. If the victim or his survivors give up the right to retaliate, or if it is impossible, the guilty party has to pay compensation or blood money to the victim. The amount payable for the death of an adult Muslim male is one hundred camels or $20,000.

Judges can also sentence guilty parties to defined or discretionary punishment. Defined punishment includes flogging, amputation, decapitation, and stoning. Murder, renunciation of the Islamic faith, and illicit sex are punishable by public execution.

253

Murder and renunciation punishments are dealt with the curved blade of the scimitar. Fornicators are stoned to death. The newspapers announce the time and location of such punishments so all may attend.

In 1982, two Filipinos who had murdered a Lebanese businessman and raped his wife were brought to the square outside the main mosque during the Friday noon sermon. The crowd streamed out of the mosque and joined others to form a circle around police armed with submachine guns. After a brief announcement, the first handcuffed Filipino was dragged forward to the cheers of the crowd and thrown to his knees. The flashing blade traced an arc through the air and lopped his head off. As the crowd yelled their approval, the blade flashed and blood spurted again as the second Filipino was dealt Sharia punishment.

Stoning is a participatory punishment. The guilty party is required to stand chest-deep in a hole. Then everybody throws rocks at the villain. Amputation is used to punish recurrent theft. First the right hand is publicly amputated. It represents a permanent loss of face as well as a disabling punishment because the thief can never again move about in public without his crime being known, and he cannot eat with others since his left hand is considered unclean. If the thief continues his life of crime, it is ended when his left hand is chopped off.

Judges can also set punishments at their own discretion. These might consist of imprisonment, exile, deportation, fines, or corporal punishment such as flogging. Prison sentences are usually calculated from the time of arrest.

Foreigners pray to be deported because Saudi prisons are for punishment, not rehabilitation. They are dark, filthy, malodorous, hot, incredibly over-crowded hell-holes. Many prisoners do not survive even relatively short sentences. Howard Johnson, an American refrigeration engineer, got boils all over his body and had to be hospitalized after being crammed in a twelve-by-twelve-foot cell with thirty other pris-oners. Other prisoners have been beaten, tortured, and starved by their guards.

During Ramadan 1984, King Fahd ordered the release of thirty Americans held in Saudi prisons for acts that were legal in the United States but were violations of the Sharia. Efforts were then made to free another twenty Americans still rotting in Saudi jails.

Other punishment can consist of reprimands, or taking action to cause the guilty party to lose face, such as shaving off his hair and beard, blackening his face, or leading him through the streets.

Sharia includes the observance of customs and rules which differ from those of Westerners and re-strict their activities. Non-Muslims are forbidden to enter mosques and the holy cities of Mecca and Med-ina. There is a gate on the road to Mecca where identification cards are checked and non-Muslims are turned away. Muslims believe that non-believers have no business in Mecca. It is widely rumored that non-believers caught in Mecca have their legs amputated to prevent them from ever setting foot there again.

These Saudi precautions are not without justification. Mecca and Medina have endured Muslim carnage and have been the targets of non-Muslims. The Islamic rules, and rumors of amputation, are sufficient to discourage most Westerners from trying to visit the holy cities.

The restrictions, though, complicate the efforts of foreign contractors in developing those areas. Some organizations tried to solve this problem by having their employees convert to Islam. In 1978, a Texas helicopter pilot was fired because he would not convert so he could fly into Mecca. A Swedish company installing a traffic control system, and a German-French consortium building the Inter-Continental hotel in Mecca solved the problem by using closed-circuit television links and shortwave radios to enable them to supervise inexperienced Muslim employees.

Public entertainment is restricted. There are no bars, discos, nightclubs, dance halls, or cinemas in Saudi Arabia. About the only legal public entertainments for Saudis are soccer games and camel and horse races. The Saudis allow movies and closed-circuit television to be shown in the large expatriate compounds. But what is considered a "PG" (parental guidance) movie rating in the United States might be considered hard core-pornography in Saudi Arabia. Alvin Levine, a Houston engineer with Aramco, spent seventeen months in prison and paid almost $24,000 in fines after being caught with a videotape of an American movie.

To counter the effect on morale because of limited recreational opportunities, enterprising expatriates have formed groups to provide their own entertainment. Amateur American, Canadian, British, and German groups stage plays and operas and hold concerts at their embassies and some of the larger housing compounds. One legendary British group called the Exit Visa wrote, performed, and taped a number of ballads about life in Saudi. Their songs, such as "Hi-Ho, Hi-He, I am a Yemeni" and "Toyota on the Hill," were widely acclaimed until the members of the group were arrested and deported, and their tapes confiscated by the government.

There are also dietary restrictions. Pork, drugs, and alcoholic beverages are strictly forbidden. The absence of pork and pork products does not bother most expatriates, and if they want it very badly, there are some stores that sell "special meat" which looks, smells, and tastes like pork. However, most Westerners avoid the hashish that is molded into the shape of sandals and smuggled in from Afghanistan and Pakistan.

Alcoholic beverages are a problem. King Abdul Aziz initially allowed the importation of alcoholic beverages for consumption by expatriates. But in September 1952, he banned them from the kingdom after one of his sons got drunk and gunned down the British consul. Most Westerners are used to social drinking in their home countries and resent the restriction. Many drink anyway.

Some drink a whiskey called *Sadeeky* (my friend). Sadeeky is distilled and bootlegged in Saudi Arabia. It comes in light and dark, and if diluted with Pepsi Cola or fruit juice, has a taste vaguely reminiscent of scotch or bourbon. Only a small quantity of Sadeeky is sufficient to cause a disabling hangover and it is rumored that some people have been blinded by it. No one seems to know the source of Sadeeky or how it is made, but it is suspected that it may be distilled from petroleum.

A small amount of scotch, gin, and vodka is smuggled in and can occasionally be obtained for about $120 per bottle if the right connection is found. It is difficult to find connections because the Saudis go to great lengths to keep contraband out of the country. Yet, there are some expatriates who go to equally great lengths to get contraband into the country. Therefore, all goods entering Saudi Arabia must clear through customs. Saudi officials unpack containers, open boxes, and conduct very thorough searches which add to extreme delays in receiving imported products. Despite the inspections, there are still those who try to bring in spirits. Several years ago, it was rumored that the British embassy received a call from a chief customs inspector who reported that "their piano was leaking." Other enterprising souls have tried to smuggle cases of scotch in small boats through the reefs to desolate beaches. Scuba diving is extremely popular in the Persian Gulf between Bahrain and Saudi Arabia where a frightened crew jettisoned their cargo of whiskey before being boarded by a Saudi patrol boat.

Many expatriates have turned into amateur brewers or vintners to slake their thirst. The brewers mix several large cans of malt and a little yeast with about fifteen gallons of water and let it ferment in large plastic garbage cans. When fermented, they bottle the beer in European grape juice bottles that have resealable, wire-held, ceramic caps. Sometimes the bottles explode, so they generally store the beer in a bathroom. The vintners make wine by mixing a liter of melted sugar and a little yeast with twelve liters of grape juice and letting it ferment in a five-gallon plastic gas can for about ten days. When their vintage wine is about a month old, they often hold wine-tasting parties.

Drinking, possessing, brewing, smuggling, and selling alcoholic beverages are illegal. The penalties for getting caught include deportation, public flogging, and up to two years imprisonment. In June 1978, seven Britons were arrested and sentenced to six months in jail for brewing beer. Two others were publicly flogged and deported. In March 1980, a British doctor was sentenced to a year in prison and his wife to a public flogging of eighty lashes for serving drinks at a party, after one of the guests attracted the attention of the police by falling to his death from the window of the doctor's sixth-floor apartment. Howard Johnson, the refrigeration engineer, fared even worse. He was sentenced to 300 lashes and two years in jail for smuggling several hundred cases of whiskey into the country. In 1983, Bob Taggert, an American at Aramco, was sentenced to two years in prison and given 200 lashes for making whiskey, allegedly following instructions and using supplies given to him by Aramco.

Expatriates violate Saudi prohibition laws and live in fear of getting caught. An American director was told that one of his crew gave several bottles of beer to some Saudi students and was warned that his company's living compound might be raided by the Religious Police. He relayed the message to his staff in case anyone had anything they wanted to get rid of. The next day, half of his staff had hangovers.

Foreigners are not the only ones who drink in the kingdom. From time to time, Westerners are invited to the home of urbane Saudis and treated to a cocktail by their hosts.

Western women are most annoyed by the sexual restrictions. There is a double standard of mores in Saudi, wherein women are restricted, protected, and shielded from men, but men are granted a wide latitude of sexual freedoms.

The Koran says that men are a degree above women. It is written that a man is responsible to himself and God, but woman is responsible to man. In Sharia, a woman has only half the legal rights of a man.

Women were believed by the Bedouin to be compulsively driven to seduce any man with whom they happened to be alone, if even only for a few minutes. This attitude influenced the writing of the Koran and subsequent interpretation of Islamic law. It still persists among many Saudi men. The Koran says a woman must "guard her private parts and fold a shawl over her bosom." If a woman thinks that her beauty would drive men insane with lust, she must cover her face.

A Saudi woman's place is in the home. Saudi women are segregated from all men except those in her family. Their houses have *majlis* (separate reception rooms) for men to entertain male guests away from the *harem* (family quarters). The houses also have separate entry halls for women to enter without being seen by men in the majlis. If women are not secluded in their homes, they must have male relatives as escorts. Women are not allowed to drive cars and cannot even take taxis alone. However, buses were recently introduced with seating areas for women, who are separated by partitions from the men. Women are separated from men in all formal gatherings. Restaurants have family sections where women can dine with their families and single sections where men must dine alone. Women are segregated from men at mosques, and hospitals are divided into men's and women's wings. Public facilities such as amusement parks and swimming pools have different hours or days for family and single use.

Women are not allowed to work without the consent of their male guardians and cannot work in places where they can come into contact with men. King Fahd emphasized this restriction in 1983 by decreeing that American firms must not allow women to work in the same offices as men. Therefore, Saudia hires all its flight attendants from abroad, and Saudi women are normally restricted to working in the medical or teaching professions. However, some Saudi women have started businesses to serve other women and, since women control over a third of the kingdom's wealth, a number of women's banks have been formed.

Saudi men are not bound by the same restrictions. The Koran allows men to have concubines and up to four wives. But if they have multiple wives they must be treated fairly. Most Saudis only have one wife. They say if they have four wives, they have four problems. Saudi men can also divorce at will, but must abide by the divorce provisions in their marriage contracts.

The Saudis actively exercise their right to have concubines when they leave the kingdom by hiring prostitutes. In London, several prestige hotels provide their Saudi clients rooms with ladies. In September 1984, a high-priced call-girl ring that catered exclusively to Saudis was busted in New York City. Inside the kingdom, Saudi men vie for the attentions of foreign women. Nurses, teachers, and visiting flight attendants are lured with gold necklaces and bracelets or offered cash payments for their charms. Saudia flight attendants, assigned to fly on royal family flights, are expected to comply with every wish of the passengers.

Many Saudi men have arranged for live-in concubines through employment agencies in the Philippines that maintain books of photographs and vital statistics of young women seeking jobs. Many of the young Filipinas hired as children's nursemaids discovered that there were no children when they arrived at the residences of their new employers. In 1982, several hundred young Filipino women who objected to the demands of their jobs were cared for by the Philippine embassy because their employers would not return their passports and they could not leave the country.

There have also been many occasions of expatriate employees being advised by their Saudi employers that salary increases or continued employment were contingent on the cooperativeness of their wives. Several employees of the German Hochtief construction company capitalized on the desires of the Saudis by marrying prostitutes and bringing them into the kingdom to augment their incomes.

Many of the sexual restrictions also apply to expatriate women with varying degrees of enforcement. They usually have the same employment restrictions, other than working as flight attendants. If an expatriate's wife is caught working without a permit, she and her husband will be deported, and the employer fined. Western women are not allowed to go anywhere unescorted, and when in public, they are expected to wear loose clothing which completely covers their body. At formal Saudi gatherings, expatriate wives are either segregated from their husbands, or else not invited to attend.

Expatriate women are not allowed to be with any

men other than their husbands. If an unmarried Western woman is caught alone with a Western bachelor, they could both be deported. An American manager of a company in Jeddah, who hired the wife of one of his employees to be his secretary, almost lost his job for driving her home after working late.

If an American bachelor is caught alone with a Saudi woman, he could be deported, killed by her male relatives, or legally beheaded. The Saudi woman could be flogged one hundred lashes, killed by her male relatives, or legally stoned to death.

In July 1977, Saudi Princess Mishaal was publicly shot to death in Jeddah. Her lover, Khaled Muhallal was beheaded. Princess Mishaal had refused to fulfill her marriage contract to another man, had an affair with Khaled while in Beirut, and later tried to leave the kingdom with him. Her grandfather, Prince Muhammad, exercised his right as head of the family to order the death of one who dishonored his family, and killed the party who made a member of his family die.

Antony Thomas of Britain interviewed a number of Saudis to learn the facts leading to the executions and made a docu-drama film called *The Death of a Princess*. It consisted of the portrayal of a series of interviews and flashbacks of scenes with dialogue describing the conflict of Islamic and Western values. It supported the legality of the executions. But it also conveyed the message that the women of the royal family were promiscuous and indifferent to Islamic values. The royal family was outraged when they saw the film because they felt it dishonored their women, defamed the kingdom, and attacked Islam. They became so angry that they tried to bar non-Muslims from entering the country and forbade Saudi women from traveling abroad to study. The Saudis also asked the British ambassador to leave the country and tried to prevent the film from being shown in the United Kingdom. As a result, diplomatic relations between the two countries were strained for almost a year.

In the spring of 1980, the Public Broadcasting System (PBS) scheduled the film to be shown in the United States. PBS was warned by oil companies doing business in Saudi Arabia not to show the film and Mobil ran full-page newspaper advertisements asking Americans not to watch it. PBS stuck with their schedule and was later sued by the Saudis for showing the film.

Sharia causes Western women to feel very repressed. Most Western women are accustomed to the freedom of driving cars and going wherever they want to go at the time of their choice. In Saudi Arabia, women are not allowed to drive; their husbands, or his employer, must arrange or provide for their transportation. In the hot Arabian climate, expatriate women prefer to wear shorts or sun-dresses and resent being hassled if they do not wear ankle-length dresses and head scarves.

It also makes living in Saudia Arabia very uncomfortable for single, expatriate men and women. The penalties are so severe that most Western men would not even think about trying to date a Saudi woman. Western men who manage to find and date single Western women must sneak around and be very careful.

Saudi Arabia is the only country that completely adheres to the Hanbali school of Sharia. The Saudis boast that they have one of the lowest crime rates in the world. They also have the largest population of frustrated expatriates!

Chapter 10

A WAY WITH WORDS

*L*awful magic is the expression Saudis use to describe the ability of spoken Arabic to influence and sway audiences. Its hypnotic effect is so strong that it affects the psychology of its users. Arabic's liquid vowels, consonants, and tonal inflections give it a melodious quality that generates and conveys feelings unrelated to the content of the message.

The process of speaking Arabic eventually generates emotions in the speaker that he did not have when he started, and causes him to convey an intensity out of proportion to his meaning. The speaker's language-generated feelings are contagious as they subliminally penetrate beyond the listeners' consciousness directly to their emotions. The moods created reduce the listeners' ability to think clearly and cause them to react more strongly to the language than they would to music. This leads to spirals of rising emotionalism which cause confusion and contribute to controversy. Consequently, discord and quarrelling are a normal part of Arab discussions.

Arabic originated in central Arabia around A.D. 200 and was widely used by A.D. 400. Its roots are based on the original Semitic Akkadian language which evolved around 2350 B.C. when the desert nomads gained control of Sumeria. Akkadian later evolved into the Aramaic language of Babylon around 2000 B.C. and into the Nabataean language, the immediate predecessor of Arabic, about 800 B.C.

As the language evolved, it was adopted as the primary means of artistic expression by the continuously moving Bedouin who were unable to acquire non-functional material luxuries. The Bedouin also developed a broad vocabulary for everyday objects, including over 6,000 words to designate things related to camels. They created heroic legends which praised the virtues of personal honor, family loyalty, and tribal raiding. Gradually, their legends grew into poetic odes which were chanted to rhythmic meters.

Arabic words are structured on a three-consonant root that provides basic meaning. Set combinations of vowels give specific meanings to the root, so a given group of consonants can have a variety of meanings and overtones. The patterned vowels provide a broad variety of rhyming possibilities which were exploited in Arabic poetry. The opportunities for creativity were so great that the criterion of excellence turned into form rather than content. Eventually, Arabs grew to love fine-sounding but often meaningless words for their own sake.

Poetry became so important that annual contests were held at which tribal poets displayed their command of phraseology. The winners enjoyed great prestige and their poems were woven into tapestries and hung in the sacred Kaaba. Because of their rhetorical skills, the poets served as negotiators for the tribes and psyched-up warriors with propaganda before battles. Eventually, rhetorical and poetic eloquence became the most admired cultural attainment in the Arab world.

Around A.D. 620, the Koran was written in a rhymed, unmetered prose form. Since the Koran is supposed to be written by Allah, it is considered to be the most perfect expression of literary or classic Arabic. Thus, the subsequent development of the language was impeded.

The fourteen hundred-year-old Koran became the sole model for vocabulary, usage, style, and grammar in classical Arabic. Since it was considered the ideal language, changes could not be made without the consent of religious scholars. Consequently, the classical Arabic vocabulary lacks words to describe modern concepts or technology.

The language also lacks clear distinctions of time. It uses an imperfective verb form which conveys the continuous present, indefinite future, and timeless past experience. Therefore, it can obscure the time of events. If a Saudi says "tomorrow afternoon," he might mean any time from noon to late in the evening on any one of the next several days.

Normal Arabic usage results in exaggeration. The Arabic word for "exaggeration" is derived from the same word root as "eloquence," and means almost the same thing. Saudi speakers use verb suffixes to give special emphasis and conjugations to provide greater emphasis. Then they use redundant figures of speech and analogies to overemphasize. Therefore, Saudis normally have to over-assert to make sure they are understood. If a Saudi wants to convince someone that he intends to do something, he states his intentions several times. But if the Saudi merely agrees to do something, it might be nothing more than a polite form of evasion.

Written Arabic was also used for artistic expression. Because of the Islamic ban on pictorial representation, the alphabet was used to create intricate, geometric-patterned or arabesque designs. Over the centuries, the script evolved into a calligraphy with precise rules of shape and proportion. Two major types of script emerged, the rounded *naskhi* and the angular *kufic*, which is used for very formal occasions.

There are three different forms of the language. Classical Arabic requires the ability to read, so only a small percentage of the population could use it. Those who could not read used colloquial Arabic for normal conversation but could not be widely understood. To overcome these problems, modern standard Arabic was developed for mass media and written communication. Its grammar is similar to classical Arabic but its vocabulary and style are different. Consequently, modern standard Arabic is used with combinations of ancient words to synthesize modern terms, and colloquial Arabic expressions are used where possible.

Arabic is the official language of Saudi Arabia, but because of its limitations, English is used as the technical language. English is the only foreign language taught in schools and its knowledge is mandatory for a number of occupations, such as petroleum engineering, aviation, and data processing. When a technical subject is being discussed by Saudis, the conversation is conducted in a mixture of English and Arabic.

Although the Saudis are forced to learn to speak English, not many English-speaking people learn Arabic. It is too difficult! Arabic is dramatically different in structure from English, which belongs to the family of Indo-European languages. Spoken Arabic is difficult for Westerners to understand because of its many tonal inflections, accents, and voice changes. It is also hard for Westerners to pronounce because so many of the sounds are formed in the back of the mouth. The written language is equally rough for Westerners to learn as its twenty-eight characters may take four different shapes depending on their position in a word, and spacers of differing lengths may be used between characters. The Arabic script consists of series of loops and swirls of different sizes which look more like shorthand symbols than English cursive characters. It takes an intensive two-year course for Americans to become proficient in the language. Consequently, it is not cost-effective to train Americans who go to Saudi Arabia on one- to two-year assignments.

Verbal communication between Westerners and Saudis can be a trying experience. English must be spoken slowly and clearly, with a limited vocabulary to enable the Saudis to absorb the message, think in Arabic, and respond in English. While communicating, Westerners are never sure if the Saudis fully understand what they are saying. While Saudis are speaking to them, Westerners have to strain to relate the words to what has been discussed and try to interpret their intent as well as their meaning, because the Saudis may be conveying "no" while describing "yes."

Written communication between Saudis and Westerners is an excruciating ordeal! Saudi law requires that Arabic be used in correspondence with the government. The majority of Western executives, diplomats, and military advisors can only speak a few dozen words of Arabic and cannot read or write it at all. They are totally dependent on others to translate and interpret for them. But not many people are good translators; it requires a person with mastery of English, modern standard Arabic, and the linguistic skills to convert words and phrases of one language into identical meanings in the other. Without this combination of skills, translation suffers.

There are no letter-for-letter or word-for-word translations from Arabic to English. As a result, there is a confusing variation of English spelling of Arabic words. For example, the holy book is spelled *Koran* and *Qu'ran*, and the seaport city is spelled *Jeddah, Jedda, Jidda,* and *Juddah*. Personal names are a special problem. The Prophet's name is spelled *Muhammad, Mohammed,* and in other forms. Two brothers may spell their last names differently in English, and English correspondence will vary the spelling of names so that identification is often uncertain. Even the holy city, which was spelled *Mecca* for centuries, is now spelled *Makkah* because a British disco used its name and refused the Saudi government's request to change it.

Most Western organizations do not have trained translation staff and professional translators are not readily available. So, someone in the organization must be reassigned from his normal job or work overtime to perform translations. Since very few of the population are qualified in modern standard and classical Arabic, and even American-educated Saudis have difficulty with English, not many persons are qualified to do even approximate translations. Although Western managers can readily ascertain the English skills of Saudis, they cannot evaluate the Saudis' proficiency in Arabic. Because of their pride, marginally qualified Saudis are not likely to admit to this shortcoming. Consequently, Western advisors and executives must frequently rely on people who are not proficient in either language to do translation work.

It can take up to a week to obtain a short translation full of omissions and inaccuracies. Several years ago, a Saudi newspaper sent a reporter to cover the introduction of a new program. The reporter spoke no English, so the article was drafted in English by an American and then turned over for translation into Arabic by a Saudi who was a graduate of an American university. His English language skills were excellent, but he labored for hours to translate the three hundred-word draft. When he was finished, another Saudi who was equally fluent in English but had no part in the translation effort read the article back in English. The retranslation was so full of unintentional distortions and misinterpretations that the project had to be started over again with the help of a professional translator.

The need for both English-to-Arabic and Arabic-to-English translation is never-ending. In a typical business cycle, Western companies receive requests for proposals written in Arabic from government ministries which must be translated into English so that the companies can learn what is required.

Western managers use Egyptians, Jordanians, and American-educated Saudi college graduates to translate government documents. Then they study the translations and question the translators to clarify inconsistencies. Even then, they cannot take anything for granted or be sure that the English translation is exactly what the authors of the documents intended.

Translated versions of Arabic government documents often provide minute details of some aspect of the communication but not its purpose or global meaning. In other cases, requirements are grossly exaggerated. Western executives are forced to review the probable intent of the translated documents and use their personal experience to try to reconstruct what was actually said. Many proposals have missed the mark because the Arabic-to-English translators thought they were using correct English and the Westerners thought the translations were accurate. If additional information is required, the companies have to request meetings with the authors of the documents and bring English-speaking Saudis with them to serve as interpreters.

After the Western companies prepare the proposals, they have to be translated into Arabic. The English-to-Arabic translations usually contain errors in descriptions of work scopes, prices, and schedules. When the translations are completed, they are bound into bidirectional English/Arabic documents which in English read from front to back, and in Arabic read from back to front. The Western managers pray that the translations are correct because they cannot review the final documents for completeness or accuracy.

When the Western companies are awarded contracts, the Saudi executives of the joint venture companies and the government representatives typically hold bargaining sessions in Arabic, after which the contracts are issued in Arabic. When the Western executives arrange to have the contracts translated back into English, they are often shocked to find contract items that are much different from their carefully prepared proposals.

Frequently, the Arabic version of the awarded contract, the binding document under Saudi law, contains items not in the proposals, prices lower than actual costs, and schedules that are impossible to carry out.

One Western consulting firm that went through the laborious process to bid on the operation of complex electronic systems for a government agency learned that they were awarded a contract for performing janitorial services and pumping septic tanks! After the company reluctantly accepted the contract, they had trouble getting paid for services rendered because the government agency did not like the Arabic wording of the monthly status reports.

An advertisement placed by the Saudis in the *Washington Post* in September 1984 illustrates the problems of Arabic-to-English translations. It read: "Saudi Arabia. Educational Project Management Specialists. The Ministry of Education in the kingdom of Saudi Arabia has open positions for Educational Project Management Specialists. Candidates have to be specialists in the management of educational projects, site, engineering, administration and cost control of big value projects. EDP used either wholly or extensively. Qualifications include Bachelor plus 15 years or Master plus 12 years in project management of which computer at a responsible level is utilized.

Arabic is a plus. The Ministry offers good salaries and infringe benefits commensurate with academic qualifications and experience. Saudi Arabia is a tax free country."

After reading the advertisement, most Americans could not tell whether the Saudis were looking for educators, computer project managers, or construction superintendents!

Chapter 11

NEED TO KNOW

Saudi Arabia is making an unparalleled effort to shift the mentality of its entire population from the seventh to the twentieth century, and to educate its people to run the country without dependence on foreigners.

Twenty years ago, Saudi Arabia had one of the lowest literacy rates in the world. Saudi education took place in the home, augmented by religious scholars. Girls were taught how to cook. Boys were taught to memorize verses of the Koran, and to count. Occupational skills were learned through imitation.

In 1970, 85 percent of its people were totally illiterate. Almost every Saudi hired by a Western company had to be taught to read and write before he could be trained to do anything else.

King Faisal recognized the problem and made education one of the highest priorities in the first five-year development plan. During the early 1970s, Saudi Arabia embarked on a gigantic, country-wide effort to educate and train its entire population. Numerous organizations were established to speed up the process. Faisal created four special agencies to set educational policies and guide the programs, and formed the Ministries of Education and Higher Education to administer the programs. Departments were also formed in the Ministries of Health, Agriculture and Water, Finance and National Economy, and Labor and Social Affairs, as well as the army and National Guard, to provide adult literacy and vocational training programs.

The Saudi government adopted the American system of education using the kindergarten, elementary, intermediate, and secondary divisions to provide basic education. It spent 15 percent of the first five-year development plan's budget to get started.

The king also established several organizations coordinated by the General Presidency of Youth Welfare to help young people fulfill themselves and satisfy the country's needs while shielding them from the attractions of the Western world. The organizations provided cultural activities and learning programs and promoted participation in sports. They built 140 sports complexes and hired Western coaches to develop their skills. Soccer became the favorite sport and soon teams from all over the kingdom vied for the national championship. By 1984, a Saudi team qualified for the Olympic games and later won the Asian Cup in Singapore.

Saudi Arabia has spent billions of dollars each year to improve the quantity and quality of education. In 1958, it had twenty elementary schools. In the 1970s, the government began opening an average of one new school each week and by 1987, the kingdom had 10,791 totally segregated schools.

The first private school for girls was quietly opened by King Faisal's wife, Queen Iffat, in 1956. The first public school for girls started classes in Buraydah in 1963. The Saudis rioted when it opened and a mob of 500 parents went to Riyadh to complain to King Faisal. Police had to guard the children and National Guard troops had to dispel the angry mobs. By 1980, over 400,000 girls were enrolled in over 800 girls' schools. By 1987, 2,000,000 children, almost a quarter of the population, were enrolled in school and Saudi claimed its literacy rate had risen to 52 percent.

In 1958, Saudi Arabia opened its first college. By 1987, it claimed to have sixty-six colleges and seven full universities. In 1975, 12,000 Saudis were undergraduate students. In 1985, there were 4,000 postgraduate students. By 1987, there were 107,000 students in Saudi colleges and 20,000 in foreign universities. Over 43,000 of the college students were women.

Saudi's first college was opened as the University

of Riyadh. This greatly expanded school, now called King Saud University, has separate men's and women's campuses in Riyadh, Abha, and Qaseem. It has an enrollment of 19,000 students in its colleges of liberal arts, science, pharmacy, commerce, engineering, agriculture, medicine, dentistry, nursing, and education.

The second college opened in 1963 in Dhahran and was called the University of Petroleum and Minerals (UPM). Instruction is in English and it has an all-male student population of 2,500. UPM is world-renowned for its architectural design and the quality of instruction in engineering, science, and industrial management.

King Abdul Aziz University started classes in 1967 and now has separate men's and women's campuses in Jeddah and Mecca. It has colleges of education, Islamic law, economics, administration, liberal arts, and science. In 1975, King Faisal University opened in Dammam and Hofuf with colleges of medicine, architecture, and agriculture.

The kingdom has two major religious educational centers, Imam Saud Islamic University in Riyadh, and the Islamic University in Medina. It has separate women's colleges of education in Jeddah, Riyadh, and Abha; military training colleges in Dhahran and Taif; and the King Faisal Air Force Academy in Riyadh. Riyadh is also the site of the College of Islamic Law, the College of Arabic Language, and the National Police Academy. Mecca is the site of the Institute of Education and the College of Legislation.

Saudi Arabia has schools for female nurses in Riyadh, Jeddah, Hofuf, and Jizan. It also has three health, four industrial, two commercial, and one agricultural higher institute for men. In addition, the Institute of Public Administration has ten vocational training centers for pre-service and in-service training.

The quality of higher education is still well below similar institutions in the West. Bachelor's degree programs are three years in duration except for pre-med which is four years, and engineering which takes five years. However, King Saud University and UPM now have master's degree programs.

Women's education is improving despite the official policy which states that "the object of educating a woman is to bring her up in a sound Islamic way so that she can fulfill her role in life as a successful housewife, ideal wife, and good mother, and to prepare her for activities that suit her nature, such as teaching, nursing, and medicine."

During the 1970s, most Saudi students dropped out of school to go to work, but were almost useless because they could not understand how to operate or maintain even the simplest equipment. The government paid for private companies to train young Saudis, reimbursed the wages paid to the trainees, and gave the employees a 50-percent bonus to take the training. But the young Saudis turned it down because there were too many other opportunities for them to make money. So the government began pushing young Saudis to complete their secondary education before entering the job market. By 1985, Saudi Arabia had opened twenty-six commercial, eight technical, and twenty-four vocational secondary schools. It had also started two technical and three commercial higher institutes and twenty-one advanced industrial institutes.

Saudi high school graduates began entering the labor force around 1980. They were much better-trained than their predecessors but still very deficient by Western standards. Part of the problem was due to the Wahhabi ban on the use of pictorial diagrams for instruction, a ban which King Faisal finally overcame. Another reason was that the education concentrated on the development of verbal skills with little emphasis on written skills. In girls' schools, for example, the students watched male teachers lecture on closed circuit television and used telephones to ask questions. There was no interdisciplinary learning and there was no encouragement for students to use their imagination or exercise creativity. When these deficiencies were pointed out in 1980, the government started developing new curricula, new teacher training methods, and new instructional methods.

Until just recently, the majority of school facilities were inadequate. Over 75 percent of the elementary schools and 50 percent of the intermediate and secondary schools in Riyadh were rented. In rural areas, the problem was much worse, and the Bedouin received almost no education. But the situation is rapidly improving.

The Saudis have a critical teacher shortage.

Teaching is an undesirable occupation to Saudi men because the pay is lower and the work is harder than most other government jobs. There is also the unpleasant possibility of being posted to teach in primitive rural areas. Since it is one of the few career opportunities open to them, women comprise more than half of the students enrolled in elementary education training.

Because of the rapid growth in education, the kingdom is heavily dependent on foreign teachers. In 1980, one-third of the elementary and two-thirds of the intermediate teachers were Egyptians, Jordanians, and Palestinians on short-term contracts. At the secondary level, four-fifths of the teachers were British and Americans. The untrained Saudi teachers taught mostly Islamic cultural subjects and social studies. By 1983, Saudi women had filled 25,000 teacher positions and the need for foreigners was cut in half.

Saudi Arabia has an attractive program to encourage young Saudis to get a college education abroad. It pays their entire tuition fees, costs of books, housing and clothing allowances, and stipends of $800 per month while they attend foreign universities. In return, the students are obligated to work for the government after they graduate, for a period equal to that spent in the university. In 1982, over fifteen thousand Saudi students were attending American universities.

A major drawback of this program is that it causes the government to be overstaffed and it does not provide candidates for private industry. By the time the Western-trained university graduates complete their government service, they have picked up inefficient bureaucratic work habits or become entrenched in their high-paying, undemanding jobs.

The government is trying to train young Saudis for the private sector through its "Saudi-ization" program. Most contracts specify that foreign companies must train Saudis to take over operation and maintenance of their projects when completed. The government also provides funds for foreign companies to give technical training to Saudis. But the Saudi-ization program has three major problems: there is a shortage of young Saudis who are interested in pursuing these demanding and average-paying careers, it is difficult to motivate them to learn, and it is difficult to actually teach them.

In one company, thirty-six Saudis were assigned to learn how to write computer programs and operate a computer. The Saudi in charge reported to the American manager of the project and coordinated the trainees. During a six-month period, the American project manager, who was responsible for their training, never saw more than five or six of his Saudi trainees at any one time. Half of the time, the Saudis were found sleeping in closets.

The American operators of Saudi military hospitals had difficulty getting their Saudi management trainees to do anything during day shifts and could never locate them during night shifts.

Young enlisted men being trained to operate electronic equipment aboard Saudi ships by an American firm quickly learned that they could avoid the rigors of sea trials by pulling wires loose in the electrical panels of vital equipment to prevent the ships from going to sea.

An Arab-owned, Western-staffed, computer services company set up a program in 1981 to teach computer technology to young Saudi high school graduates. It was a very simple course to prepare the Saudis for on-the-job training. The first class included business and technical English, and basic work ethics. One-third of the class dropped out during the two-month course. After the final examination was completed, it was learned that all of the remaining students had cheated and it was impossible to assess how much they had learned. Then, about a dozen of the more promising graduates were assigned to development projects for on-the-job training. Some of the trainees were absent more often than they went to work; the others were tardy every day; and none of them were dependable. Their absorption proved to be so low that the Western project managers were only able to train them to do the simplest of tasks.

The same company had responsibility for training three groups of government employees, one of which was composed of college graduates. In each case, the level and amount of training provided was minimal compared to the actual job requirements, but was geared to what it was believed the students could learn. It was found to be impractical to try to teach technical principles or the reasons behind procedures because the students' basic conceptual comprehension level was too low. Instead, the training concentrated on teaching them how to operate equipment under specified conditions.

In all four cases, attendance, punctuality, and motivation were problems. The students were all courteous, well-meaning, likeable young men who were handicapped in learning by their previous education and cultural values.

The only organizations with notable success in training Saudis to replace Westerners are Aramco, which has spent fifty years and hundreds of millions of dollars in the effort, and Saudia, which has been working at it for thirty-five years; and they are both still heavily involved in training Saudis. It is a slow process.

Educational opportunities for expatriate children are of a different caliber. The schooling is extremely scarce and is available only through the equivalent of the ninth grade. Expatriate high school students must attend school outside the kingdom. The Saudis do not provide schools for expatriate children and will not allow many to be opened. Those permitted are sponsored by large foreign companies or interested parent groups.

English language schools are either based on the American or the British systems. Students from one system who attend the other system's school while in Saudi Arabia usually encounter problems when they return home. The quality of education is high, but the schools are very expensive. The annual tuition per child at the Saudi Arabian International Schools in Dhahran and Riyadh is $4,500. The tuition at the American Parents Cooperative School in Jeddah is $8,500; yet, it has very few vacancies for new students and cannot accommodate all the requests for admission.

Most companies that allow their employees to bring their families provide tuition assistance or an educational allowance for dependent school age children. But company allowances are nowhere near the cost of the American school in Jeddah. In a few special cases, companies have increased the educational allowances of critically needed employees, but that is the exception rather than the rule.

Children's education is a source of many problems for American expatriates. Most American families want to have their school-age children with them in Saudi Arabia, unlike many British families who send their children to private boarding schools in the United Kingdom. The cost and lack of available schooling have caused many expatriates to quit their jobs and caused other families to separate so the mothers could bring the children home to be educated.

These problems are of little concern to the Saudis. They are concerned with getting their own children educated. As Dr. Ghazi Algosaibi, the former minister of industry and electricity, said, "We must not depend on foreigners to run the machinery of our country. They neither understand nor care about our culture. We are blessed with revenue, but unless we develop skills, money will not solve our problems."

Chapter 12

CAMELS AND CADILLACS

*F*ive years after men orbited the earth in space-craft, the vice president of the Islamic University in Medina published an essay denying the existence of the solar system. He stated that the sun revolves around the earth and that anyone who believes otherwise "is guilty of falsehood toward God, the Koran and the Prophet." Saudi Arabia has come a long way since then and is acquiring new technology so rapidly that many conditions change dramatically from year to year. As could be expected, the technology is not uniformly applied and a weird combination of the ancient and the ultramodern coexists in the magic kingdom. Sail-driven, wooden dhows are handmade from teak logs on the shores of waters patrolled by jet-powered hovercraft; nomads ride donkeys alongside roads traveled by huge diesel trucks; and Bedouin pitch their tents under the flight paths of jumbo jet aircraft.

Acquiring technology is one thing; using it and maintaining it is another. Saudis do not have either the technical knowledge to make repairs or the interest in doing anything so demeaning. Technicians have to be imported at great expense to make repairs, an expense Saudis have difficulty justifying. Most automobile dealers in Saudi Arabia regard repair shops as an unnecessary overhead.

Until five years ago, Saudi Arabia was a throwaway society. If something broke, it was abandoned, including cars, trucks, airplanes, computers, and buildings. These derelicts were everywhere. Fully-loaded trucks were left where they stopped running, and construction cranes still towered over buildings after they were completed. Cars which were involved in accidents or had stopped running were just pushed to the side of the road and abandoned. Near the ports, giant stacks of wheat and flour were left to rot. Piles of vegetables rotted on the piers and scores of dead cattle lined the roadside near the docks. Because of the construction debris that littered the area, Riyadh was referred to as the Garbage Capital of the East. In 1982, ten thousand wrecked cars were picked up during the first two weeks of a $5 million clean-up campaign in Jeddah. Pakistani sanitation crews now try to keep it clean.

Not all of the debris was litter; some people lived in it. The cities were surrounded by shanty towns constructed from tin cans, packing crates, and cardboard, inhabited by lower-class Saudis and foreign workers. The nomads who migrated to the cities built these shanties in the manner of their desert tents because there was no other housing that they could afford. Although the government built 500,000 low-income housing units, shortages still persisted in many areas.

The government now provides all adult Saudis with a plot of land and a loan of $80,000 with which to build a home. In 1988, 347,260 people took advantage of the loans.

Although housing is a problem for lower-class and poorer Saudis, the situation is quite the opposite for the upper class. When money started flowing into the kingdom, the upper class imported craftsmen and materials to build houses that reflected their status. The homes of sheikhs, wealthy businessmen, and the royal family resemble resort hotels in size and appearance. Many are very beautiful and novel. There is even one house in Riyadh that rotates to follow the sun.

Housing for expatriates is another matter. The Saudi government segregates expatriates from its citizens and forbids foreigners to build or buy houses. Employers must provide housing for their expatriate employees. Companies rent housing, but if they have more than one hundred employees, they must build housing compounds in previously undeveloped locations. Compounds can be blocks of apartments in a building, walled-in areas holding several mobile homes, or walled-in areas containing groups of single-family villas and possibly a swimming pool and a clubhouse. On the large side, the compound for Saudia in Jeddah is almost a mile square and houses over 17,000 people. The Aramco compound in Dhahran is a city almost twice that size and contains houses, trailers, commissaries, a grassless golf course, and a private beach.

To rent housing, companies must pay a year's lease in advance. In the mid-1980s rental costs ranged from $12,000 for poor-quality, two-bedroom apartments to $43,000 for livable, three-bedroom villas. A good four-bedroom villa in a better residential neighborhood cost $75,000 per year!

Available housing is generally small and very poorly designed, constructed, and maintained because it was built to make quick profits. Many Saudi entrepreneurs obtained one-time construction loans from the government's Real Estate Development Fund (REDF) which were discounted 30 percent if paid back early. By 1982, the REDF had loaned $17 billion to build 266,000 houses and 20,000 apartment buildings. The demand for building lots caused land prices to skyrocket, increasing in value several times per year. By 1982, land cost was about $175 to $300 per square yard, enough to add about $60,000 to the cost of building a modest residential house. The building boom created a surplus of rental properties in the cities but did not lower the rents.

During the building boom, Saudis approached the challenge of rental housing construction in a variety of ways. Some hired construction companies from third world countries which had no experience in building houses. Others hired European and Oriental companies with home building experience. Some even hired architects. The construction companies then did their own thing, free from the restrictions of building codes or the interference of inspectors. Contractors used surplus building materials from many countries, but their most popular building material was concrete, even for inside walls. The entrepreneurs built until their money ran out. The end result is amazing by American standards.

There is no consistent architectural style, and most rental houses are either drab or gaudy. On the same unpaved street, four-story buildings faced with bright blue Italian ceramic tile may stand several feet away from sagging, three-story buildings built of unevenly laid, painted concrete blocks. The interiors of many apartments have electrical wiring tacked to the walls, connected directly to an external line without fuses or circuit breakers. Water heaters are hung on kitchen walls near the ceilings. Plumbing generally runs down the exterior walls. Carpeting, if any, is laid without regard to seams or patterns, and windows are frequently nailed shut.

In August 1981, a fifteen-story, poured-concrete building under construction in Jeddah collapsed and killed about twenty construction workers. Saudi engineers subsequently examined government buildings and found massive cracks in their foundations. Many private houses were also found to have huge cracks running from roof to ground.

Westerners living in older company compounds complain that the housing units are plagued with exploding hot water heaters, malfunctioning toilets, leaking pipes, electrical shorts, broken air conditioners, and inoperable appliances. They have great difficulty in getting repairs made because they cannot find anyone who is either willing or capable of doing them, and they cannot find the parts to do the repairs themselves.

There are also some beautiful, Western-designed town houses of concrete block construction with painted stucco exteriors and wood trim, that face grass courtyards with swimming pools, squash courts, shrubs, and trees. The interiors of these houses are the same as those in suburban America, but they are very scarce and extremely expensive.

By 1980, master plans had been created for the growth of major cities. Regulations for residential construction were issued to control the materials used, ensure compliance with Islamic building styles, and make the houses pleasing in appearance. Many of the houses constructed since then have been interesting and attractive. The dynamic former mayor of Jeddah, Sheikh Muhammad Said Farsi, even persuaded developers to donate statuary for placement adjacent to their construction sites, and wound up with many interesting and unusual statues.

The expatriate housing shortage was so severe for a while that companies had to delay the arrival of new employees because there was no place to put them. In 1982, a Jeddah-based company prepared to start a project in Yanbu and learned that there was no family housing available or under construction. It was forced to hire only single men, or married men in unaccompanied status, and arrange for them to live in dormitories. As is to be expected, housing is a sore point with many expatriates.

Temporary housing is also a problem. In 1988, there were 246 hotels in the kingdom with a total of 22,298 rooms. Holiday Inn, Sheraton, Marriott, Intercontinental, and Hyatt all have fine hotels in Riyadh, Jeddah, Yanbu, and Taif. But there are very few accommodations in the smaller towns and villages. Even in the cities there are still severe shortages of hotel rooms, particularly in Riyadh. At times, travelers without reservations are not able to find rooms anywhere in the capital and even those with confirmed reservations are turned away or forced to sleep in chairs in the lobby.

Reasonably priced, adequate office space is also in short supply. Companies frequently obtain consulting contracts from Saudi organizations and then find that there is no space for project personnel to work in, so they are forced to use old villas as offices. Much of the available office space is poorly constructed, is inadequately wired for electricity and telephones, and is not plumbed for rest rooms. One company with offices in Jeddah had a staff of forty men sharing one residential-type bathroom in which the water was turned off for three hours every afternoon.

Public services are less than Westerners are accustomed to. Mail is delivered to employer's post office boxes because there is no home delivery. It normally takes two to three weeks for mail to travel between the United States and Saudi Arabia. During Ramadan, it can take five to six weeks. Since the lengthy turnaround is impractical for business correspondence, most companies use telex to send short messages, and couriers to send documents. Expatriates usually pool their personal correspondence and have friends leaving Saudi Arabia mail it from the first place the plane lands to speed its delivery.

During the past decade, the telephone network has been upgraded to a sophisticated system using coaxial cables, microwave relays, and satellites. But it is too complex for the Saudis to maintain. It can take months to get a new telephone installed in a residence, but then it might not work because of improper installation. It takes weeks to get it fixed.

Telephone circuits to the United States and Europe are usually overloaded during the Western business day and it can take hours to get calls through. It takes days or weeks to get calls through to Egypt or Jordan. Because of the delay, it is common practice to send a telex to the party to be contacted asking them to try to call into Saudi because it is impossible to call out.

Saudi Arabia has thirty combination power generation/desalination plants which produce over 3,000 megawatts of electricity and 500 million gallons of water per day. The plants burn natural gas to boil sea water, creating the steam which spins the turbines to generate electricity. The steam condenses as distilled water. The kingdom has extensive electrical service in the cities and is rapidly expanding rural electrification. Newer areas have 110-volt, 60-cycle service, while older areas have 220-volt service. Many expatriates burn out electrical appliances while learning which is which. Severe voltage fluctuations can burn out sensitive appliances. The service is also subject to frequent failures, during which it gets very uncomfortable without air conditioning.

Despite the desalination plants, the water is not potable. The water mains which connect wells and desalination plants to buildings are contaminated. Tap water is laden with bacteria and microorganisms which cause dysentery. Expatriates must use bottled water for drinking, cooking, brushing their teeth, and washing dishes. A one-liter bottle of water costs about a dollar, almost four times the cost of a gallon of gas!

There is a variety of radio and television broadcasts, but they are mostly in Arabic except in the Dhahran area, where Aramco broadcasts in English. Two radio stations broadcast the Koran in Arabic twenty-four hours a day. Because they are the only stations with continuous broadcasts, they are used by Westerners for setting clock radios. The two radio and television stations of the Ministry of Information broadcast in English 5 percent of the time and are dominated by religion. English language news broadcasts are provided by the Saudi Press Agency, but most expatriates use shortwave receivers to listen to the Voice of America and the BBC to learn what is really happening in the world.

Arab music is repetitious and incomprehensible to Westerners. Most expatriates buy cassette players and cassettes for their musical listening enjoyment. Pirated cassettes are sold in the suqs for about $1.50 each. Many expatriates also buy video cassette recorders and swap tapes with each other.

Health is a major concern of all Western expatriates. The government has allocated a large portion of its development budget for improving health conditions and the Ministry of Health has made fantastic progress, considering that it started from absolutely primitive conditions.

While Dr. Jonas Salk was perfecting the polio vaccine in America in the 1960s, most Saudis believed that diseases were caused by evil spirits that could be warded off by wearing blue beads or replicas of the human eye around their necks. Some Saudis still believe this, but most appear to have accepted the germ theory of disease causation. Now all they have to do is stop the spread of germs. Water supplies and sewage networks in urban areas are major health hazards. There is also widespread ignorance of basic hygienic practices and home health care.

In Saudi society, people eat with their hands instead of silverware. They are supposed to wash their hands before dining; then everyone reaches into a common bowl with their right hand and eats from their fingers. Several diseases are spread by this custom. Saudis also ritualistically wash their hands in mosque pools before praying; the pools can become infected and spread disease.

Herds of goats wander loose and eat garbage in the cities. Wild dogs fight over scraps of meat. They occasionally kill each other and their remains lie in the sun to fester. Wild cats are everywhere, many of them infected. A British woman adopted a stray kitten and got the worst case of ringworm ever seen by her doctors.

There are few drains for rainwater. When it rains, water lies on top of the ground for weeks, breeding mosquitos. Hotels, offices, and new buildings have toilets which generally drain into septic tanks. Waste matter from the septic tanks is pumped into large trucks which unload the effluent into public gardens. There are many places in the older sections of towns where public toilet facilities consist of an open hole in the ground. Many people do not even bother with those, but relieve themselves by the roadside.

Tuberculosis, malaria, dysentery, cholera, bilharzia, syphilis, and trachoma are widespread. To counter the spread of disease, the government provides smallpox and tuberculosis immunization and promotes anti-cholera clean-up campaigns twice a year. The Red Crescent organization, the Islamic version of the Red Cross, assists in disease control during the hajj. Although there was a widespread cholera epidemic in Jordan and a typhoid epidemic in Bahrain in the mid-1980s, no major epidemics have occurred in Saudi for several years.

If an epidemic starts, the Saudis will receive free medical treatment and hospitalization. By 1987, the kingdom had 149 hospitals with over 26,000 beds, 1,480 clinical dispensaries, and over 4,000 doctors. Their prize facility is the King Faisal Specialty Hospital in Riyadh which was completed in 1975 at a cost of $200 million. It has computerized nursing stations, kidney dialysis machines, a radioisotope laboratory, and all other modern technologies.

Some of the newer major hospitals are operated by American, British, Canadian, and European companies. Most of the other hospitals are staffed with questionably trained Egyptian and Pakistani doctors and Asian nurses, many of whom do not speak English. The results are unpredictable. An American technician went to a clinic to get a smallpox vaccination, but the Chinese nurse misunderstood and gave him a cholera injection instead. He had to cancel his trip, but was glad he had not gone to the clinic for minor surgery!

The spectacular improvement in health care during the last decade has raised the life expectancy of urban Saudis to fifty-four years. But the Bedouin, far from towns, still use spells and charms, set their own broken bones, put camel dung on infections, and sear wounds with heated knives.

Transportation has improved dramatically since the first pier was built in Jeddah in 1949. The kingdom now has 170 ship berths in Red Sea and Persian Gulf ports and offshore terminals at Jubail and Yanbu to load the very largest crude oil tankers.

Saudi ports are among the busiest in the world. Large tankers arrive empty and depart filled with light Saudi crude oil. Container and break-bulk dry cargo ships arrive heavily laden and depart empty. Petromin-owned tankers load crude oil at Ras Tunurah and carry it to a refinery at Jeddah. Even with all its new berths, pier space at some locations is inadequate to accommodate the traffic. Some ships must wait days before they can unload their cargo and have it inspected by customs. Dozens of ships lie at anchor off Yanbu, waiting for pier space, while shipping companies impose a 90-percent surcharge on their cargos because of the delay. In the past, the delays added almost 40 percent to the cost of imports and created serious material shortages in the kingdom. There were numerous cases where new automobiles were delivered months after the next year's models were introduced. But Saudi Arabia now claims to be able to unload and clear cars through customs in forty-eight hours.

A crude airstrip was marked in the sand near Jeddah in 1938 to accommodate planes carrying pilgrims from Egypt. In June 1981, the 40-square mile King Abdul Aziz International Airport was inaugurated in Jeddah at a cost of over $10 billion. In November 1983, the world's largest airport, at 110 square miles, opened in Riyadh. A third new airport is being built in the eastern al-Hasa province.

The national carrier, Saudia, is the tenth largest airline in the world. It provides service to forty-seven cities on four continents from international airports in Jeddah, Riyadh, and Dhahran. Its fleet of more than one hundred jet aircraft carry over 10,000,000 passengers per year. For international service, it has twenty-three Boeing 747s, seventeen Lockheed L-1011s, and eleven French Airbus A-300s. It also has twenty Boeing 737s, six Boeing 707s and other aircraft to serve twenty-three locations in the kingdom. The airline monopolizes the best routes and schedules into Saudi Arabia and is the mandatory carrier for all travelers doing business with the government. Saudia does not serve alcoholic beverages. However, other airlines that serve the kingdom, like PanAm, British Airways, SAS, Air France, Swiss Air, Lufthansa, Olympic, Iberia, Italia, and AirMoroc, offer alcoholic beverages on international flights.

Despite the new airplanes and beautiful computerized airports, air travel is a trying ordeal. Most international flights depart between midnight and four in the morning. Travelers must check in two hours prior to an international flight and one hour prior to a domestic flight, or lose their reservations. International flights are frequently three to four hours late, and even after a traveler boards the aircraft he may be bumped off to accommodate a member of the royal family. In the terminals, it is very easy for Westerners to get lost as ticket counters and gate areas are poorly marked and most announcements are made only in Arabic.

Confusion characterizes flight arrivals. Buses bring passengers to the wrong gates and luggage is sent to the wrong carousels. After arriving on international flights, passengers must endure long queues for immigration and customs clearance. At the customs stations, airport personnel who are indifferent and almost hostile to travelers open and thoroughly search all baggage for alcoholic beverages, drugs, pornographic materials, and other contraband.

Ground travel also has its problems. There are not many maps of Saudi cities, and those available are generally out of date. Up to 1985, maps were not very helpful because the Arabic spelling of the few streets with names were indecipherable, and buildings did not have numbers. Westerners navigated by landmarks such as water towers, bridges, statues, and signs. This was somewhat effective during daylight hours, but it was extremely difficult at night. However, there could also be problems by day, as discovered by a company in Jeddah which leased an apartment building but had to cancel the lease because no one could find it.

There are only about 560 miles of railroad, so two million trucks are used to haul freight inside the kingdom. Five-ton Mercedes trucks, assembled in Jeddah, dominate the highways. The Bedouin drivers paint their entire trucks with bright-colored patterns and adorn them with chrome and reflectors. The kingdom has bus service, but cars, over two million of them, are the primary mode of passenger transportation. The cities suffer from severe traffic congestion and a critical shortage of parking spaces for the cars that do make it to their destinations.

But many cars do not reach their destinations. Car accidents are said to be the second major health problem in Saudi Arabia, but most Westerners will swear that they are the primary problem. There is nothing deadlier than a Bedouin driving a twenty-ton water truck. About 20,000 people a year are killed in car crashes; one for every 250 Saudis. In the typical month of September 1981, 42 pedestrians were killed in the city of Jeddah alone. Up until three years ago, it was not uncommon to see five or six accidents during a five-mile drive. Sometimes, bored expatriates went to busy intersections or parking lots just to watch the crashes. Many of the accidents were spectacular and resembled Hollywood productions. Along the highway from Jeddah to Yanbu, totally demolished new cars used to lie along the side of the road at 500-yard intervals. In 1977, there were 80,000 wrecked cars in or around the city of Jeddah. It has been claimed that the highway connecting Jeddah and Riyadh is the bloodiest road in the world.

Driving is on the right hand side of the road, but there are many violations of this law. Saudis drive on the wrong side of the road, over median strips and curbs, and on sidewalks. They drive the wrong way on one-way streets. They pass on either side and on hills, curves, and into oncoming traffic. They routinely run through stop signs and red traffic lights without even slowing down. Drivers propel their cars as fast as they will go and then lose control of them. They disregard painted lines, warning signs, and the laws of physics. They appear oblivious to the fact that they are going to have accidents. When Saudis were asked why they run past stop signs at blind intersections, they replied that "Caution does not alter the decree of fate." They say nothing will happen to them unless it has been written by Allah, but if it has been written, there is nothing they can do to change it.

Many third-world nationals driving in Saudi Arabia never saw a car before arriving in the country, which may partially explain the absolutely bizarre driving. Westerners cannot help but imagine what it would be like if alcoholic beverages were not banned from the kingdom!

Everyone has his own version about the worst accident he has seen in Saudi Arabia: twenty-ton water trucks plowing through cars stopped at red lights; huge cement mixer trucks completely flattening yellow Toyota taxicabs; Mercedes cargo trucks sailing through space after taking out guard rails on mountain roads; head-on collisions on desert roads; or cars aimed at pedestrians on city streets. But all Westerners agree that they live in constant fear of being involved in traffic accidents. Some are afraid to drive, and stay away from busy streets. Those who drive are forced to acquire combat driving skills, constantly anticipating threats in every direction in preparation for taking evasive action. It is even dangerous driving on desert roads with no other cars around because two thousand-pound camels walk right out in front of onrushing cars and block the road!

What Americans call Saturday night is Sunday night to a Saudi. Each day begins at sunset and day follows night. Until fifteen years ago, all clocks and watches were set at twelve o'clock each day at sunset. The embassies used sun time and the military used Greenwich Mean Time plus three. The resetting practice was finally discontinued because it was impossible to coordinate long-distance communication or transportation with any other part of the kingdom. Saudia had a particularly difficult time trying to prepare or stay on schedules.

The official calendar is the Islamic Hegira calendar. The Western method of designating Hegira calendar dates is by the abbreviation A.H., for *Anno Hegirae*, which means the "year of the Hegira." The Hegira calendar started on A.D. 16 July 622, the date Muhammad fled from Mecca to Medina.

The Hegira calendar is based on the lunar year. One lunar month, the cycle between two new moons, contains 29 days, 12 hours, 44 minutes and 2.8 seconds. A lunar year of twelve months contains 354 days and eleven thirtieths of a day. The eleven extra days in every thirty-year cycle are inserted into the calendar as leap years of 355 days by adding the leap day to the last month of the year.

In theory, the even-numbered months contain thirty days and the odd-numbered months contain twenty-nine days. But it does not always work out that way because the length of each month depends on when the new moon is actually sighted, since this marks the beginning of the new month and the end of the old month. Sometimes the position of the sun prevents the new moon from being seen until a day or two after its arrival.

The lunar year is unrelated to seasons because, compared against the Western Gregorian calendar, each year begins ten or eleven days earlier than the previous one. So, the months of the Islamic year progressively skip forward in relation to the solar seasons.

Since the Islamic calendar is the official calendar in Saudi Arabia, all correspondence to or from the government uses Hegira dates. All Westerners use Gregorian dates; so, when a document is received from the government, it must be converted from Hegira to Gregorian. Conversion from the 354/355-day Hegira calendar to the 365/366-day Gregorian calendar of the West is very difficult. For example, A.D. 1 January 1982 was A.H. 6 Rabi'Awwal 1402; and A.D. 4 July 1982 was A.H. 13 Ramadan 1402. Meeting dates and work schedules which were estimated us-ing Gregorian dates must be converted to Hegira dates in correspondence with the Saudi government.

To add to the confusion, all dates in both systems are written numerically as day, month, year in Saudi Arabia. Therefore, 4 July 1990 is written 4-7-90, which Americans would commonly read as April 7, 1990. The difference in calendars has caused all kinds of problems for both Saudis and Westerners.

Photography can be risky in Saudi Arabia. An

American project manager took a picture of a window display of gold jewelry as he was strolling through the suq with his Egyptian assistant. He heard a sudden cry in Arabic and turned to see a filthy little red-bearded man pointing at him. When he asked his companion what was happening, the Egyptian took him by the arm and said, "Let's get out of here." After winding through about a block of alleyways, they were surrounded by four men in olive drab combat fatigues—and the dirty little man. As the project manager opened his mouth to inquire why they were being hemmed in, the four fatigue-clad men leveled their submachine guns at him and pointed to his camera. The project manager trembled as he handed it over and prayed that the police, or whatever they were, would stay calm.

Wahhabi Muslims consider it blasphemous to make pictorial representations, and the more ignorant villagers are afraid the camera will take their spirits. It is illegal to photograph defense facilities, ports, airports, and palaces for military security reasons. Saudis are offended to have Westerners snap photos of picturesque old buildings because they feel that they are being ridiculed. The Islamic practice of hiding women and the Saudi sense of honor discourage photography of women. Therefore, Westerners have to be careful when and where they take photographs. If caught, their film can be destroyed, their cameras can be confiscated, or they can be arrested.

Chapter 13

*M*IND SET

To Westerners, Saudi behavior appears that of a paranoid schizophrenic. This is because the Saudi mind set is based on Bedouin values, and feelings about the West are ambivalent. Saudi behavior patterns differ from those in the West in eight major, interrelated areas: pride, sensitivity, distrust, emotionality, vengefulness, perception of time, intentionality, and dishonesty.

During the summer of 1984, the kingdom was proud that its soccer team participated in the Olympic games held in Los Angeles. It was so proud that it purchased dozens of American television commercials which described their accomplishment. It also arranged to have a major American television network show a two-part propaganda film produced by Saudia and the Saudi Olympic Committee.

Saudis are extremely proud. They derive great self-esteem from their manly virtue, their families, their language, and from being Arabs. They are proud of their life-style and the glorious history of Islam. They are also proud, to the point of arrogance, that they own a third of the world's oil and a vast supply of money.

The dignity or self-esteem of Saudis depends on their public esteem or reputation. If Saudis have a good image, they can command the respect of others and gain face. Thus, they are driven by their sense of honor to do things which will impress others with their good qualities, like buying American television time to show commercials which brag about Saudis having free medical care and education.

Their sense of honor compels them to do whatever is necessary to save face. The Saudis can save face even if they commit shameful acts or fail at something —as long as nobody learns about it. Late in the summer of 1984, 150,000 Iranian Shiites and their supporters staged anti-American demonstrations in Mecca. The Saudis, who are charged with maintaining order at the holy place, tried to save face by not reporting the riots. But the Iranians did. So the Saudis suspended the rule against non-Muslims entering Mecca to invite Western newscasters to film the peaceful hajj and thus regain face.

The need to save face is so great that the Saudis are extremely sensitive and susceptible to having their feelings hurt. Saudis are very protective about their image and are easily offended by the innocent remarks or actions of others. They cannot stand to be contradicted, corrected, or argued with, even in the most well-meaning, pleasant manner. Any critical comment will be taken as an insult.

They cannot tolerate bluntness in any form. To a Saudi, "getting to the point," "telling it like it is," or "putting the cards on the table" is rude, pushy, and demanding. To be reminded of milestones, deadlines, or promised actions that they have agreed to is also offensive. For the Saudi to retain his dignity, others must always speak softly, make points subtly or indirectly, and maintain an attitude of politeness, even if the Saudi himself is having a temper tantrum. If the others do not, the Saudi will feel slighted or offended and his sense of honor will make him act to save face.

Saudis are also easily insulted by innocent breeches of protocol or custom. If a Westerner exposes the sole of his shoe, a Saudi will take offense. If it is done in front of others, the Saudi's dignity is threatened and he will become openly aggressive. Saudi princes and ministers have left meetings with Westerners who crossed their legs and inadvertently turned the bottoms of their feet in the direction of the Saudis.

They also have a xenophobic distrust of foreigners and a suspicion of all things that are different. The fear and distrust of strangers originated in the desert where anybody who was not a friend was assumed to be an enemy. This fear carried over socially into the Saudis' love for privacy. High walls with locked gates are everywhere. Houses are built around closed courtyards and have high roof parapets to prevent others from looking inside. The windows are covered with ornate wooden shutters to allow those inside to look out without being seen.

Yet their respect for privacy disappears in public. They routinely push and shove their way into the front of lines in airports and stores because it is beneath their dignity to wait for others. They believe that whoever demands attention will get it. In banks, several Saudis will elbow their way to the teller window as money is being paid out, much to the consternation of Westerners. Saudis also crowd the personal space that Westerners normally leave for each other, and will stand toe-to-toe and stare directly into the eyes of whomever they talk to.

The Saudis believe that they have been treated unfairly and as inferiors by the West since the Christian Crusades. They believe they were exploited by the West during World War I and deceived by conflicting British promises of Arab independence and the creation of a Jewish state. In recent years, they have been distrustful of the United States because of its support of Israel.

They also distrust the West in a commercial sense. During the contract bidding for the second five-year development plan, Faisal Bashir, the deputy minister of planning, suspected that they were being cheated. He complained that there seemed to be three sets of prices, one for the West, a higher one for OPEC countries, and a still higher one for Saudi Arabia.

The distrust and suspicion of new things was incorporated into the religion by the Wahhabis who strongly resisted change. This has complicated the Saudi government's attempts to improve living conditions of the people in many ways. One of the more frustrating attempts concerns housing. The government built huge, mile-square, high-rise apartment complexes in Jeddah and Dammam containing thousands of expensively furnished apartments. Yet, despite the acute housing shortage, the Saudis have continuously refused to move into them.

Saudi men are very emotional. As a United States foreign service officer advised, "If you will think of the emotional and sexual roles as reversed of ours, you will do much better out here." Men hold hands while they walk together and kiss each other when meeting or departing. They have a tendency to generate data subjectively, on the basis of their feelings about past experiences; to superimpose personality onto issues; and to reject facts if they do not like them.

Since their actions are guided more by emotions than by reasoning and their emotional states may vary in the same situations, their behavior is unpredictable. They are extremely volatile and any event outside their normal routine can trigger an outburst of temper. Family quarrels are so common that it is said, "At each meal a quarrel, with each bite a worry."

When the Saudis lose their temper, they vent their fury on anyone around. They blame their mistakes on others and call on Allah to curse the person and his ancestors. They often lose their tempers at the bearers of bad news, make impossible demands, and refuse to back down if they are wrong.

It is fairly common to see Saudis crash into cars by running past stop signs, then lose their temper and blame the driver whose car they hit, even if the other car was not moving. On the business scene, it is not unusual for them to refuse to pay for a piece of equipment they ordered, and then get angry because it is not delivered.

Sheikh Muhammed al-Fassi lost his temper on many occasions during the summer of 1982. The sheikh promised to give the city of New York $200,000, but reneged because he was snubbed by the mayor. He then promised a check to the Skinner Boys Club in Orlando, but tore it up because he did not like a newspaper editorial about his generosity.

In business, Western managers frequently arrange to have subordinates deliver bad news to Saudis and suffer their displeasure, rather than deliver it themselves and jeopardize working relationships. The head of a Saudi company refused to cooperate with a leading American company on several occasions when it would have been to his distinct advantage to do so, because of a disagreement that had occurred two years previously.

The Saudi mind set is programmed for vengeance. For thousands of years, the Bedouin khamsah was the

vehicle for retaliation. When the Bedouin were converted to Islam, the Sharia provided for retaliation as
the "right of man." Retaliation is used to save or
regain face, to right wrongs, and to get even. It is the
motivation for verbal attacks, physical attacks, murder, raids, and war. If a Saudi feels that he has been
insulted or slighted, he will seek revenge. It is his
right, his tradition, and his duty!

The time perception of Saudis constantly exasper-
ates Westerners. Their short-term perception is un-
clear; their long-term perception is very blurred. This
vagueness causes disregard for punctuality and
makes it extremely difficult for Saudis to visualize the
time dependencies of future scheduled events.
Saudis are generally late for appointments and other
commitments. They cannot really appreciate the
need for schedules and the value of using time effi-
ciently.

To a Saudi, anything beyond one week is the indefinite future. Specific thinking of exact future
times is difficult for Saudis. The Arab economist,
Sayeigh, criticized this characteristic of his people
and described it as "the sloppy or cavalier attitude
toward time that upsets industrial organization."

In the West, everything runs by clock and calendar—schools, churches, businesses, governments,
transportation, athletic events, and entertainment. If
people are tardy, they are penalized by having to stay
after school, having their pay docked, being denied
admission, or paying fines. Westerners begin thinking in precise time frames at a very early age and do

so all their lives. They take it for granted that others have the same perception of time as they do, and act accordingly.

Western executives are responsible for scheduling activities and directing and controlling events to assure that they are completed on time. In Saudi Arabia, however, advisors and managers are severely hindered by Saudi concepts of time. Coordination meetings called by the Saudis are routinely cancelled when the parties that called the meetings do not show up. Contract signing is frequently delayed for weeks or months, and payments for work performed are equally delayed.

Western companies are not the only parties which suffer the consequences. Many of the projects of the kingdom's five-year development plans ran to higher costs because of the imprecise scheduling. The Saudis spent double the amount budgeted for their first five-year plan, exceeded the budget of the second plan by $18 billion and overspent for the third plan by $50 billion within the first two years.

If a Saudi says he is going to do something at a certain time, he may well not do it. He may not do it because he is not conscious of time. He also may not do it because of intentionality: the tendency to state intentions of taking actions or make threats and then do absolutely nothing to carry them out. It is as though the act of saying that they are going to do something relieves the Saudis of the mental burden of actually doing it. Behavioral psychologists attribute this phenomenon to Bedouin child-rearing practices. Bedouin mothers breast-fed male children until long after they learned to talk, so that whenever the boy was hungry, all he had to do was ask for the breast. They claim that mothers also threatened the little boys but never carried out the threats. Whatever the cause, Saudis frequently state that they are going to do things and then forget about doing them, or even that they said they would do them.

Numerous examples of Saudi intentionality have been reported in the press. Sheikh al-Fassi was evicted from a Miami hotel in August 1982 for non-payment of a $1.5 million bill. Later, a Miami judge ordered al-Fassi to stop writing checks after a $20,000 check he gave to his attorney was not honored by the bank it was drawn upon. The sheikh explained that he intended to pay the hotel bill and to transfer funds to cover his bouncing checks.

It is fairly common for Saudis to renege on agreements and contracts through intentionality. Saudis have been offended when expatriates requested that contracts be put in writing, because they felt that verbal agreements should suffice. However, the expatriates insisted on written agreements because they frequently observed the reluctance of Saudis to honor verbal agreements. An American director of a Saudi-owned firm reported that whenever he discussed the status of something his Saudi boss promised to do for his employees, the Saudi boss denied having said it!

The problem with intentionality is that the victim does not understand what is happening, so intentionality is easily confused with lying; and lying is permissible and expected of Saudis.

Saudis have no moral compulsion to tell the truth as practiced in the West. Honesty, to a Saudi, is not a matter of black and white, but a series of shades of gray. A man is expected to lie in order to save face according to Bedouin ethics, and Islamic law directs a man to deny his guilt if confronted. It is also permissible for a Saudi to lie by being less than emphatic in the use of his language, and it is customary for a Saudi to evade the truth rather than risk controversy which could lead to confrontation. So, Saudis have a tendency to be evasive and deceptive. They will give noncommittal answers to requests rather than say no, make promises that they do not intend to keep, or lie if it suits their purpose.

The history of Saudi Arabia is strewn with broken promises, promises made with the clear intention of not honoring them unless forced to. The United States and other Western governments, companies, and expatriates have been affected by Saudi evasiveness. The United States government was impacted when the Saudis promised, but did not deliver, the oil required for the United States strategic reserve. American oil companies were infringed on when the Saudi government reneged on their contracts and declared participative ownership of their shares in Aramco. Expatriate employees have had their salaries and other benefits withheld despite contracts to the contrary. It is extremely difficult to work in good faith when the two parties have different understandings of the concept.

The Saudis have been accused of being primitive and medieval. Their response has been, "Be fair, we came a long way in a short time." In fact, the speed of change has been so fast that many Saudis have experienced future shock as their culture changed around them. Many Western-educated Saudis are caught in a cultural ambivalence. They are attracted to Western culture and, at the same time, they fear and distrust it. They love their country, yet despise the backwardness of its people. They enjoy the grandiloquence of the Arabic language, yet admit that it is inadequate for modern communication. They cherish Bedouin values, yet try to avoid personal contact with the dirty nomads. They love their leisure but work longer hours. The Saudis want Western technology, productivity, and management expertise so they can become a leading industrialized nation by the year 2000; but they want to retain their traditional values.

The Saudis ask not to be judged by Western values. To them, their culture is normal and right and the Westerners are strange *khuwujis* (outsiders). To the Saudis, Westerners are nationalistic foreigners who come from countries which have had the natural advantages of mild weather, plentiful water, and abundant food and materials. Westerners are spoiled, self-indulgent people who do not have to continuously sacrifice and fight for their very survival. They are people who have strong rich countries but have let them deteriorate because of the confused thinking of their leaders.

In their view, Westerners come from huge, densely populated cities where people are indifferent to each other and criminal violence is commonly accepted. Westerners have no appreciation of their ancestors and little or no loyalty to their families. They are a very large group of people whose women want to behave like men.

As they see it, Westerners have strange election rituals which allow candidates to publicly insult each other and later pretend to be friends and to make promises they forget to keep if they are elected. Western governments use many types of taxes to take wealth from those who have worked for it and give it to those who refuse to work.

To Saudi Muslims, Westerners have a wide range of conflicting religious beliefs which they only practice one morning each week. They also appear to be fascinated by faith-healing mystics who are shown on television. The Western religions tolerate the use of mind-clouding substances like alcohol and allow women to run wild and flaunt their sexuality.

In their eyes, Westerners have thousands of conflicting laws. Their legal systems are so complex that they have to hire specialists to represent them in order to obtain simple justice. Their laws stifle individual initiative and interfere with their ability to conduct business. They pamper criminals and provide them with more privileges and rights than their victims.

To the Saudis, Westerners have strange values and offensive behavior. They are emotionally cold

322

and insensitive. They are blunt and outspoken and have no appreciation for subtlety. They are always in a hurry and have no sense of dignity. They are pushy and demanding in their rush to get things done.

East is East and West is West and where the twain meet, there are differences. Saudi values are not going to change much and Westerners cannot change the Saudi mind set. Westerners have to adapt to the Saudis as they are, and learn how to deal with them as effectively as the Saudis have learned to deal with the West.

Chapter 14

ENSHALLAH BUKRA

It seemed like a dream come true. The Saudis had more money than they knew what to do with. They wanted to buy everything, and price was no object. What a place to do business!

In 1974, so much money began pouring into Saudi Arabia that it started a gold rush. The top 400 American companies and the thirty-five largest banks swarmed into the country to get the billion-dollar contracts being awarded. Those that got contracts scrambled to hire people to work in Saudi Arabia. American and European newspapers, trade journals, and magazines ran advertisements for managers and technicians of all disciplines.

Aramco ran double-page magazine spreads which promised engineers that they could earn enough money to allow them to retire in six years. Siyanco offered "free housing, medical care and transportation and a very attractive tax-free salary." Trainex promised "40 days vacation a year, two paid R & R periods." Parsons Company said, "Claim a rare opportunity to work on a timeless project." Bechtel promised "a chance for career challenges and responsibility that will allow you to earn unmatched rewards...the chance of a lifetime." Charter Medical advertised, "Explore Europe, the Mediterranean and Africa as you take advantage of generous leave time." HE International promised "the opportunity to travel to some of the most intriguing cities in the world." Litton offered "an opportunity to travel to foreign lands, visit ancient cultures, be involved in exciting work and challenging projects, and be rewarded generously." McDonnell Douglas said, "If you're looking for adventurous living in a foreign land...and substantial rewards, we're looking for you. For many, it's a dream come true."

The advertisements were alluring enough to make anyone consider the possibility of working in Saudi Arabia. For some, it meant a chance to see the Acropolis in Athens, the Pyramids of Egypt or the wild game of Kenya. For most, it was a chance to escape the quicksand of inflation, and an opportunity to pay off the mortgage, buy a new car, send the kids to college, or start their own business.

Many accepted the challenge and by 1983, there were over 800 American companies and 30,000 Americans in the kingdom. They found themselves in an environment so totally different that it was like being on another planet.

After a fatiguing two-day trip, the new arrivals suffered immediate culture shock caused by sudden differences in time, weather, language, food, water, transportation, money, customs, and behavior. The lack of family and friends combined with the anxiety of the journey was enough to awe even the most adventurous.

Following the trauma of not being able to make people understand them, being shoved around by foul-smelling people in strange clothes, having their baggage ransacked at the airport for contraband, riding through town in uncontrolled traffic, finding themselves assigned to decrepit housing, learning that their job was not what they expected, feeling dreadfully homesick, and being told to surrender their passports, many Westerners quit their jobs during the first week.

Most of those who stayed were given very little orientation and were left to sink or swim. They were forced to work in semi-primitive conditions and learn how to do things differently. Most of what they needed had to be imported at considerable expense with great delay, so they either made do with what they had, or they did without. They could not count on business practices that were accepted as constants in the West.

The first thing that Western managers missed was the efficient support of a female secretary. If they were provided any clerical assistance, it was usually in the form of a sullen or confused Pakistani or Egyptian man who spoke a limited amount of British English, could barely type, knew little about Western business, and had no contact with the Saudis. If a manager was lucky, he got a highly competent, English-speaking Filipino secretary. But Westerners did not usually receive the level and quality of administrative support that they needed.

Business support services, such as marketing research firms, recruiting agencies, customs clearance brokers, international law firms, real estate agents, consumer credit companies, and printing shops are practically non-existent. The few services available are either non-English-speaking or not worth using.

There is an acute shortage of accurate business data. It was believed that counting was an ostentatious display of wealth which Allah would punish, so Bedouin did not count their camels and merchants did not calculate exact amounts; they used approximations. The Saudis may still believe this, because they maintain such strict financial secrecy that even their own employees do not know their status. Annual company reports, industry indicators, statistical abstracts, performance ratings, and stockholder reports do not exist.

Data produced by the government or its agents are usually inaccurate, obsolete and filled with translation errors. All data must be carefully analyzed to ascertain the reliability of the source, the date of its collection, and the compilation methods used.

Statistical reports are often found to be internally inconsistent and contradictory to other reports on the same subject. No two sources of information contain the same Saudi Arabian population estimates. Sometimes, the estimates are inflated to make it appear that the country is less dependent on foreign labor. Other times, the statistics are lowered to make per capita estimates more impressive. Therefore, any statistic based on population figures is probably wrong.

Financial data expressed in dollars can be misleading because of the fluctuation of currency exchange rates. The data are useless unless the statistics contain the exchange rate current at the time of computation. Annual data are often inconsistent because of the difference in the number of days between the Gregorian and Hegira calendars and the consequent overlap of time periods.

Very few directories are printed in English, including telephone books. If an American is fortunate enough to come across one, he finds that placing a call is like playing roulette. If he gets lucky, an American, Briton or Canadian will answer and he can communicate. More often, an Egyptian or Ethiopian will answer who understands some of what he is saying. If it is not his day, he will get a non-English-speaking Saudi. Gestures and pantomime do not help much over the phone. After the American expends most of his Arabic by saying, "Marhaba, maffi inglesi?" (Hello, do you speak English?) he is likely to hear the Arab say "la" (no), and something he does not understand, just before the Saudi hangs up.

To make matters worse, there are no standard working hours in Saudi Arabia. Government offices, shops, and banks all keep different hours. The odds are against reaching all the people who have to be contacted during the same time frame. Thus, it is almost impossible for a person to make a few quick phone calls to solve a problem.

Placing calls outside the kingdom is also difficult because of the differences in workweeks and time zones. There are only three common workdays for office-to-office communication with the United States or Europe. Saudi time is three hours ahead of London, eight hours ahead of New York, and eleven hours ahead of Los Angeles. So, most overseas calls have to be placed between four and eight in the evening, Saudi time, on Mondays, Tuesdays, and Wednesdays.

The difference in workdays is a continual problem for Westerners. After working for many years from Monday through Friday, it is very difficult to adjust to working Saturday through Thursday. They find that they are oriented toward thinking in terms of weeks, and to them the start of a new workweek is logically Monday and the end of the week is Friday. Therefore, when speaking among themselves, expatriates frequently refer to "logical Monday" to designate Saturday, and "logical Friday" to designate Wednesday.

It also takes Americans some time to get used to

thinking in terms of riyals and handling the varied-sized currency. The Saudi riyal fluctuates in value against other currencies, so the expatriate must constantly be aware of the daily exchange rate. Many foreigners have salaries quoted in their native currency but are paid a fixed amount of riyals. At times, their pay can be 10 to 15 percent less than they were hired for. Managers have to be careful that products they buy from another country do not actually cost 20 percent more than they thought they were paying.

The largest denomination of riyal note is SR 500, which in mid-1990 was worth about $133. When expatriates cash their monthly pay checks, the stack of money they receive is too thick to fit in a wallet or billfold. But most of them do not take cash. They convert it to their native currencies as quickly as possible and remit it for deposit outside the country to protect against loss, should the government restrict the transportation of money from the kingdom.

But these are minor annoyances. The Westerners are constantly frustrated by working with the Saudis. The more they interact with Saudis, the more they are affected. They have to overcome Saudi suspicions and cope with Saudi attitudes, work ethics, philosophies, and management styles.

Because of their different attitudes, Saudi expectations of Westerners are different than those understood by the Westerners. The Westerners find that what works for them at home does not work in Saudi Arabia.

They discover that the Saudis have a trading mentality and are always bargaining and making deals. They have a tendency to bargain for everything, including equipment, labor contracts, materials, and even taxi fares. The bargaining must be done according to their rules and they must have the last word. Saudis are very shrewd bargainers and alert to many possibilities. They may pay the asking price but take the advantage in interest rates, financing terms, transportation arrangements, storage fees, handling charges, or some other unexpected aspect.

Many Saudis are deal-making opportunists who will invest in anything to make large, quick profits with minimal effort, and get rid of their business at the first sign of a declining market. They concentrate more on forming joint venture companies and obtaining contracts than on performing the contracts. Some joint venture companies exist only because the foreign partner offered a good deal and paid cash in advance to form the company. There are notable exceptions, however, such as the Juffali brothers, the Gosaibis, the bin-Ladins, the Alirezas, and the Olayans, who are very effective.

Another form of bargaining is *baksheesh*. This is payment for favors sought or received, similar to "greasing the palm." Baksheesh payments are expected by public officials to expedite visa requests, avoid traffic tickets, or obtain priority service. But they must be given in a way that allows the recipient to maintain his dignity. A public attempt to give money to a government official, in a way that might insult him, could result in the arrest of the donor!

A Canadian engineer tells of trying to ask permission at the airport to go from the transit waiting area to a nearby snack shop in the main terminal. As he was talking to an armed guard at the connecting doorway, he noticed that the man was winking and wiggling his fingers at his side. After pressing the equivalent of two dollars in the guard's hand, he was able to enter the country without showing a passport or visa.

It is said that doing business in Saudi Arabia is like breeding elephants: "It's a laborious process and it takes a long time before you see results." Part of the difficulty is the cultural difference in management philosophy.

American managerial philosophy is based on the Protestant work ethic and the virtue of thrift. It is assumed that hard work will be rewarded with prosperity, and that individual initiative, if given the opportunity for self-gain, will result in the common good. Great emphasis is placed on personal freedom, the sanctity of contract, and the service obligation of those in authority. It relies on competitive market forces and does not tolerate much government regulation.

The Saudis neither believe in the Protestant work ethic nor subscribe to the virtue of thrift. Instead, the population is largely dependent on government largess, and it is assumed that individual initiative, if given the opportunity for self-gain, will result in the good of the individual.

The Saudi philosophy that "hurry is the devil's

work" is just the opposite of the American Protestant work ethic. Saudi productivity is about half that of Americans. They move and work at a slow pace because they would lose face if they rushed. They do not want to appear busy because status is derived from not having to work hard. There are only limited types of work that the Saudis are interested in doing. They will not work with their hands, carry even small parcels, perform menial tasks, or do dirty jobs. They are reluctant to work long hours because they love their leisure time. Their normal response if asked when they will complete a task is *enshAllah Bukra!*

It is customary for Saudis to take a three-hour break in the middle of the workday, a time when most Americans are very productive. While Americans hustle to meet deadlines, their Saudi counterparts take a nap or drink coffee with their friends. Toward five in the afternoon, when the Americans wind down and get ready to leave, the refreshed Saudis begin to call meetings.

Western executives are frustrated by the way their Saudi partners manage their organizations. Their management styles reflect the practices of Bedouin sheiks and merchant traders, and the fact that slavery was practiced until the mid-1960s. Management styles are the ways managers plan, organize, staff, direct, and control people to accomplish objectives.

Planning, the foundation of management, consists of establishing objectives, selecting alternatives, and scheduling the activities necessary to achieve the desired results. The plans are then used to direct and control all the activities of the organization.

Saudis believe that planning is blasphemous, as it is the responsibility of Allah who has preordained every man's destiny. Any attempt to influence or change the outcome of events is considered offensive to Allah. Because of this conviction, the Saudis do not like to make decisions and prefer to delay them as long as possible. Numerous Saudi proverbs warn about the futility of making plans or efforts to provide for the future. One proverb advises, "The provision for tomorrow belongs to tomorrow"; another states, "To each moment its decision."

Many Saudi executives have overcome their religious convictions against planning, and realize the value of a tool which provides direction. However, they are still not committed to the use of plans and are generally reluctant to make them. Saudis do not like to commit themselves in advance and are liable to change their minds at any time for no apparent reason. They do not like to put things in writing if they can avoid it. It symbolizes commitment and increases the chance for controversy and confrontation if they decide to change their minds. It also enables someone else to study the information and find errors which could lead to loss of face.

When Saudis are forced to make plans, they are prone to describe what they would like to happen without consideration of the conditions that must exist before they can happen. They are equally prone to factor in wished-for events or activities. Saudi plans contain many elaborate details but are generally incohesive. They lack priority assignments and definitions of responsibility, and gloss over errors and omissions with impressive, unsupported claims. They are also generally incomplete, too tightly scheduled, and underbudgeted.

These factors make it extremely frustrating for their joint venture partners who are involved in the planning process. The partners foresee the difficulties of trying to implement Saudi plans, but they cannot express their concerns without offending the Saudi executives.

A former United States government official explained: "Five-Year Plans are a wish list...they put down hundreds of items in the plan with less than a dozen actually going through. That leads to a misunderstanding. We say they don't mean what they say; they say that...does not mean the East lives in a fantasy world; only that the time frames are less precise."

After plans are made, it is necessary to organize the work, the workplace, and the work force. Labor is divided into a formal hierarchy of defined positions which assigns authority to issue orders and responsibility to carry out those orders.

Most Saudi companies are owned and controlled by one or two families. They are complex organizations which combine the finances of several dissimilar enterprises. It is not unusual to find the same company combining engineering services with brokerage, real estate development, transportation, import agencies, and distributorships.

Authority is concentrated at the top of these organizations, in positions held by family executives. Their span of control is very broad because they are reluctant to relinquish authority. Delegated authority is soon bypassed if the family executive becomes emotionally involved in matters supervised by a junior manager. If a real or imagined threat is perceived in a subordinate manager, his authority is quickly removed.

The family executives demand extreme loyalty from their employees. Security and advancement are based on loyalty and sociability rather than technical competence or managerial performance. When a Saudi enters into an employment or other contract, he considers it merely the starting point of building a business friendship. Only after the friendship has developed will the Saudi trust the other party.

Decision-making by Saudis is highly personalized and is based on the principles of the Bedouin majlis. The Saudi manager will consult with several people to gain a consensus. During the process, he will give the greatest credence to those he trusts most as friends, and consider their opinions over experts'.

Saudis are accustomed to believing only what they hear from friends, so the best advertising is by word of mouth. In most cases, foreign businessmen cannot obtain access to senior Saudi business and government managers without the help of another influential Saudi.

Once a foreign executive has access to an influential Saudi, he has to court him as he would a prospective wife. The foreigner must frequently visit the

Saudi's office and drink coffee with him and his associates. If the Saudi feels comfortable and the foreigner does not rush the process, he may be accepted as a friend. Once this stage has been reached over a period of weeks or months, the foreign manager is able to discuss business. He must start by describing the concepts and how they can benefit the Saudi. After the Saudi shows interest, the foreigner can talk about specifics, changing his strategy until the Saudi hears something that appeals to him. Only then can the foreign executive prepare an outline for the Saudi to discuss with his family, and for the foreigner to use as a basis for eventually developing a proposal.

Many Western companies made the mistake of writing a proposal at their headquarters and sending a sales representative to Saudi Arabia to try to close the deal in a few meetings. All they received were vague encouragements as they waited unsuccessfully to be notified that they had gotten the contract.

Status is very important. If a Saudi has a title, he expects to be called by that title. Abdul Turki, Ph.D., would expect to be called "Doctor Abdul" by his close subordinates in very informal situations, and "Doctor Turki" in more formal settings. If a Saudi is a sheikh or an engineer, he expects the title to precede his name. A man cannot supervise another person with more education than himself. Expatriates meeting with titled Saudis are at a disadvantage unless they hold equivalent titles or rank. Saudi executives find it offensive if junior expatriates are sent to deal with them. The meetings demand the dignity of equals meeting as equals.

In family-controlled businesses, positions of responsibility are built around individuals with whom the senior executive feels comfortable. Delegated authority is frequently reassigned to reward individuals who happen to be in favor at that moment, thus creating overlaps of responsibility and eliminating accountability for actions.

There is very little teamwork, group cohesion, or company loyalty. Employees tend to rally around individual managers, who are expected to look out for their immediate subordinates. In businesses staffed by large numbers of foreigners, chauvinism can further divide the organization when one nationality group feels it must compete with, or defend itself against, the threat of other nationalities.

After an organization has been defined, staffing begins. This consists of recruiting and placing qualified personnel in positions where they can work most effectively. With the critical labor shortage that exists in the kingdom, this process is fraught with problems.

Most Saudis are not attracted to industry They would rather capitalize on the numerous get-rich-quick opportunities than risk Allah's displeasure by attempting to plan a career. The glamor of the armed forces and the prestige of government employment also attract many young men. This is because the government pays more and demands less of Saudi employees than private industry, and leaves them enough time to run their own businesses on the side.

The restrictions placed on women working with

men keeps half the potential work force out of the job market. This work force could be used to fill clerical and semi-skilled jobs which are thought to be beneath the dignity of Saudi men. Even if Saudi companies could devise a way to isolate women from men in the workplace, the arrangement would probably create additional bottlenecks in the flow of information. As it stands now, it is necessary to hire young, untrained Saudi men and to import expatriate labor.

Senior Saudi managers hire all the members of their family who want jobs and give them preferential treatment. Many organizations are overstaffed by family members who do nothing but sit around reading newspapers and drinking tea.

The rest of the employees are expatriates. The lead time for acquiring an expatriate is at least three months from the date the need is identified. In many cases, especially during the Ramadan-Hajj period, it can take four months or longer.

Labor-related costs are extraordinary. Each expatriate employee is about three times more expensive than in the United States. Employers are required by law to provide everything necessary for their employees to live, including furnished housing and medical facilities. Additional expenses for expatriate employees include visa processing, pre-employment physical examinations, relocation and expatriation air fare for the employee and his family, children's schooling, local transportation for the employee and his family, thirty days of paid vacation, eleven paid holidays, and government social insurance. If the work site is in a remote area, the employer must also supply the employee's food.

The provision of these benefits by the companies places many additional pressures on expatriate managers. They must plan for and administer the benefits and involve themselves with the employees' well-being during non-working hours. Busy Western managers may find themselves spending as much time dealing with broken air conditioners in employee housing, late school buses, and wives' shopping trips, as they do on business matters. In Saudi Arabia, it is all part of the job.

After the venture has been organized and staffed, it becomes necessary to direct the people to achieve the goals. Direction includes assigning tasks to subordinates and motivating them to perform their work as scheduled.

Because of the multinational composition of the staff, a variety of supervisory techniques is used. Most managers are American, British, or European, and use supervisory methods which they learned in their home countries. As most expatriates plan to stay in Saudi Arabia only between one and three years, management training programs are impractical, except for the largest, most affluent organizations such as Aramco and Saudia.

Western managers find themselves in the dark when it comes to practicing participative management. Saudi executives refuse to share information and rarely issue policy statements which define organizational goals, strategies, and priorities. If these are known to the Saudi executive, he will keep them to himself in most cases and not even tell his senior managers until his intentions are fait accompli.

Foreign managers must ask the Saudi executive to explain current goals, and what is expected of them. If no direct answers are obtained, the manager is left to second-guess the head man and work in a reaction mode. During meetings with Saudi executives, expatriates can sometimes gain insight into Saudi priorities by observing how much time an executive spends in discussing specific topics.

It is difficult for foreigners to get undivided attention because Saudis do not respect closed doors or the privacy of meetings. They constantly barge in and interrupt the expatriate's train of thought. If an expatriate tries to prevent Saudi colleagues from entering his office during private meetings, the Saudis will be offended.

A business meeting with Saudi executives is a test of patience. The meetings are generally delayed by the late arrival of the Saudis, who shake hands, rub noses, kiss each other on the cheeks, and profusely greet each other prior to getting down to business. Next, coffee is brought in small cups, and there is a period of discussion devoted to non-work-related subjects. After the obligatory three cups of coffee are finished, business may begin.

Once in session, meetings are constantly interrupted as the Saudis take telephone calls and greet others who enter the room to talk about different subjects concurrently with the meeting. It is not un-

common for families and friends to enter and participate in the meeting as Saudi executives sit and finger
their beads or pick their toes. So many other visitors
may be present that the meeting turns into two or
three overlapping conferences concerning different
subjects. During this period, while visitors are entering and leaving the room, the serving boy may offer
little glasses of tea. The meetings may ramble on
without the original subject ever being discussed, and
can end abruptly without accomplishing anything.

Motivating employees in Saudi Arabia is more
difficult for the Western manager because he has staff
members from many countries, all of whom respond
to different motivations.

Psychologist Abraham Maslow theorized that
Americans are motivated by five levels of need satis-
faction, each of which must be fulfilled before the
next level becomes a motivating force. The five levels
are the physiological need for food, clothing and shel-
ter; security; social affiliation; prestige or ego satisfac-
tion; and the highest level, the need for achievement.

Compensation and job security are motivating
factors to expatriates from all countries, and all respond to managerial recognition. North Americans,
Britons, and Europeans are also motivated by job
challenge. However, Saudi employees are very difficult to motivate. The government supplies their
physiological and security needs and their families
supply their social affiliation needs, so these are not
managerial motivating factors. Achievement, to a
Saudi, would be not having to work at all.

Threats by expatriate managers are counterproductive and could prove detrimental to the expatriate if reported to Saudi authorities. The only motivational factor left is the Saudi need for prestige. Western managers must work with Saudi employees on a highly personalized basis and appeal to their egos and sense of pride. They must offer special incentives or favors to Saudis for expected performance in ways which allow Saudi employees to receive social recognition from their peers.

The final management practice is control. Control consists of monitoring and measuring performance and initiating action as needed to ensure that planned activities are carried out as specified in terms of quality, quantity, timeliness, and cost.

Control by Saudi executives is unsystematic, only partially effective, and varies from periods of no control to periods of overcontrol. Schedules, if made, must be frequently revised. United States Air Force maintenance advisors found that monthly schedules of activities for Saudis were worthless; only a third of weekly schedules were carried out; and only half of the daily schedules were met. Schedules for expatriate employees are also subject to slippage because of unplanned changes and long periods of absence. The productivity of expatriate employees is only ten months per year, after deducting vacation, holidays, and sick time. Adherence to tight schedules is almost impossible to achieve.

Financial control is also a problem. There are no standard financial reports required by the government, no standard accounting procedures are used, and no standard accounting principles are followed. The accounting systems are maintained in Arabic and expatriate managers may never receive budget performance reports from which to monitor actual costs against estimates. Late deliveries, currency fluctuations, and slipped schedules all cause Western executives to overrun their budgets. Budgets that were prepared or approved by Saudi executives are frequently too low. When expatriates request previously budgeted funds for expenditure, they could be refused if the Saudi executive has changed his mind.

After studying Americans working in Saudi Arabia, anthropologist Solon T. Kimball dryly reported that there were "cultural differences that led to considerable misunderstandings," and "restrictions placed upon their behavior, contrary to American habit, which resulted in greatly lowered productivity."

American productivity was reduced to a fraction of that in the United States. It was impossible to realistically estimate schedules or budgets because of the uncertainty and high risks involved. Contingencies had to be provided for currency exchange rate fluctuations, material import costs, productivity of third world personnel, commissions, bribes, breakdowns, delays in transportation, penalty clauses in contracts, and uncompensated changes in contractual specifications. Western managers were constantly forced to use previously allocated resources to deal with unforseen, culturally caused problems. As a result, it took three times as much effort, time, and money to accomplish a given objective as it would have taken in the United States.

The constant frustration of coping with cultural problems led to very high stress levels and caused managerial burn-out within three to six months after arrival. When American managers first arrived in Saudi Arabia, they worked for long hours to maintain their United States performance levels. However, they soon felt the sense of futility described by United States Army officers in a study submitted to the Defense Systems Management College: "About two to three months after arrival, advisors tended to experience a tremendous drop in expectations and a resulting frustration and bitterness concerning the possibility of accomplishing anything, no matter how slight." The Americans gradually lowered their standards, refused to allow themselves to be bothered by the decrease in their personal productivity and just tried to survive. By the end of six months, their morale had hit rock bottom.

Their work was so frustrating and living was such an ordeal that about one-third of the Americans who went to Saudi Arabia decided that it was not worth the effort and left before the expiration of their contracts. Ross Perot, founder and former president of Electronic Data Systems, said that he would never do business in the Middle East again.

The Saudi government observed that traditional Saudi management styles and practices were not able to achieve the levels of productivity that it wanted. The government tried to create a new work ethic by changing the welfare system. It even mandated, in the third five-year development plan, the goal of improving productivity by 27 percent through the use of sophisticated management techniques. But most Saudi companies did not change, and some went bankrupt when the economy slowed down. The Saudi government is still trying to improve Saudi management practices. But until then, it is business as usual, *enshAllah Bukra*!

Chapter 15

WINDS OF CHANGE

The winds of change are always blowing, and in
Saudi Arabia they could change direction as drastically as the winds of the monsoons. They have
shifted one direction and brought a recession. They
could blow from another direction and bring war.
The winds of change could also bring rebellion of the
educated youth or the women who want more freedom.

The Middle East has a long history of instability
and continues to be a powder keg with many fuses lit
by the Soviet Union. The religious fanatics Muammar
Qaddafi of Libya and Ayatollah Khomeini of Iran

openly fomented revolution and used terrorist tactics to create dissension. Syria, Iraq, and Libya were all heavily supported and armed by the Soviets. Jordan and Kuwait turned to Russia to buy modern weapons systems. Iraq and Lebanon are internally unstable because of their mixture of religions and sects, and are ruled by minority groups. Lebanon continues to be divided and crippled by its civil war. Then there is the Palestinian issue and the cold war against Israel.

Iraq used its armory of sophisticated weapons to invade Iran, blast Iran-bound tankers, and reduce Iranian oil revenues. The Iranian people grew tired of a war of attrition and finally agreed to United Nations cease-fire conditions after their airliner was accidentally shot down over the Persian Gulf. The new ayatollahs want to rebuild Iran. The Iraqis did not win, but emerged as the most powerful country in the Middle East with a large, combat-seasoned army. The scene was set for Iraq to again try to seize Kuwait. If the Soviet leadership changes, the Russians, with Iraq covering their flank, could again send their troops into Iran.

Lebanon may never again function as an independent state. The Syrians are dug into the north and the Israelis are entrenched in the south. The Lebanese government is as fragmented as its culture and cannot force them out. No outside power has been able to do so either.

The Palestinian issue will not go away. It will continue to fester until the Israelis give part of the

West Bank back to the Palestinians to form their own state. The Israelis are afraid to do that because it would weaken their ability to defend the country against a major Arab attack.

An Arab-Israeli war is a low probability because the Egyptians and Jordanians are not interested. Syria would like to attack, but will not do so alone; it has been beaten by Israel too often. Qaddafi would like to attack, but cannot put his army into position without getting it cut to shreds. So, continued terrorist activity seems most likely.

Russia continues to be a long-term threat. As the world's oil supply becomes depleted, the Middle East and Saudi Arabia will increase in strategic importance. The Soviet Union is well positioned to launch a campaign to control the Middle East oil supply.

The West is in poor position to stop such a campaign. Britain has token forces in Oman and France has a base at tiny Djibouti. The United States has a strong naval presence, but has very little influence over the Arabs and is opposed by Syria, Iraq, Libya and Yemen because of its support of Israel. The Saudis depend on United States military assistance but are afraid to allow American forces to be permanently based in the kingdom because they would lose the respect of other Arab nations. Therefore, the Saudis will continue to delicately balance their foreign affairs as they have for the past two decades, and continue their cold war with Israel.

Saudi Arabia's continued development depends on continued high oil revenues. Unless a safe, clean, alternative form of energy is developed soon, or another gargantuan oil field is discovered somewhere else, the Saudi oil reserves will become increasingly important during the next fifty years. As oil reserves in other areas become depleted, there will be greater demand for Saudi oil and higher prices offered for it.

But in the meantime, the demand for oil will fluctuate as will prices. OPEC lost most of its power after its members followed Iran's lead and cheated by dropping their prices and producing more than had been agreed. The price war that followed almost forced prices down to $10 per barrel.

The OPEC production cutbacks did not work and Saudi oil production stayed at about four million barrels per day. If Saudi Arabia can sustain this level of production, it can generate the revenue it needs and supply most of its gas requirements.

With continued oil production levels and diminished but still large financial reserves, the kingdom will continue to improve its defense, develop diversified industries, implement state-of-the-art automation systems, and train its people.

Saudi Arabia spent close to $100 billion to develop light industries and petrochemical plants, and has diversified downward into the production of plastics and plastic products. Although some of the petrochemical products can be used as raw material for manufacturing in Saudi Arabia, most of the products have to be sold outside Saudi Arabia in already oversaturated markets. The success of Saudi Arabia's petrochemical venture links it to the stability of the world's economy.

The winds of change will also be influenced by two forces building within the kingdom: an educated society and frustrated women.

The Saudis poured billions of dollars into education, sent tens of thousands of young Saudis to American universities, provided advanced technical and vocational courses in industry and the military, and educated the masses. Over half the population is under twenty-one years of age, and there are over 2,000,000 children in elementary and secondary schools and 100,000 in colleges. Their education is improving in content and quality as universities add new colleges and new majors to their curriculums. The national literacy rate will continue to climb as Saudi teachers graduate and teach the children of the villagers and the Bedouin.

The graduation of millions of Saudis from high schools and hundreds of thousands from universities will change the Saudi culture. They are being taught to work, think, question, and learn and are being exposed to all kinds of knowledge the Saudi people have never had before. Education has also given them the opportunity to sample and acquire a taste for material possessions and Western life-styles.

These trained Saudis will take their place in the labor force and fill critical shortages in education, medicine, business, and technical trades. The English-speaking Saudi graduates will overcome many of the translation problems and further expand their awareness of the West.

353

Consequently, the Saudis will acquire a partially Western work ethic. They will become more productive, and government and business will become more efficient. As the increasing number of graduates who have been exposed to the West gain more influential positions, government will become more tolerant of the West and its ideas. The graduates will also tire of the traditional practices and will become more Westernized. They will then challenge the Sauds and Wahhabis for more freedom, and press for more say in government policy and a less strict interpretation of Islam.

There is also trouble brewing behind the veils. Until recently, most Saudi women believed that marriage was the only reason for their existence and derived their identity through their husbands. They accepted their second-class status and put up with their husband's treatment because they did not know any better. Now that they are becoming educated and exposed to Western ideas, they are challenging their traditional role. Saudi women argue that their status has nothing to do with Islam, but with male chauvinist attitudes that have been institutionalized over the centuries. The women want to use their education and are defying tradition. In 1981, they balked against "blind marriages" and gained the right to see their prospective grooms once their engagements were announced.

As more women become educated, they are going to demand more independence. There are over 1,000,000 girls in elementary and secondary schools

and over 30,000 women in colleges. The present generation of Saudi women are aware of women leaders
like Corazon Aquino, Benazir Bhutto, and Margaret
Thatcher, and want more say about what they will
become. They are going to demand the rights enjoyed
by women in other Arab lands such as Jordan, Bahrain, and Egypt, where women have cast aside their
veils and are allowed to wear Western clothing, drive
cars, and work at jobs of their choice. They want a
chance to work in the fields of law, engineering, data
processing, and science, to enter government and to
become managers.

They also want the right to decide if they should
get married, and to choose their husbands. Many
Saudi women who hold jobs do not want to get married because their husbands would make them quit
their jobs. Saudi men say educated women do not
make good wives, and refuse to be neglected by a wife
who works. But as men become more educated and
open to Western ideas, these attitudes will change
slightly. Already, women appear in public with
shorter abayas and open veils. Some young married
couples have mixed, rather than segregated, social
gatherings. Occasionally, unmarried people are invited to the mixed gatherings so they can meet and,
perhaps, select their own partners. Changing life patterns will also affect the family. As men work harder
and women become more educated, the divorce rate
will continue to increase.

As more Bedouin move into cities to get jobs, the
society will become more settled and less nomadic,

and tribal influence will decrease. The society will change in other ways. The Bedouin, too, will receive training and their children will become educated. The Saudi labor force will shift further from agriculture and construction into industry and services.

As more people move to the cities, work at jobs, and earn more money, they will miss the freedom of the open desert and demand more time for leisure. As this pressure builds, the government may be forced to reduce the workweek to five days.

An expanded, better-trained, more productive local work force will reduce the kingdom's dependency on foreigners. There will be greater emphasis on managers, professionals, technicians, and special educators, as well as menials to do the jobs the Saudis do not want to perform. Saudi Arabia will continue to need about 200,000 Americans and Europeans to help complete its development and military modernization programs.

The internal forces of social change will arouse responses from the royal family, government, and the ulama.

The government will continue to maintain its cultural sensitivity and fear foreign corruption of its values. Because of the strong threats by neighboring Islamic countries, it will continue to be reluctant to implement a constitution which would give the people the right to criticize it. The government does not think its people have enough knowledge or experience to vote for their leaders. But, as university graduates swell in number, the king may finally establish a consultative council composed of elected representatives to serve as the people's advisory organization.

Social benefits provided by the government will continue to increase and reach more of the people, but at a much slower rate as most of the people's basic needs have already been provided for. Corruption will decrease for there will be fewer opportunities for big deals, and the regulations already decreed will take stronger effect. The public trading of private company stock will further reduce corruption. The government may require annual filing of standardized financial reports by publicly traded companies which list the holdings of the owners and officers, such as the reports required by the United States Securities and Exchange Commission.

Wahhabi ulama will continue to strenuously resist social change and will vary their pressure for strict conformity to Islamic principles to match the forces of change. The more the Iranian Shiites and Qaddafi denounce the Saudis, the more pressure will be exerted for strict observance. Security procedures will be further tightened for the hajj to reduce the denunciations and demonstrations by foreigners. But if the external criticism is reduced, the ulama can be expected to make concessions to the royal family for liberalization, as they have in the past.

The royal family is facing its greatest challenge. After a decade and a half of spectacular success which the Saudi people have come to expect, the economy has cooled off and people are disappointed. In addition, King Fahd is not yet the father figure the Saudis have come to identify with their king. The Saud family knows it has problems and has increased its propaganda to reaffirm its image. Fahd's image and power will increase as more progress is seen under his rule.

The desert dynasty should stay intact. It has the evidence of United States support to keep it in power, a broad power base from tribes, influential families, and the ulama; and it holds all key government positions. It is also a large family. If something should happen to Fahd, there are still twenty-six sons of Abdul Aziz younger than Abdullah who could be appointed crown prince or king. Prince Bandar Sultan, the Saudi ambassador to the United States, would probably be the front runner for crown prince; but three of Fahd's brothers are also ministers and six others hold important government positions. There are also many eminently qualified grandsons of Abdul Aziz who are ready for more responsible positions.

But the royal family will have to yield to the masses of Saudis who are becoming more qualified to think for themselves and less ambivalent in their views toward westernization.

The royal family and other government officials will complete the large construction projects and continue to extend electricity, telephone service, running water, and paved roads to the rest of the kingdom. More desalination plants and irrigation systems will be built to increase agricultural capacity.

Unless the economy skyrockets again, the Saudis

will continue repairing things instead of just throwing them away. As construction is completed, they will clean up more of the country. Increased emphasis will be placed on clean-up operations of all kinds, both to improve sanitation and health in the kingdom and to make it more pleasing to the eye. Healthcare will show continued improvement, first as the medical facilities are completed, and later as qualified staff are trained to run them. Housing will improve in quality as it ceases to be a speculative venture and as regulations control design and construction. The availability of housing for expatriates should improve as the number of expatriates decreases. The country will continue to acquire state-of-the-art labor-saving devices and systems as fast as they can be absorbed, to reduce their dependency on outsiders.

Business will change. There will be fewer opportunities for overnight wealth and the environment will become more competitive. The government is already forcing competition and the regulation of performance. Salaries paid to expatriates have dropped significantly from the boom-period high and many government contracts have imposed ceilings to hold down costs. More support services will become available because entrepreneurs will see them as money-making opportunities. Companies will become increasingly managed and staffed by Saudis as college graduates enter the labor market. The graduates will bring more management skills to the companies, enhance Saudi ability to plan and control, and increase efficiency.

The future of Saudi Arabia depends on the direction of the winds of change. If the Saudis can stay out of war, keep their fellow OPEC members in line, and deal with the challenges of an educated citizenry and liberated women, their future looks rosy. If not, *Alhamdulilah*, there are too many things that could happen for speculation.

SELECTED BIBLIOGRAPHY

Al Awaji, Ibrahim Mohamed. "Bureaucracy and Society in Saudi Arabia," *Dissertion Abstracts International*, 32 (1972), 6525A (University of Virginia).

Atlas of Saudi Arabia: London, Edward Stanford, 1978.

Bowler, Rosemarie M. "Expatriates in Saudi Arabia: Stress, Social Support, Modernity and Coping," *Dissertion Abstracts International*, 41 (1980), 405B (Wright Institute).

Davis, Stanley M. *Comparative Management: Organizational and Cultural Perspectives*. Englewood Cliffs, NJ: Prentice-Hall, 1971.

Doing Business in Saudi Arabia. New York: Price Waterhouse & Company, 1979.

Fisher, Sydney Nettleton, ed. *Social Forces in the Middle-East*. New York: Greenwood Press, 1968.

Gibb, Hamilton A.R., and J.H. Kramers, eds. *Shorter Encyclopedia of Islam*. Ithaca, NY: Cornell University Press, 1965.

Henle, Paul, ed. *Language, Thought and Culture*. Ann Arbor: University of Michigan Press, 1958.

Hobday, Peter. *Saudi Arabia Today: An Introduction to the Richest Oil Power*. London: Macmillan, 1978.

Holden, David, Richard Johns and James Buchan. *The House of Saud*. London: Sidgwick & Jackson, 1981.

Hopwood, Derek, ed. *The Arabian Peninsula: Society and*

Politics. Totowa, NJ: Rowman and Littlefield, 1972.

Jeddah Old and New. London: Stacey International, 1980. Reprinted, 1981.

The Kingdom of Saudi Arabia. 4th ed. London: Stacey International, 1979.

Lipsky, George Arthur. *Saudi Arabia: Its People, Its Society, Its Culture.* New Haven, CT: Human Relations Area Files Press, 1958.

Mayton, Joseph H., Jr. *Cultural Factors in Managing an FMS Case Program: Saudi Arabian Army Ordinance Corps (SOCP) Program.* AD-A052 105/4GA. Fort Belvoir, VA: Defense Systems Management College, November 1977.

Mostyn, Trevor, ed. *Saudi Arabia: A MEED Practical Guide.* London: Middle East Economic Digest, 1981.

Nawwab, Ismail, Peter C. Speers, and Paul F. Hoye, eds. *Aramco and Its World; Arabia and the Middle East.* Washington: Arabian American Oil Company, 1980.

Nyrop, Richard F., and others. *Area Handbook for Saudi Arabia.* 3d ed. Washington: Government Printing Office, 1977.

Patai, Raphael. *The Arab Mind.* New York: Scribner, 1973.

Pesce, Angelo. *Jiddah: Portrait of an Arabian City.* London, Falcon Press, 1977.

Philby, H. St. J. B. *Saudi Arabia.* New York: Arno Press, 1972.

Shiloh, Ailon, ed. *Peoples and Cultures of the Middle East.* New York: Random House, 1969.

Smith, Wilfred Cantwell. *Islam in Modern History.* Princeton: Princeton University Press, 1957.

Terpstra, Vern. *The Cultural Environment of International Business.* Cincinnati: South-Western Publishing Company, 1978.

Twitchell, Karl Saban. *Saudi Arabia.* 3d ed. New York: Greenwood Press, 1969.

U.S. Department of Labor. Bureau of Labor Statistics. *Labor Law and Practice in the Kingdom of Saudi Arabia.* Washington: Government Printing Office, 1972.

Westlake, Howard J.H. *Saudi Arabia.* Guides to Multinational Business, No. 1. San Francisco: Four Corners Group, 1977.

Index

220-221, 350

Libya, 192, 194, 200, 202, 206, 220, 350, 351

Mecca, 27, 70, 77, 78-79, 81, 82, 83, 87, 91, 94, 99, 100, 101, 104, 106, 107, 108, 111, 115, 210, 212, 255-256, 273, 312

Medina, 27, 78, 79, 80, 81, 99, 106, 107, 115, 218, 221, 256

Muhammad, 27, 67, 77-83, 84, 85, 86, 95, 98, 107, 218, 252, 273, 308; *see also* Islam

Muslims, 67, 81, 87-88, 89, 132, 194, 199, 203, 207, 218, 255; *see also* Shiite Muslims; Sunni Muslims; Wahhabis

Nadj, 104, 106, 107, 108, 109, 110, 119, 123

Nasser, Gamel, 126-127, 128, 129- 130, 131, 132, 185, 186, 187, 189, 190, 191

National Guard, 130, 133, 139, 141, 215, 216, 280, 281

nomads, 41, 42-43, 293; *see also* Bedouin; Bedouins

North Yemen, 128, 129, 132, 189, 190, 197, 221

oil, 29-30, 112, 119, 134, 146, 168, 174, 187, 195, 201, 220, 232, 351; companies, 119, 123- 124, 146-147, 148, 154-155; concessions, 123-124, 146-149; embargoes, 134-136, 155-157, 171, 193, 223, 243; fields, 150, 152, 206-207; industry, 12-13, 213; prices, 119, 135-136, 151, 155- 157, 159, 162-163, 168-169, 172, 175-176, 180; pro-

duction, 11, 135, 139, 141, 146, 149, 152, 154-155, 156, 162, 168, 169, 170, 171-172, 173, 174-176, 220, 352; refineries, 166-167, 171; reserves, 145-146, 179, 352; revenues, 16, 157, 175, 176; taxes, 154; *see also* Saudi Arabia

Oman, 104, 107, 109, 119, 124-125, 126, 137-138, 190, 191, 202, 207, 221, 223, 351

Organization of Petroleum Exporting Countries (OPEC), 19, 135, 152, 154, 155-156, 162-163, 170, 171, 173, 174-176, 201, 315, 352, 360

Ottoman Turks, 89, 91-92, 104, 106, 107, 108, 109, 110, 111, 112, 113-115, 116, 233

Palestine, 115, 116, 117, 118, 182, 183, 184, 185, 203, 217, 218, 219

Palestine Liberation Organization (PLO), 188, 189, 190, 194, 204- 205, 206, 219, 221, 243

Palestinians, 185, 189, 206, 219, 350-351

Persia, 71-72, 73, 83, 116, 181; *see also* Iran

pilgrims, 98-101, 146, 147, 180, 201, 212

Qaddafi, Muammar, 190, 191, 349, 357

Qatar, 106, 109, 121, 123, 124, 131, 192, 202, 207, 221

raids, 46, 47, 50, 81-83, 104-105, 110-111, 112, 118, 120, 122, 123, 186, 204

Ramadan, 81, 95-97, 100, 230,

255, 298, 340
Religious Police, 68, 93, 95, 96, 129
Riyadh, 26, 110, 132, 148, 153, 294, 303

Sadat, Anwar, 134, 191, 193, 197, 203
Saud family, 15, 102, 103-144, 145- 153, 156, 158, 159, 169, 172, 173, 175, 177, 181, 183, 185-186, 191-192, 193, 195, 200, 202, 203, 205, 209, 212, 213, 214, 219, 223, 227, 239, 240, 241, 242, 255, 261, 264- 265, 304, 356-358; *see also* Saudi Arabia
Saudia, 161, 262, 294, 304, 341
Saudi Arabia, 185, 189, 190- 191, 194-195, 196, 203, 207, 208, 209, 210; boycotts, 233- 235; business practices, 327- 347, 354, 359; censorship, 243-244; climate, 25- 26; clothing, 34-35; crime, 252- 254; culture, 11, 13, 54-56, 300; currency value, 150, 169, 172, 173; customs, 57- 59, 300-301; development programs, 12, 134, 137, 140, 141, 153 154, 158, 159, 160 162, 163-168, 173-174, 176- 177, 232, 280, 314-315, 318, 356; economy, 11-12, 14, 16- 17, 169, 170, 173, 177, 357, 358; employment, 12-13, 37, 63-65, 325-347, 353; enemies of, 216- 218, 219-221; family life, 44-46, 54-56, 57-59; for- eign policy, 180-181, 201- 203, 317-318; geography, 14-15, 21-25, 26-29, 118-119, 179, 181; government 14, 15,

16, 17, 217-128, 129, 150- 151, 153-154, 158, 160, 175, 225- 250, 315, 356-357, 359; government corruption, 126- 130, 230-234, 357; gross na- tional product, 145, 157, 173, 175; health care, 300-302; his- tory, 37-42, 51-54, 67-72, 73- 84, 84- 93, 103-144, 216-218; housing, 293-297, 315; infra- structure, 29, 153, 158, 160- 161, 162, 163-164, 169-170, 176-177, 291-306, 358- 359; marriage, 54-56; military, 15, 159, 176-177, 180, 185, 196, 197, 200, 201, 203-204, 208, 210- 211, 213, 214, 215- 216, 223; per capita income, 145, 157; physical appear- ance, 33-34; population, 36, 37, 179-180; press, 242, 300; punishment, 253-255; reve- nue, 146, 151, 157-158, 168- 169, 170; sexual mores, 260-266, 354-355; social be- havior, 64-65, 311-323; social classes, 35-36, 63-65, 293; so- ciety, 15, 33, 35-36, 39; suqs, 59-62, 300; technology, 14, 17-18, 291-292, 298-308, 352; traffic laws, 248 250, 306- 307; transportation, 302-307; tribal life, 46-49, 54; use of alcohol, 257-260; values, 13- 14, 310, 311- 323; visas, 244- 247; wars and battles, 103-123, 181; work permits, 247-248
Saudi Arabian Basic Indus- tries (SABIC), 166, 167, 170- 171, 172, 228
Sharia, 16, 226, 227, 233, 240, 249, 251-266, 317; *see also* Is-

lam
Shiite Muslims, 36, 84, 85, 87,
101, 111, 121, 139, 188, 198-
199, 200, 203, 207, 208, 217,
312, 357
South Yemen, 137-138, 189,
191, 196, 197, 206, 219
Soviet Union, 107-108, 109,
111, 122, 181-182, 183, 185,
186, 187- 188, 189, 190, 191,
192, 193, 194, 195-196, 197,
199, 202, 206, 211, 219, 220,
221, 349, 350, 351
Standard Oil Company of
California (Socal), 123-124,
146-147, 148, 171, 172
Standard Oil Company of
New York (Mobil), 148, 149,
171, 172, 204, 265
Suez Canal, 108, 132, 153,
186, 187, 197
Sunni Muslims, 35-36, 69, 84,
85, 87, 216-217
Syria, 116, 117, 118, 134, 180,
183, 184, 186, 187, 188, 189,
191, 193, 194-195, 200, 202,
204- 205, 206, 207, 208, 219,
221, 350, 351

Texas Oil Company (Texaco),
147, 148, 171, 172
Trans-Arabian pipeline (TA-
Pline), 148, 149, 153, 190, 217
Trucial States, 107, 109, 118,

121, 124, 126, 192; *see also*
United Arab Emirates

ulama, 68, 69, 127, 130, 131,
141, 226, 356, 357, 358
United Arab Emirates, 136,
192, 202, 221; *see also* Trucial
States
United Nations, 183, 184, 187,
211- 212, 213
United States, 12, 125, 131,
134, 138, 139, 145, 147-148,
150, 157, 159, 168, 180, 183,
185, 187, 192, 193, 194, 196-
197, 199-200, 201, 203-204,
205-206, 208, 209, 210-211,
213-214, 221-223, 314, 351

Wahhabis, 92-93, 105, 110,
122, 130, 132, 140, 141, 284,
310, 315, 357; *see also* Ikhwan
wars and battles, 85, 87, 88-
91, 131-132, 155, 157, 193-
194, 186- 187, 188-196, 199,
200-201, 204- 205, 206-207,
208-214, 217; Saudi, 103-123,
181; *see also* Arab-Israeli
War; Iran-Iraq War
Work and Workmen's Regulation, 237- 239

Yanbu, 28, 29, 73, 115, 160,
164, 217